THE

VOYAGE

HOME

THE

VOYAGE
HOME

· A NOVEL ·

PAT BARKER

DOUBLEDAY NEW YORK

www.doubleday.com

DOUBLEDAY and the portrayal of an anchor with a dolphin are
registered trademarks of Penguin Random House LLC.

Cover illustration by Sarah Young
Cover design by Emily Mahon

LIBRARY OF CONGRESS CATALOGING-IN-PUBLICATION DATA
Names: Barker, Pat, 1943– author.
Title: The voyage home : a novel / Pat Barker.
Description: First Edition. | New York : Doubleday, 2024.
Identifiers: LCCN 2024003321 (print) | LCCN 2024003322 (ebook) |
ISBN 9780385549110 (hardcover) | ISBN 9780385549127 (ebook)
Subjects: LCGFT: Novels.
Classification: LCC PR6052.A6488 V69 2024 (print) |
LCC PR6052.A6488 (ebook) | DDC 823/.914—dc23/eng/20240125
LC record available at https://lccn.loc.gov/2024003321
LC ebook record available at https://lccn.loc.gov/2024003322

MANUFACTURED IN THE UNITED STATES OF AMERICA

1 3 5 7 9 10 8 6 4 2

First American Edition

In loving memory of Alice Stott

THE

VOYAGE

HOME

1

She had yellow eyes. At times, particularly by candlelight, they scarcely looked like human eyes at all. Calchas, the priest, once said they reminded him of a goat's eyes: that she had the same numbed look of a sacrifice. *I* never saw her like that. She reminded me of a sea eagle, a common enough bird on the coast where I grew up; the sailors call it "the eagle with the sunlit eyes." And its eyes are beautiful, but it doesn't do to forget the brutal beak, the talons sharp enough to tear living flesh from bone. No, I didn't see her as a victim, but then, I knew her better than most. I was her body-slave, or, to use the common, vulgar term slaves themselves use, her catch-fart. And I hated it.

That day, the day we finally abandoned the Greek camp and set sail for "home," I was feeling really fed up with her because she'd kept me awake half the night praying—if you could call it praying. To me, it sounded more like a married couple having a row. Apollo didn't say much—in fact, nothing that I could hear. *She* was saying, "Home? *Home?*" over and over again, as if it were the worst swear word in her vocabulary. I knew what she meant, because whatever unimaginable place our Greek captors were taking us to it certainly wouldn't be home. Home, for me, had been a little white house on the side of a hill, the back garden so steep I had to cut terraces into it to grow my herbs. I loved that garden.

There were goats at the top of the hill, so my days were punctuated by the clanking of bells. For Cassandra, home had been first a palace, then a temple, both, now, in ruins, just like my house—a shared misfortune that should probably have brought us closer than it did.

Leaving Cassandra with the cart and the baggage, I walked round the hut for the last time, checking to see we'd left nothing behind—or that she'd left nothing behind. I didn't have anything to leave. The floorboards were gritty under my feet, the sand already starting to encroach. Normally, sweeping that out every morning was one of my jobs, but the last few days I hadn't bothered. What was the point? The sand would be everywhere soon, piling up in corners, wedging doors shut; and after that the winter storms would begin, finding cracks in walls, blistering paint, warping wood until only a few spars would remain, scattered across a beach that had swallowed everything else. There was a bitter satisfaction in knowing that the ruined marble palaces and temples of Troy would endure for centuries to come while in a few short years the Greek camp would vanish without trace.

Being alone like this, even for a few moments, was a luxury. For the past two months, I'd shared the hut with Cassandra, who'd been in a state of "divine frenzy" when she arrived, clothes ripped, skirt bloodied and stained with semen. Nobody who saw Cassandra in those first days ever forgot it. Holding two blazing torches above her head, she whirled around the overcrowded hut, hair and skirt flying, shouting, "C'mon, get up, what's wrong with you all? Dance!" Her mother and sisters cowered away from her. "C'mon, what's the matter with you?"—she was kicking her mother's shins at this point—"Get up, dance! DANCE!" And Hecuba, desperate to calm her demented daughter down, shuffled her scaly old feet from side to side. A further moment of horror in the old queen's life, seeing her daughter reduced to this: a pathetic creature with spittle on her chin and garlands of dead flowers drooping from her neck.

"Come on, all of you. Dance at my wedding!"

What wedding? Like every other woman in the camp, Cassandra was facing a lifetime of slavery. Royal birth, her status as a high priestess of Apollo, none of that would be enough to save her. Like everybody else there, like her own mother, she wasn't an important person anymore; in fact, she wasn't any kind of person. She was a thing, because that's what a slave is—and not just in other people's eyes, the people who own her, and use or abuse her; no, it's worse than that. You become a thing even in your own estimation. It takes a strong spirit, a strong mind, to resist the stripping away of your old identity. Most of us can't do it. And yet here was Cassandra, who if half the stories were true was as mad as a box of snakes, prophesying that she was about to become the wife of a great king.

"Rejoice!" They all had to rejoice with her, not because she was going to marry the richest, most powerful man in the Greek world, but because her marriage would lead directly to his death. *Look at him,* she was saying, *riding in triumph over dead children, king of kings, lord of lords—and yet this hero, this mortal god, will die the death of a stuck pig on a slaughterhouse floor.* Her own death was of no importance. She'd go down into the darkness crowned with laurels, having done what her brothers, for all their strength and courage, had failed to do: bring Agamemnon's head level with the dirt.

Deluded. I don't remember anybody saying the word, but then, it didn't need to be said. Her sisters exchanged pitying glances, though I noticed that not one of them tried to console her. Even surrounded by the women of her own family, she was completely alone. She wasn't despised exactly, but nobody believed her prophecies; in fact, nobody listened to a word she said.

But then—and this was as unexpected as a flash of lightning in a clear blue sky—Agamemnon chose her as his prize. I was there. I felt the ripple of surprise, even consternation, that spread around the arena. Afterwards, as the crowd dispersed, I overheard a couple of Greek fighters talking: "Bloody hell, I wouldn't want that in my bed." "No, you'd never dare sleep." "Did you see her with them torches? Bloody near set the place alight." "Well, I suppose if all else fails they'll just tie her to the bed."

As it turned out, he wasn't far wrong about that. For her own safety, she was kept locked up, and I was the lucky soul sent to take care of her. The ranting, the raving, the spitting and pissing, went on as before, but behind closed doors. I followed her sisters' example and ignored the rants—no easy matter when they're being shouted in your ear in the middle of the night. What I couldn't ignore was the obsession with fire. Every minute, she was watching me, waiting for me to go to sleep so she could get out of the hut and grab torches from the sconces that lined the path outside. I'd wake and find the door wide open, cold night air streaming in, and Cassandra outside on the path whirling torches in great arcs of flame above her head. No doubt, in her poor crazed mind, they were the torches of Hymen that light a virgin bride to her marriage bed.

Hour after hour, I lay awake, staring at the rafters, afraid even to close my eyes in case I dropped off to sleep. "Divine frenzy" people called it, but to me, supervising her every waking minute, combing her hair, washing her face, changing her bloody clouts—even that she couldn't do for herself—there was nothing "divine" about it. When, finally, she began to calm down, when she no longer paced the floor for hours on end, spit flying, fingers snatching empty air, when she sat up in bed and accepted a cup of cold water, having slept non-stop for fifteen hours, I was broken. As close to physical and mental collapse as I've ever been. But curious too. Despite the weeks of enforced intimacy, I felt I didn't know this woman at all, and I wanted to.

Unfortunately, almost everything I'd learned about her since then repelled me. And—in so far as she bothered to notice me at all!—she returned the dislike. I'd seen her at her worst, dribbling and drooling in urine-soaked sheets. You can dress it up whichever way you like, but the simple fact was, I'd seen too much. I knew too much. Sometimes, I think, she found it difficult to be in the same room as me.

"Ritsa? RitSA!"

That was her now. One last look around the empty hut, one final blessed moment of peace, and then I had to go.

"What *have* you been doing?"

She was standing beside a cart loaded with her possessions, a great heap of them—not bad for a woman who'd arrived in the camp with nothing but the rags she stood up in.

I held out my hand. "I found your earrings."

Her hand went to her earlobes. "Oh. I can't think how they got left behind."

They were nice earrings too: solid gold hoops, a gift from Agamemnon. God knows what poor girl's ears they'd been ripped out of. Cassandra didn't thank me. I watched her climb into the cart beside the driver and then, with a snap of the reins, they were off, leaving me to trudge along behind, carrying a bag of "special" clothes. What was special about them I had no idea; she'd packed that bag herself. It was heavy, I knew that, inexplicably heavy if all it held was clothes. I was also carrying her jewellery case, containing the various presents Agamemnon had given her, including a beautiful silver necklace set with fire opals. I had my own reasons for wishing to keep *that* safe.

So, there I was, stumping along behind the cart, my horizon bounded by the bullocks' shit-caked backsides and swishing tails. Had I really sunk so low? *Yes*—the only possible answer. I was Cassandra's catch-fart—well, be honest, would you want that on *your* headstone? No, me neither. Not that I was likely to get one—a headstone, I mean—or even a grave. In the camp, the bodies of women who died were thrown off the cliffs, or added—as kindling, you might say—to a fighter's funeral pyre. I lost count of the number of good women I saw leave the world that way.

At the end of the track, the driver reined the bullocks in because going any further would risk getting the wheels stuck in loose sand. Jumping down, he walked round the back of the cart, considered the number and size of Cassandra's boxes, sighed, ostentatiously, and went off to find somebody to help. Cassandra didn't seem to notice his departure; like me, she was staring out across the bay.

For the past few days, ever since the wind had changed direction, the harbour had been filling up with brown, fat-bellied cargo ships, sitting low in the water, holds stuffed with loot from ruined Troy, rising and falling on the choppy waves like a puddle of disgruntled ducks. They were surrounded by the black, beaked warships that were waiting to escort them home.

Closer to where I was standing, shadows of clouds chased each other across the wet sand. Dwarfed by the immensity of sea and sky, knots of Greek fighters stood around, some of them still singing the same stupid song they'd been singing for weeks: *"We're going, we're going, we are going HOME!"* Home. And what about us, the women of Troy and its satellite cities, where were we going? There were many women on the shore, hundreds; some of those who were holding little girls by the hand would be mourning the loss of their sons. Men and boys dead, women of child-bearing age shared out among the conquerors, some already pregnant with their children. What we were witnessing on that beach was the deliberate destruction of a people.

The long lines shuffled forward, a few feet at a time. Those at the front were being encouraged, by prods from the butt ends of spears, to wade into the sea and climb the rope ladders that dangled down the ships' swollen sides. I watched their uncertain progress and saw no comfort anywhere. It felt like the end of everything. *Was* the end. And then, suddenly, one of the women began to sing, though it was a while before I identified the singer. An old woman, past child-bearing age, had chosen to sing, not a song of defiance, but one of loss. A lament, but stoical rather than self-pitying. She gave a voice to those hundreds of silent women. You don't always need hope; sometimes it helps just to have your despair recognized, and shared.

Cassandra said, "Do you think he's ever coming back?"

Meaning the driver, I supposed. A minute later, she'd jumped down from the cart and was striding across the beach, looking straight ahead of her, neither to the right nor to the left, like a young warrior eager for battle to start. Lugging the heavy bag, I stumbled and floundered after her. As we got closer to the shore, I saw that a small group had gathered to wave me goodbye. These were women from other compounds whose kings were not yet ready to sail—and among them, my closest friend, Briseis, who'd already spotted me and, despite her pregnant belly, was jumping up and down and shouting, "Good luck!"—doing everything she could to urge me forward into my new life. But I didn't want a new life, I wanted the old life back. And I don't mean my previous existence as a freewoman in Lyrnessus; I'd long ago accepted the loss of that. No, I just wanted a few more months in the Greek camp, because then I'd still have *her*, and I'd be able to help her through the birth of her child. I stared long and hard at that little group of friends, though mainly at her, trying to fix this last sight of her in my mind so I'd have something to turn to in the blackest hours of the night when time just doesn't pass.

But Cassandra said, in a slightly prissy, bossy tone of voice, "Come on, Ritsa, don't dawdle, we've got to get on board."

Why did we? I couldn't think of a single reason, but it didn't rest with me. And so, long before I was ready, I had to turn my back on Briseis, who was like a second daughter to me, and face the sea and the ships.

Cassandra raced ahead. Slithering down the last steep slope of shingle, she dislodged an avalanche of pebbles that peppered in her wake. I followed her down more cautiously, telling myself, every time my right foot hit the ground: *last* time, *last* time, *last* time . . . I was desperately trying to nudge myself into feeling something, anything, but I couldn't. From the moment I turned my back on Briseis, every emotion seemed to dry up.

The ship we were about to board was easily the biggest in the cargo fleet, possibly the oldest and certainly not the best preserved. Why on earth was Agamemnon sailing home in this battered old sick bucket? *Medusa*, she was called. Fortunately, the figurehead was pointing out to sea—not that I had anything to fear from her gaze: I was already stone.

There was a gangplank. Nobody seriously expected Agamemnon to wade into the sea and scramble up a rope ladder, though presumably during his years as a fighter he'd done just that many times. But rumours were circulating about his health. In the last two months, he'd rarely been seen in public and when he did appear he kept his distance from the crowds. I hoped he was ill; I hoped he was dying, but I wasn't holding my breath. Even then, I'd lived long enough to see the wicked prosper, reach a ripe old age and die in their beds.

Cassandra *ran* up the gangplank—boldly, though I have to say, not gracefully. She wasn't a graceful woman, Cassandra. None of her movements was ever precisely the right movement and so, wherever she went, she left a trail of minor destruction behind her. I was forever picking up after her. On this occasion, just as she neared the top, she stumbled. I caught my breath, though she was never in any real danger—anonymous hands quickly reached out and pulled her on board. She was Agamemnon's . . . Well, what was she? Concubine, I suppose you'd have to say. Were there rumours of a secret wedding? I didn't know, and I didn't dare ask. But whichever way you looked at it, she was valuable cargo. You wouldn't want that landing in the drink on your watch.

Now, my turn. The bag of "special" clothes weighed a ton and I had the jewellery case clamped to my side.

"You can leave that with us, love," one of the sailors said. "We'll look after it."

Aye, bet you will. Dozens of boxes and bags were piled up round his feet. I added the clothes bag to the heap, but not the case—no way was I going to let go of that—and began to edge cautiously up the gangplank, trying not to look down at the waves rushing past beneath my feet. Two thirds of the way up, I wobbled to a halt, knowing I could never reach the top. My predicament was spotted by the sailors below—much to their amusement—and one of them bounded up the gangplank, nearly dislodging me in the process, planted both hands squarely on my arse and, to the accompaniment of ribald cheers from below, pushed me the last couple of yards onto the deck.

I was intact, even if my dignity wasn't—though I made everything worse by tripping over the hem of my tunic and falling flat on my face.

"Hey up, lass."

Calloused hands hauled me to my feet and dusted me down. My rescuer was saying something, but I was too flustered to take it in and thanked a blur of chest and red beard. All the same, even in that first moment, something snagged my memory. His voice? Somewhere or other, I'd heard that voice before, but it was only a fleeting impression, and he'd already moved on.

I stood for a moment, struggling to take in this strange new world. The deck was crowded with sailors; two were shovelling what looked like sheep shit off the boards, while others gathered by the rowing benches and rubbed chalk into their hands. Obviously, Agamemnon was expected on board at any minute. Everybody looked nervous. One young lad stood not far away from me, fingering a pipe, even raising it to his lips and giving a little, tentative *toot*. Apart from that, my overwhelming impression was of the stink of animals. There were sheep in a pen and a couple of small goats, tossing their heads from side to side, clanking their bells—a dolorous sound at the best of times, one that always reminded me powerfully of home, but especially so at that moment. I was a good sailor, a calm sailor, but I was frightened of this voyage. Listening to the goats' bleating, I felt in my own legs and belly the terror of the tilting deck.

Cassandra was standing in the stern, staring across the beach and the battlefield to the ruins of Troy. They say if you look back you turn to salt, but what else could she do? Her father and brothers, her baby nephew, were all buried in that soil. Glancing sideways, I saw she'd stuffed the edge of her veil into her mouth, perhaps to stop herself crying out loud, or cursing Agamemnon, whose procession was now winding its slow, glittering snail's trail along the shore. A splendid sight—or so it must have seemed to the Greeks. Blaring trumpets, battle horns, beating drums, sunlight flashing on helmets and spears and, high above, the red-and-gold standards of Mycenae straining in the wind. Right at the end of the procession came Agamemnon, marching in the shade of a huge square canopy; priests swinging censers walked ahead of him to sanctify his path.

I expected Cassandra to remain on deck to greet him, but she spat out the hem of her veil and turned away.

"Come on, let's see where they're putting us to sleep."

She called out a question to the man with the red beard, who indicated a low door on the opposite side of the deck. We had to bend nearly double to get through it. Blinded by the sudden gloom, we groped our way down a flight of stairs—it was a proper staircase, I was pleased to see, not just a glorified ladder—and into the deeper darkness beneath. A sweet, rather sickly smell with a stench of decay underneath, like the water in a vase where lilies have been left to rot. Even Cassandra, often so lost in her own thoughts she was oblivious to her surroundings, wrinkled her nose in disgust.

As my eyes adjusted to the light, I saw we stood in a long passageway with doors on either side. Voices shouted on the deck above us, but down here we might have been the last people left alive. The floor tilted and swayed—I was more aware of the ship's movement here than I had been on deck. We looked at each other, not knowing whether to press on or return to the deck and ask for more directions, but then a man came up behind us, holding a storm lantern whose shuddering light sent shadows fleeing along the walls.

"Hello, ladies," he said. "Lost, are we?"

"Yes," Cassandra said.

"Don't worry, we'll soon get you sorted out."

A wheedling, insinuating tone; this was a man who inspired instant distrust, but at least he seemed to know where he was going. So we followed him. About halfway down the passageway he pushed a door open and stood aside to let us past. Small, that was my first impression. Dingy was the second.

"I'll bring your bags and stuff down later."

Looking round, I said, "There's nowhere to put anything."

"There's pegs."

There were—two—on the back of the door.

"Look, I know it's a bit tight. When you get your things, just take out whatever it is you think you'll need and then give us a shout. The rest's got to go in the hold." He glanced at Cassandra. "Sorry, love, that's just the way it is." He pulled a bunch of candles from his tunic and handed them to me. "Go canny with 'em, mind. They're not cheap."

"Can't we have a lamp?" Cassandra asked.

"Sorry, love, Captain's orders."

Cassandra's face was a picture. This was probably the first time she'd been *sorry-loved* in her entire life.

Our guide was leaning against the door now, settling in for a chat. "See, if a candle's knocked over, nine times out of ten it's dead before it hits the deck. Whereas a lamp, now . . . that'll go on burning. Ship this age . . . Phuh, well, she's firewood, basically. Any little spark and *whoosh!*"

"If the ship's that dry," I said, "why does everything feel so damp?"

"Does it?"

"These blankets are virtually wet."

"She's an old lady, she leaks." He nodded over his shoulder. "Wind gets up, that passage is awash."

Cassandra said, "More to the point, how long will it take to get there?"

"Nobody can tell you that, love. Because everything depends on the wind. Case you haven't noticed, this is a *sailing* ship, because it's too bloody far to row."

"Two nights," I said. "With a following wind." I turned to him. "That's right, isn't it?"

"'Bout right."

By now, I was almost pushing him out of the door. It was a relief when that over-intimate, somehow slightly threatening voice was cut off.

With him gone, I looked more closely at the cabin. Water had gathered in puddles all over the rutted floor. There'd been no recent stormy weather, so perhaps that had been left behind after a last-minute attempt to clean the place up. The ceiling was low, too low to allow Cassandra to stand upright, so she paced up and down between the bunks like a predatory bird. I hoped she wouldn't go on pacing all night—it had been known. Even praying was better than that. What worried me wasn't so much the discomfort of damp blankets as the size of the place. The hut we'd shared had been cramped enough to get on her nerves and it was ten times bigger than this. But, give credit where it's due, she uttered not a word of complaint. After a minute or two, she sat down on the right-hand bunk and bounced a little, though you could see without testing that the mattress was lumpy and hard. Horsehair, I was guessing— possibly straw. She'd be sleeping on goose down, though, since she spent most of her nights in Agamemnon's bed.

After a moment's hesitation, I sat down on the other bunk. The space between us was so narrow our knees bumped awkwardly in the middle and I had to shuffle along.

"*Well*," she said.

She sounded amused rather than angry, and I realized all this must have seemed trivial to her. From the moment she'd arrived in the camp, she'd been prophesying Agamemnon's death, and her own. Yes, yes, I know: fantasies, wish fulfilment, a traumatized woman's delusory dreams of revenge. But the point is, *she* believed them, and they determined the way she reacted now. Why make a fuss about the size of your cabin? However narrow it is, it's likely to be wider than your grave. I probably minded the constriction more than she did.

And I did mind. The dim light and the smell of damp wool made me feel submerged. I knew we hadn't walked far to reach the cabin, really no distance at all, and yet in the semi-darkness I'd lost all sense of where we were; for all I knew, we might be below the waterline. Perhaps what lay on the other side of that mottled wall was not light and air, but mile upon mile of the grey, heaving, voracious sea. Not a comforting thought—particularly as some parts of the wall were cracked and flaking, resembling nothing so much as the hide of an ancient whale.

Cassandra stirred restlessly.

"You all right?" I asked.

"I'll be fine once we get going."

Somewhere above our heads a drum began to beat. Shouted orders, a slap of running feet, followed by a cacophony of pipes, whistles, trumpets, drums: Agamemnon coming on board. Cheers—formal, organized cheers—and then, after a short pause, footsteps coming along the passage outside. I heard Agamemnon's voice, affable, charming—oh yes, believe it or not, he could be charming!—followed by a different voice entirely: curt, brusque, self-consciously down-to-earth, a man forced to play the role of courtier and knowing it didn't suit him. Again, I felt I knew the voice; and it wasn't just the accent, though that was a large part of it. I thought I recognized that mixture of aggression and . . . I couldn't think of the right word, but there was something both prickly and vulnerable in that voice. A few seconds later, they'd gone past.

Almost immediately, there was a great rattling of chains as the anchor was raised. The drumbeat started again, more measured now, marking time as the rowers bent to their oars. I pictured the ship pulling slowly away from the shore, the blades dipping and rising. Cassandra and I looked at each other. We were leaving our homeland for the last time and simply as Trojans we shared the pain of that moment. The cabin felt very dark. She'd gone back to sucking her veil and that tore at my nerves. I'd rather she'd howled like a wolf that's seen her cubs killed, anything would have been easier to bear than that babyish clinging to a piece of saliva-stained cloth—which was making me feel helpless too. Perhaps I could persuade her to go on deck, to watch the land disappear, confront the reality of loss, but just as I was about to suggest it, the drumbeat stopped.

For a moment, the ship floundered—Cassandra's knuckles whitened as she gripped the side of her bunk—and then, above our heads, there were rhythmic cries of *heave! heave!* and a further rattling of chains as the sails were raised. This was it, we were leaving, and we'd never be able to go back.

2

The ship leapt forward and then, as it left the shelter of the bay, began to shoulder its way through heavy seas.

We'd hardly got used to the change in motion when there was a hammering on the door and our guide appeared, looking even more unprepossessing than I remembered. He wore his hair scraped back in a long, greasy ponytail, despite being very bald at the front of his head. He probably had a tough time of it since the Greeks pride themselves on their long, thick hair. Pale eyes, almost colourless in the dim light, darting here and there for opportunities of one kind or another. He pointed to Cassandra's boxes and pushed the biggest inside the cabin. "Ten minutes." He held up the fingers of both hands as he spoke, as if I might not know how to count. Typical Greek arrogance—they really do think of us as barbarians with barely sense enough to wipe our arses. "Not long enough," I said, and slammed the door.

Opening the box, I took out a richly embroidered dress—yellow, a colour Cassandra was fond of, though it didn't suit her—a couple of plainer, more serviceable tunics and a thick woollen shawl for walks on deck, and . . . ? What else was she likely to need? Further down, tucked away beneath a blue dress, was a linen bag containing her clean clouts. As I hung the bag on one of the hooks, I was doing mental arithmetic and I suppose the calculations must have shown on my face because Cassandra said sharply, "I'm not late."

"No." Seeing her face, I said it again. "No, of course not."

She was late. I knew that for a fact because it was my job to wash the clouts—but it never paid to contradict Cassandra, so I just got on with shaking out the creases in her tunics and hanging them on the back of the door. She'd been on her period when she arrived in the camp, and she definitely hadn't been since. Of course, in one way she was right: five, six weeks, it was nothing. Women in the camp, many of whom had witnessed the deaths of their sons and husbands, often went five or six months without a period. I've had many a girl come up to me crying her eyes out, begging and pleading for something to bring it away, and yet, when I examined her there was nothing there. On the other hand, a missed period isn't the only sign. I dressed and undressed Cassandra, bathed her, slept in the same bed: I knew how her breasts had changed.

Behind me, the silence went on curdling.

"You think I am, don't you?"

She was adept at reading people's thoughts. I've never known anybody do it better, before or since.

"You can't wear this," I said, running my fingers down the yellow dress from neck to hem. "It's damp."

"I'm wearing it."

"You'll catch your death . . ."

"I won't need to run very fast."

I hated the way she teased me about her bloody prophecy. She knew I didn't believe in it.

"I daresay you'll live as long as your mother. That's always the best guide."

Turning away, I tried to hang the shawl on top of the tunics, but it kept sliding off.

"You can give that to me."

She wrapped it around her head and shoulders, snuggling down into its sea-green folds—a colour, incidentally, that suited her far better than the saffron yellow of the dress. After I'd used all the available space—two hooks, for god's sake!—I dragged the box outside to await collection. Then, since Cassandra's eyes were closed, I lay down on my bunk, telling myself I mustn't go to sleep, though I was tired enough.

There was a new noise drifting down to the cabin from the deck above: the thrumming of the wind in the rigging. To me, it sounds like a mind at the end of its tether, as if the rigging ropes are nerves. I can hardly bear to listen to it, but cooped up as we were in that foetid little box, I had no choice. Was the sea getting rougher? I was aware of the ship's every movement, the laborious climb to the crest of a wave, the shuddering shock of its descent. Glancing across at the other bunk, I saw Cassandra had gone very white.

"You'd be better off on deck, you know. Get some air in your lungs."

"I can't, you know I can't. I've got to be ready in case he sends for me. Oh, and that reminds me, I'm going to need hot water for a bath."

Hot water? A bath? Apart from anything else, where did she think we were going to put the bath? Still, I got up at once, glad of any excuse to leave the cabin. Closing the door behind me, I saw that the boxes had been collected, though I hadn't heard anybody come for them. The passage was empty, nothing but a long, dark tunnel. I hesitated, not knowing which way to go, but then somebody opened the big double doors at the far end and a tall, broad-shouldered man came out. His face was in shadow, but when he turned I caught a glint of gold at his throat and in his hair. Agamemnon. Instinctively, I flattened myself against the wall. For a moment, he seemed to be looking straight at me, but then I realized he was peering beyond me into the darkness. I turned to follow the direction of his gaze, but I couldn't see anything, just more doors, more darkness. A man's voice called from the lighted room behind him and, after a quick, dismissive glance at me, he went inside and shut the door.

I was left alone with the murky light and the heaving floor. No railings to hang on to, but still, somehow, I had to find hot water, so using an arm to steady myself, I scuffed along the wall towards the double doors. A short passage led off to the right. As I hesitated, a door at the far end of it opened, belching steam, and an enormously fat man carrying a tray of cups emerged, his face slick with sweat.

"Oh, hello," he said.

"My mistress would like some hot water."

"Would she now?"

"And a bathtub."

"We've only got the one, and *he's* in that."

I repeated the request, trying to sound assertive, but it made no impression. "Tell her she can have a bucket of *warm* water in half an hour, same as every bugger else." Meanwhile, he said, I should go back to my cabin and lie down. "Wind's getting up—and you can see for yourself there's nowt to hang on to. Wouldn't want you breaking a leg now, would we?"

A wolfish grin. I suppose, to be fair, we none of us choose the length of our canines.

"Is that lamb?" I offered a placatory smile. (God, I despise myself sometimes.) "Smells nice . . ."

"You tuck in, love, because that wind's rising—can you hear it?—and there's nowt worse than chucking up on an empty stomach."

Defeated, I returned to the cabin to find Cassandra sitting on the side of her bunk.

"Hot water?"

"On its way."

I had no faith whatsoever in the arrival of water of any temperature, though I was wrong there. A bucket of reasonably warm water was delivered about thirty minutes later. I undressed her, washed her, began brushing her hair . . .

"I can't be."

It took me a second to grasp what she meant. "Well, you could . . ."

It didn't seem to occur to her that a young, healthy woman having sex every night was likely to get pregnant, that it might even be rather surprising if she didn't. Looking down at the sunless white of her neck, I felt a twinge of pity for her, for this clever, convoluted woman, this prophet, this seer, who'd somehow managed not to foresee what any fourteen-year-old scullery maid could have told her to expect.

"You know, if you told him you were pregnant, he might leave you alone."

"No, he wouldn't. And anyway, I'm not."

That was a stupid thing to say. I didn't even know that she wanted to be left alone. She hadn't chosen a celibate life; her mother had taken the decision for her. After weeks of enforced intimacy in the hut I'd felt I knew everything about Cassandra—only to realize as the state of "divine frenzy" receded that I knew almost nothing. Did she derive any pleasure from Agamemnon's pawing and groping? I found that hard to imagine. She never complained, but then she wouldn't, not to me. One of the surprising things about Cassandra, the virgin priestess, was how incredibly foul-mouthed she could be, how matter-of-fact about sexual practices you might think she'd never heard of. She'd told me once that her bedroom in the temple had overlooked an alley where prostitutes took their clients. Every night her maidenly prayers were interrupted by urgent demands on one side and hard bargaining on the other.

"It was no life for a priestess," she'd remarked, with one of her sudden returns to primness. "You could have asked to change rooms," I'd said. But as far as I know she never did. So, it had gone on: *How much for this? How much for that? What about . . . ?* She'd listened, she'd learned. And perhaps it wasn't such a bad preparation for Agamemnon's bed, after all. He liked to experiment, he liked games, he could be very, very rough. Many's the split lip I washed and patted dry—and on girls a lot younger than Cassandra. All the same, poor woman. No marriage, no sex, no children—a life spent poring over the stinking entrails of sacrificed birds looking for "signs." During all the years when other young women, her contemporaries, were giving birth to their babies, Cassandra was giving birth to a string of still-born prophecies—all of them true, according to her; not one of them believed.

"He kissed me," she'd said, meaning Apollo. "He kissed me on the lips to give me the gift of true prophecy, and then when I still wouldn't go to bed with him, he spat in my mouth to make sure I'd never be believed."

What was I supposed to make of that? Really, what was anybody supposed to make of that?

"Would it be such a terrible thing if you were pregnant?" I asked. "I mean, I'm not saying you are . . . But if it was a boy, you'd be safe." Safe, I meant, from being handed over to his men. During my time in the camp, more than one woman had been thrown out of his huts and left to fend for herself around the cooking fires. "Even if it's a girl, it's still his child." No response. I tried again. "You could have a life."

"What sort of life? Just thinking about it makes me feel sick— his brat sucking my tits like a bloody leech? No, thanks. You know when your friend Briseis came to see me? Do you remember? Well, I looked at her belly and I thought, *That's Achilles's child in there. He murdered her brothers, he murdered her husband—and there she is, carrying his baby.*"

"What choice did she have?"

"There's always choice! If it was me, I'd have got the biggest carving knife I could find and cut the bastard out of me."

I couldn't stomach her contempt for Briseis, who was kind and brave and honest—and, in my estimation, worth a hundred Cassandras. But there was no point getting into an argument about it. I picked up the brush and in stony silence finished doing her hair.

And not long after that, the striking of a gong announced that dinner was ready.

3

Cassandra wouldn't look at me, perhaps fearing that in criticizing Briseis she'd gone too far (she had). But no, I don't suppose for a moment she was worrying about that. I doubt if it even occurred to her that I had feelings that might be hurt. We'd started this voyage in a rancorous spirit, with Cassandra determined to keep me in my place, and, so far, there'd been no sign of softening on either side.

Anyway, whatever the cause of her silence, it soon passed. Within minutes of the gong sounding, she was striding along the passage as if she hadn't a care in the world. Of course, she was a priestess, and priestesses, unlike other women, have status, a public role, even a certain amount of power. When a priestess speaks, people listen, even men listen, if only because her voice is believed to be the voice of a god. You don't stick your fingers in your ears when Apollo speaks. So, obviously, she'd learned long since to disguise her doubts and fears—if she had any. What did she really feel walking along that passage to have dinner with Agamemnon? I had absolutely no idea. I certainly didn't expect to be going with her, but apparently, I was. It was unthinkable to Cassandra that she should appear in public without a maid to wait on her.

The room we entered was a blaze of light, dazzling after the gloom of the passage. Cassandra marched straight to the head of the table and sat down next to Agamemnon's empty chair. Immediately opposite, making a sketchy attempt to rise, was Machaon, the king's personal physician: my previous owner. Possibly still my owner. Nobody had ever bothered to explain the transaction to me. I wasn't even sure there'd been one. Perhaps I was just on permanent loan?

Once Cassandra was settled, I took up my position behind her chair. At unpredictable intervals, the floor tilted . . . I stood with my feet well apart, gripping the back of Cassandra's chair to brace myself against the movement. She'd taken a crust of bread from the basket in front of her and was nibbling the edges. Perhaps starting to feel sick? I certainly hoped so.

A minute later, the doors were thrown open and the man who'd scraped me off the deck came in. He stood on the threshold, his small, fierce, blue eyes blinking hard as he took the situation in, then set off to the head of the table, as confidently as Cassandra had done, only to check himself and take a chair further down, below Machaon. Again, he looked familiar—well, except for the beard. Pity about the bow legs—because without that, he'd have been a fine figure of a man. That phrase, popping unexpectedly into my head, brought my grandfather roaring back. *Fine figure of a man.* That was his usual tribute to men whose bearing he particularly admired, though fine figures of women were more to his personal taste. My poor grandmother, she had a hell of a lot to put up with, though, to be fair, she gave as good as she got—her *and* her sisters, all of them fine figures of women, and so straight-backed you'd think somebody had shoved a poker up their arses. Nobody messed with *them.* God knows what they thought of me: their catch-fart descendant.

The captain—and he was very obviously the captain; you could tell by the way he looked around the table—seemed to be unhappy with his situation. He was sitting with both hands spread out in front of him, the veins as blue as drowned worms. This was his ship, his room, his table—and king or no king, that place at the top was rightfully his. He certainly wasn't inclined to talk. Machaon did his best, and succeeded in extracting a name, at least. Andreas. I rolled it round and round my head hoping for echoes, but none came.

We waited, and the longer we waited, the more Agamemnon's empty chair dominated the room. The arms were carved with lions' heads—the lions of Mycenae—and the back, gleaming softly in the lamplight, was inlaid with ivory and gold. This chair went wherever he went, serving as a kind of mobile throne. From long association, it had acquired something of his power to intimidate. What could be keeping him? Machaon, who was on edge—I knew him well enough to know that—kept glancing at the cabin door. Once or twice, I thought he was about to stand up, go and check what was going on. Cassandra fixed her gaze on her plate; she was rolling a pellet of bread between her thumb and forefinger until, noticing how grey it had become, she gave a little disgusted *tsk* and flicked it away from her.

Finally, the cabin door opened and Agamemnon appeared. Everybody rose; I was already standing, of course, but instinctively switched my gaze to my feet out of some ridiculous notion that if you don't look you won't be seen. I felt his approach, though only a shadow darkening my lowered lids revealed that he'd arrived at the head of the table. Once there, he took his time, leaving everybody standing just long enough to remind them that he could, before settling himself into his chair and waving them to theirs.

Somebody must have been peeping round the door because immediately several young men carrying platters of roast meat erupted into the room. The smell made my stomach growl. I wouldn't be getting any of it, of course. A few scraps if I was lucky; I certainly wasn't counting on it—more like, a bowl of barley porridge tomorrow morning. My immediate problem was how to cut up Cassandra's meat without letting go of her chair. I wasn't managing very well, and I could tell she was getting irritated. And then, abruptly—no warning—Andreas let out a great roar. "For god's sake, woman, sit down. If there's one thing I cannot abide, it's *hovering.*"

I didn't know what to do.

"Go on, you heard me, SIT DOWN!"

Cassandra jerked her head to one side, indicating I should take a chair at the foot of the table. Feeling every eye on me, I sat down, opposite an empty chair and with another empty chair on my right. Andreas pushed the bread basket down towards me, a friendly gesture for which I was grateful, though I didn't think I'd be able to eat anything. But the conversation started up again and gradually I relaxed. When, a few minutes later, a plate of food and a cup of wine were set down in front of me, I couldn't believe my luck.

Slowly, I took stock. I was sitting next to Andreas, on the captain's right hand, no less, and I remembered from the voyages I'd done with my husband what a position of honour that was. No wonder Cassandra looked as if the next mouthful would choke her. Not that Andreas was exactly a comfortable neighbour; he seemed out of sorts with everybody there and most of all with himself. I got the impression he despised us, not personally, perhaps—more a seaman's genial contempt for landlubbers—and yet, at the same time, he was feeling overawed by his company and furious with himself for being overawed. All this combined to produce a manner alternately arrogant and obsequious. More than once he spoke sharply to the servers, who were admittedly a clumsy bunch, but then they weren't trained for this, they were sailors. You could see that in the way they effortlessly adjusted to the ship's pitches and rolls, while we held on to the table, which, being nailed to the floor, was the one fixed point in a gyrating world.

After a while, the pace of eating slowed, though the drinking never faltered. Now we were merely picking at our food, the silences became more awkward. Once, the double doors crashed open and we all looked up, expecting to see a server come in, but there was only a blast of colder air from the passage outside. We could hear the wind howling through the rigging.

"Whoa," Machaon said. "That's getting up a bit."

"Yeah, we're in for a blow, I'm afraid," Andreas said. And then, unable to restrain himself a minute longer: "You'd all be better off in your bunks."

"By a blow, do you mean a storm?"

"Kind of."

"There won't be a storm," Cassandra said.

Andreas switched his attention to her. "You know that for a fact, do you?" You could tell he wasn't used to being contradicted by a young woman, not on any subject, least of all on the prospect of a storm at sea. "Just as a matter of interest, what do you think that is?" He nodded at the open door and the howling of the wind.

"Lord Agamemnon will have a swift and safe voyage home." She was speaking in a Daddy's-little-girl voice, the kind that some men find mysteriously attractive and makes every woman within earshot want to slap you. "The gods require it."

"Well, I don't know much about the gods, love, but I do know a fair bit about the sea and I'm telling you we're in for a bloody rough night and you'd all be better off in your beds."

Cassandra ignored him, leaning towards Agamemnon, whispering, almost crooning—how the gods favoured him, how he and he alone of all the kings would be granted a safe passage home. All the others, without exception, would face the most terrible dangers. Ajax was already dead, his ship splintered on the rocks. A devouring sea monster waited for Idomeneus. And as for Odysseus, shining Odysseus, the cleverest of them all, he would descend into Hades and while he still lived and breathed walk among the heroic dead.

Agamemnon, as credulous as a little boy, was drinking it all in. "Who does he see?"

For the first time, Cassandra seemed to hesitate. "Well, Achilles, of course, and Patroclus, and Ajax—both Ajaxes—oh, and his own mother. You know, she died while he was at Troy? And . . . and I can't see any of the other faces," she said, her gaze fixed on Agamemnon's face. "It's dark down there, you wouldn't believe how dark, darker than any moonless night on earth."

"But he does get out?"

"Oh yes, he gets out, though his troubles aren't over even then. He's still got to sail between Scylla and Charybdis. Oh, and then he orders his men to tie him to the mast so he can hear the song the sirens sing—"

"What do they sing?"

Machaon muttered, "A load of bollocks, I expect."

"Don't mind him," Agamemnon said, quickly. "He doesn't believe in anything, he's famous for it."

They were looking at Machaon, laughing—the two of them, together. Agamemnon pulled her closer, so close she collapsed, giggling, against his chest. More than once, she'd told me she couldn't tell lies, that this was part of Apollo's curse, but she was lying now and lying well. The collapse was a lie, the giggling was a lie, even her contempt for Machaon was a lie. She didn't despise Machaon; she feared him. Straightening up, she smiled directly at him. "You might think because the sirens are women with naked breasts that they must be singing about love. But it's nothing to do with love. They're singing about Troy, that's what draws men to their doom. Because nobody who fought at Troy will ever manage to forget it."

An awkward pause, but they recovered quickly. Agamemnon was drinking heavily, but then he always did. He seemed to be all right talking and laughing about things that had happened during the war. Cassandra was hanging on his every word, saying just enough to prompt the next story, the next boast. He was stroking her arm.

Once or twice, I thought I saw her start to pull away, but she always checked herself and, within seconds, was smiling again.

Only then, gradually, as the evening wore on, as more jugs of wine were produced and drunk, Agamemnon's mood darkened. He kept glancing in my direction, not looking directly at me—thank god!—but at the wall behind me. I wanted to look over my shoulder, but didn't dare. Away from the table, where lamps basked in pools of golden light, the room was dark and crawling with shadows. Suddenly, Agamemnon fixed his bleary eyes on Andreas. "I'm surprised you allow women on board."

"Women? There's no women on board this ship, Sir—except for the two ladies here."

Two ladies? Cassandra must be loving this.

"What do you mean, *no women?* I saw one in the passage just now."

"Be one of the kitchen lads, Sir."

"I'm telling you I saw a woman. Good god, man, do you think I don't know the difference?"

But he looked suddenly unsure of himself, even confused. There was no sound in the room, except for our jaws munching apples— rather wormy apples, I have to say, though sweet. Agamemnon pushed his plate away, took a gulp of wine, or rather tried to—the hand raising the cup to his lips meandered and lost its way. None of us spoke, because nobody could think of anything to say. Small incidents became shocking. A jug got knocked over and rolled from side to side, spewing red wine across the table until one of the servers had the wit to grab it, mopping up the spillage with the white cloth he wore around his waist. Agamemnon ignored the incident; I doubt he was even aware of it. He was peering into the shadows behind my chair, now and then darting a surreptitious glance at Machaon, as if expecting him to comment. *There, did you see that?*

The words remained unspoken, though every one of us heard them. Machaon stared stolidly at his plate. As did I, though it was harder and harder to ignore the prickling in my scalp.

At last, Agamemnon burst out, "So what do you call that, then? I suppose *that's* a boy, is it?"

"What, Sir?"

"*That.*"

Andreas twisted to look behind him.

"Don't tell me you can't see her."

"I don't see anything, Sir."

"Then you're either a liar or blind."

Andreas looked affronted. I got the feeling you could say pretty much anything you liked to him, but call him a liar . . . ? *No.* He sat back in his chair and folded his arms. Agamemnon looked around the table, from one face to the next, reading in our carefully blank expressions that we couldn't see anything either.

Bewildered, he turned to Machaon, who slid a hand under his elbow. "I think we're done here," he said, quietly.

Cassandra pushed her chair back. Agamemnon looked up at Machaon and, obediently, like a small child, stood up. Andreas and I scrambled to our feet, bowing deeply, as Agamemnon, supported by Machaon and followed by Cassandra, stumbled across the room.

At the last moment, Cassandra glanced back at me and then she turned and followed them into the cabin, letting the door swing shut behind her.

4

Immediately, Andreas raised his hands to the skies. "Thank you, gods!" Flinging himself back into his chair, he turned to look at me. "I thought that was never going to end." He picked up the jug and held it out to me, but I covered my cup. "Fuck's sake, woman, have a drink!"

"Aye, go on then." I watched him pour, took a long, deep, satisfying gulp and wiped away what I suspected might be a red moustache. Looking up, I saw him watching me. "It's not often I get the chance."

"No need to justify yourself to me, love. If anybody deserves a drink, you do." He leaned closer. "What's the matter with him?"

"I don't know."

"Well, something is."

I should have pulled him up on that, advised him to keep quiet, though I don't suppose he'd have listened if I had. Even when he'd been speaking directly to Agamemnon, the words had been deferential enough, but his colour had risen. Oh, he was a right little bantam cock, this one—he'd take anybody on. But people who took Agamemnon on didn't usually survive.

He was grinning. "Can't place me, can you?"

"I know I know you."

"The *Artemis*?"

Just the name was enough: it all came flooding back. "Oh my god, yes." I tapped my chin to indicate his beard. "You didn't have that then."

"I was fourteen!"

"Eeh, it's not that long ago, is it?"

"Bloody is."

"I wasn't long married, I know that. It was your voice I remembered."

"That's a first. Generally it's me legs."

Behind the casual words, a lifetime of pain, of always making sure he got his joke in first.

"No, it was your voice. The minute you scraped me off the deck, I thought: *I know that man.* Mind, that's going back a long way."

"Now when a woman says—"

"Aye, I know, she's fishing for compliments. Well, save your breath, lad. I'm under no illusions. Must be, what . . . thirty years?"

"More."

"You used to play dice with my husband."

"I did—and he beat me every single time. Though to be fair, we did talk as well. Wasn't all gambling and drinking."

It was all coming back to me. A cripplingly shy lad, so bad he was almost mute, always blushing, covered in spots—even his spots had spots—and bullied unmercifully, of course, mainly about his legs, but not just that. It was so easy to get a rise out of him, the other lads just couldn't resist. Those games of dice after dinner had probably been the only peaceful part of his day. Mixed in with jokes and loud accusations of cheating, my husband had slipped in a bit of good advice. And all this at the end of a hard day, sometimes, but that was Galen all over: kind-hearted almost to a fault. Too soft to make backsides of, my mother used to say, but then she was a hard woman, my mother; nobody could have made a backside out of her.

"He was a good man, your husband."

"He was."

Strange how grief pounces on you when you're least expecting it—sometimes, years later. Suddenly, I was choked. Andreas reached out and touched my arm, which was nice of him, even if it did set me off howling fifty times worse than before. He waited patiently while I sobbed and sniffled and hiccupped my way back to some sort of composure.

"Good man. And a good healer."

That might have set me off again, if he hadn't added, "He worked miracles with my piles. That cream he give me shrank them right down. Mind you, he always said—I remember him saying it, you were stood not five feet away—he said, 'One of these days she'll be better than me.'"

"What, a better healer? Oh, I don't think I could claim that."

"That's what he said."

At that moment the door to Agamemnon's cabin opened and Machaon came out. Within seconds, Andreas was on his feet. "Aye, well, better be off."

He nodded to Machaon, bowed to me and slipped out of the room. Unlike everybody else, he was careful to close it behind him.

Machaon had slumped into his chair. I poured a cup of wine and set it down in front of him. We sat in silence for some time—not that being silent with Machaon ever bothered me, I was used to it. Most evenings, after a long and often distressing day in the hospital tent, he'd fetch a jug of wine and we'd sit together at the workbench, looking out over rows and rows of cowhide beds. Some men, the lucky ones, fast asleep, others wide awake, tossing and turning, a few crying out in pain. Very little was said on those evenings, sometimes nothing at all, but still, I took comfort in his presence. I suppose that sounds strange, given that I was a Trojan woman, a slave, and he was my Greek owner, but that didn't feel odd to me because, crucially, we were both healers. Rather naively, I suppose, I thought that mattered.

Machaon had asked for me as his prize of honour because I had a reputation and he thought I'd be useful to him in the hospital. And I was. I was useful. Admittedly, when I started, I knew next to nothing about war wounds, but I knew a lot about fevers, infection, pain relief. As for the men's injuries, when he saw I was eager to learn he put an enormous amount of effort into teaching me. And he had one or two surprising tricks up his sleeve. *Machaon's little helpers.* They were one of them. I remember the day he brought some in; he opened the box and there they were: a seething, wriggling, writhing mass of maggots. We had a man whose left leg had been amputated; somehow, thanks to Machaon's phenomenal speed and dexterity, he'd survived, but the stump was a mess. Machaon sprinkled his "helpers" onto a poultice and tied it into position. I must have looked slightly sceptical because he laughed. "Just wait, you'll see."

He was right. The maggots went in thin, they came out fat—and the wound was noticeably healthier. Oh, he was good, Machaon, better than good—and he cared. Last thing at night, first thing in the morning, always there, always sharp—sharp as a sea eagle's talons, I used to think—and it didn't seem to matter how much he drank. He was kind to me. I always felt he was on my side, and I needed that, because it wasn't easy working in that hospital, a Trojan woman dealing with young Greek men, hurting them, when they were already in pain. I had to do saline irrigations twice a day and, honestly, they are not pleasant. I remember one lad in particular— *very* young, I doubt he was sixteen—in severe pain, and frightened, and ashamed of being frightened, and, of course, trying to cover it all up by acting big in front of his mates. He gave me a really hard time, until one day Machaon came up behind him, witnessed some of his cockiness and cuffed him, very gently, on the back of the head. "Hey you, wash your mouth out, this lady's trying to help you."

"*Lady!*"

Machaon raised a finger. "*No.*"

Nothing more, just one word, but I didn't have a bit of bother with him after that.

So now, when I think about Machaon, and I often do, I try to remember how much I owe him. I wish that was the whole story, but it's not.

In those early days, before I got a bed in one of Agamemnon's weaving sheds, I used to sleep in the storeroom, surrounded by sacks of roots and tubers. My "bed" was three empty sacks spread along the floor, close to the wall. I'd filched a few burned-down candles from the hospital and at night I arranged them in a protective semicircle around me, their tapers protruding black and fragile from slippages of melted wax. Sleep never came easily, no matter how exhausted I was. The minute I closed my eyes, my mind flooded with images from the fall of Lyrnessus, sounds too: Achilles's war cry ringing round the walls, blood on the white stones of the marketplace where I used to shop, the slop and slap of cold seawater in my groin as we were forced to board their ships—behind us, a red wall of flames roaring into the night sky as our houses burned. Sometimes, right on the edge of sleep, I'd be jerked awake by the sound of the battering ram splintering the city gates—and I don't mean the *memory* of that sound, I mean the sound itself, there, in the storeroom, a few feet away from me. Whenever that happened, it took a long time to settle myself down again. I used to soothe myself by reciting the names of herbs and other medicinal plants. Perhaps I'd have done better praying to the gods, but they seemed a long way away. The herbs, I could touch and smell.

I don't know what happened next. Or rather, I know exactly what happened next—but I can't understand it. And I won't try.

Machaon had a girl who lived in his hut. I used to see her some-times: very young, pale, a moist mushroom bloom on her skin and a habit of blinking hard—perhaps shutting out sights she didn't want to remember. Anyway, for whatever reason—perhaps she was ill, perhaps she was on her period, I don't know—she wasn't available that night and so, after hours of carousing at Agamemnon's table, shouts, laughter, singing, you could hear them all over the camp, there, in the storeroom, suddenly: Machaon. My protective half-circle of candles had long gone out, but he brought a lantern in with him and set it down on the floor. I sat up on the soil-smelling sacks, shielding my eyes against the light, thinking, I suppose, if I thought at all, that a particularly badly wounded patient who'd been brought in that afternoon must have taken a turn for the worse.

What hurt—and, to be honest, still hurts, even after all these years—was that he did it doggy fashion, and I knew he was doing it like that so he wouldn't have to look at my face. I say "to be hon-est" but it's laughable really, because I've never managed to be honest about that night, never told anybody about it, even. And in one way there was nothing to tell. Every woman in that camp had been raped. I just tried to blot it out, and most of the time I succeeded. So it was a surprise, that first night on board the *Medusa*, that the memory should come back to me so vividly. I kept looking at Machaon's hands, at the sparse, black hairs on the backs of his fingers, thinking: *Why now?* Looking back, I can see that was the moment when things began to change.

We might have gone on sitting in silence for an hour or more if the sea hadn't intervened, but just then a particularly alarming lurch had us clutching the edge of the table. It soon passed; Machaon went back to swishing wine around his cup, but I could see him listening intently and, sure enough, a snorting noise came from behind the cabin door.

"Has he had his sleeping draught?" I asked.

"Yes, but they don't work as well as they used to."

I'd been hoping I might be able to go back to our cabin and snatch a few hours' sleep, but then Agamemnon cried out, and the cry was followed by more snorting—the sound people make when they're trying to escape from a nightmare. Next came Cassandra's voice, murmuring something reassuring, or so I assumed—I couldn't make out the words. Machaon had crossed the room and was unashamedly listening outside the door, though after a few minutes he came back, managing to walk in a more or less straight line until the tilting deck caught him off balance and threw him hard against the table.

"You all right?"

He sat down, flexing his wrist. "Just about. Looks like Andreas was right about the storm."

The ship was making all kinds of noises: creaks, whistles, bangs, crashes, groans. The groans sounded almost human and for some reason the strangeness of that freed my tongue. "Who does Agamemnon see?"

"He doesn't *see* anybody!"

That was a snarl. I went very quiet.

A second later: "I can tell you who he *thinks* he sees. He thinks he sees his daughter. Iphigenia."

He glanced at me, perhaps wondering if he needed to explain. He didn't. Along with probably a few hundred thousand other people, I can tell you exactly where I was when I heard the news of Iphigenia's death: Lyrnessus, the marketplace, queuing for bread on a bright, cold morning with black shadows knife-sharp on white flagstones and vicious little gusts of wind blowing grit into my eyes and sand-blasting every inch of exposed skin. My stomach had rumbled whenever the smell of freshly baked cinnamon buns drifted to the back of the queue. Several places in front of me, a big, gobby woman with pendulous breasts and blue, bulging eyes had been telling anybody who cared to listen that Agamemnon had sacrificed his daughter—*his own daughter*, mind you—to get a fair wind for Troy.

As she spoke, a murmur of unease travelled from the front to the back of the queue, like a shiver running down our collective spine. Everybody knew that ships from all over Greece—more than a thousand, some people said—had gathered at Aulis, ready to invade Troy. But the wind was against them; they were stuck on the beach, waiting for it to change. Our priests said the reason the Greeks couldn't get a wind was because their cause was unjust. They were being punished by the gods—and, if half of what we heard was true, it did sound a bit like a punishment: drinking water running out, latrines overflowing, fever spreading through the camp—and the kings quarrelling and threatening to take their ships home. Not that there was anything unusual in that. We had a saying in Lyrnessus: put two Greeks in a room, you've got a quarrel; one on his own is an argument. At the beginning I don't remember anybody being frightened. Somehow, despite the size of the army massing against us, it had never really felt like war. Were they really going to fight and die to give that whore Helen back to her fool of a husband? Oh, they might set fire to a few isolated farmhouses up and down the coast, burn crops, steal cattle—but they did all that anyway, bloody pirates.

Only now, out of the mouth of that gobby woman, one stark, undeniable fact: Agamemnon had sacrificed his own daughter to get a fair wind for Troy. That's when the fear started. You could almost hear people thinking: *If he's done that, what else is he prepared to do?* That was the moment when the city gates, the high stone walls that had protected us all our lives, started to seem fragile, insubstantial.

My own daughter, Ione, had been waiting for me at home. "I haven't got any," I said, dumping my bag on the table. "They've put their prices up again—I can't afford it."

She was already rooting about in the bag. "Got them!" She waved the cinnamon buns under my nose. "Can I have one?"

"No, you'll spoil your appetite. Oh, all right, go on, but just the one, mind."

Only a few days after that, she caught the sweating sickness: alive and well when I set off to see a patient who lived on the other side of the city; dead by the time I got back. And ever afterwards the deaths of those two girls, the young Greek princess and my own dear daughter, had been inextricably linked in my mind, along with a gritty wind and the smell of cinnamon buns.

"It's all he ever talks about."

I'd been so lost in memory that, for a second, I couldn't understand what Machaon was saying.

"Iphigenia. It's like the last ten years never happened. All that suffering. All those deaths. Somehow, it just seems to have *shrunk*." He brought his forefingers closer together, till there was no space between. "I lost friends, good friends. We all did."

Some of us lost everything.

"Oh, I wouldn't worry too much, I expect he's just frightened of his wife."

"*Frightened? Of his wife?*"

"Well, she's hardly going to jump for joy at the sight of him, is she?"

"She'll jump if he tells her to!"

Pure reflex that, an automatic assertion of the rights of men, of husbands and of fathers: as instinctive and uncompromising as a clenched fist. After a little while, he went on, more gently: "Remember, she's had ten years to get over it—and she has other children. A son, another daughter. She'll have put it behind her."

Like hell she would. For once, I felt my authority more than equal to his. I tried to imagine Clytemnestra waiting inside the palace for her husband's return and it was surprisingly difficult. I conjured up a tall, stately figure, diamonds flashing in her ears and at her throat, all the trappings of royal status, but the face was a perfectly smooth oval, no eyes, no mouth, no nose. Instead, what flitted into my mind was a fat-bellied spider sitting at the centre of her web, all eight feet alert for the vibration of a fly landing.

I realized Machaon was waiting for me to speak. When I remained silent, he said, "Ah well, I think I might turn in, see if I can get some sleep. I've a feeling I might be up again before dawn."

He finished his wine, wiped his mouth delicately on his napkin and set off for the door. I say "set off" because the ship was now rocking so badly that even the shortest trip was hazardous. With one hand safely on the latch, he turned to look back. "You know, people say she went to her death willingly—they say in the end she sacrificed herself for the honour of her family. It's not true. She fought them every step of the way. They had to gag her in the end, they were so frightened she'd curse him with her last breath. Though even with the gag in you could still make out some of the words. 'Father,' she kept saying—and then, right at the end, she—"

There he stood, stuttering to get the words out, a man who never hesitated over anything.

"She s-said . . . *D-Daddy.*" A supreme effort. "*Daddy.*"

He ducked his head, an odd little movement, like somebody dodging a blow, and then he went out into the night.

Left alone with the groaning of the ship, I stared at a litter of empty cups, greasy plates, crusts of bread, scraps of meat curling at the edges and islanded in fat—and it all looked like the wreckage of so much more than a meal. Spreading my arms wide, I swept the whole lot off the table and on to the floor. One second of glorious relief, followed immediately by terror, as a big jug spewing wine began to roll backwards and forwards across the floor, making, to my ears at least, enough noise to wake the dead. I lunged at it, but it slipped out of my fingers and skittered out of reach. In reaching out to grab it, I landed on the floor too and waited, heart pounding, for Agamemnon to erupt from his cabin and demand to know what was going on. Or, worse in some ways, Cassandra. She might possibly believe the storm had caused this devastation, but not if she found me sitting on my fat arse in the middle of it.

With one last, terrified glance at the bedroom door, I struggled to my feet and fled.

5

Cassandra jerks awake and lies staring into the darkness, trying to identify the noise that woke her, but all she can hear is the creaking of the ship's arthritic joints. Poor old *Medusa*. She's so inconceivably ancient, it's easy to imagine her breaking up altogether, seawater flooding down the passage into this room. Years from now, their bones, hers and Agamemnon's, jumbled together, will be picked over by shoals of curious fish. She tries briefly to give these pictures the authority of a vision, but it's no use: they're nothing like. That's not how their story ends.

Something woke her. She can't get up to investigate, because Agamemnon's fallen asleep on top of her, as he often does. Wriggling, she manages to free the fingers of one hand, but even that slight movement causes him to stir and smack his lips before sinking back to sleep. She waits, tries again, this time gets a whole hand free and begins to explore, a mouse venturing out into the vastness of night. All she can see are purple and orange flashes on the inside of her lids, but they're not real, they're not like this patch of bedsheet she's managed to recover—that's real, that's outside herself. Real, unreal; inner, outer—always debatable land to her. She can only marvel at the lives of others for whom these are clearly established, undisputed borders.

And Agamemnon? How does he experience these things? Is he

secure in the world of touch and smell? Lying underneath him in the dark, his fuck-sweat clammy on her skin, she finds it difficult to credit him with any kind of inner life, but he obviously has one. He sees his dead daughter. What's that if not a disputed boundary? His cum's tightening on her thigh. *Is* she pregnant? No, she can't think like that: a baby's a future and there is no future. Dare she risk trying to reclaim another inch? No, not yet. He's a light sleeper—you mightn't think so, with all the snoring and snorting and gagging that goes on, but he is. And this bed, which looks so narrow in the lamplight, in the darkness becomes as vast and wide as the windswept plains of Troy. Often, she'd stood on the battlements by her father's side, to watch the day's fighting. There was always something hideous in the proximity of the city to the battlefield: women watched their sons and husbands die; old men watched their sons and grandsons fall and rise no more. Of course, they could have spared themselves the suffering by staying away, but who could resist the fleeting glimpse, the face turned towards you for the last time before it vanished for ever? And she, who had neither husband nor son, followed her brothers' plumed helmets across the field, day after day, year after year, as one by one they fell. She'd known, to the day, to the hour, when Hector's appointed time had come.

No, you didn't know, her mother's voice says. *How could you possibly know?*

I did know. It's true, she did. She saw Achilles standing there, glittering like a god, and she knew. After the fight, he'd strapped Hector's body to his chariot wheels and dragged it three times around the walls of Troy until there was nothing left of the man they'd known and loved—just a bloody lump of flayed skin and splintered bone.

Oh, thanks for reminding me. I was on the battlements too, you know? I saw all that.

She's fully present now, as real as Agamemnon, indeed slightly more real since, unlike him, she's visible. Straight from the black night of Hades, the lesser darkness of the upper world has no power over her. There she sits—though it's by no means obvious what she's sitting on—white-haired, haggard, her face as old as the walls of Troy and at least twice as hard.

Why is it always you who comes?

Oh, I've no doubt you'd rather see your father.

He was always kind.

And I wasn't?

You sent me away. I never wanted to be a priestess.

No, but you made the best of it. The fact is, it suited you. Everybody hanging on your words. Of course, it helps if you can tell a good story. Oh, yours was good: Apollo kissed you to give you the gift of true prophecy and, when you still wouldn't sleep with him, spat in your mouth to make sure you'd never be believed.

Which bit of the story don't you believe?

All of it!

You don't want to believe I'm a seer, do you? Because that makes you a hen that's hatched an eagle.

Oh, I'm a hen now, am I? Good god, listen to the woman.

Her mother sits there, sucking her gums and sulking.

Ritsa says I'm pregnant.

Pregnant? By him? My god, girl, you've fallen on your feet.

He's going to die, Mother.

You think far too much about death.

Difficult not to, talking to your mother's ghost.

Who says I'm a ghost?

I don't know what else . . .

But she's gone. Infuriating, as always, leaving an unanswered question behind her, because what else can she possibly be, if not a ghost?

The voice in your head that won't be silenced, the voice that sneers: Of course you're not a seer. You're just a nasty little girl who wets the bed and tells lies. That's what your prophecies are. Lies, lies, lies.

She tries to wrench herself out from under Agamemnon's sweating body, but his powerful arm reaches over and falls across her chest. All that painfully regained territory gone in an instant. His sweat's changed too: it's fear-sweat now, which has its own distinctive smell. He'd be ashamed if he knew. His arms are flailing, his fist pummelling the mattress, and then, although nothing else about him changes, she knows he's awake. His hands move up and down her body, though not in lust; he's simply trying to identify this strange object he's found lying beside him in the bed. Abruptly, the exploration stops; she feels the mattress sag and lift as he gets out of bed.

She hears him go into the room next door—for more wine? When he comes back, he's holding a candlestick, the candle burned right down, its flame barely surviving in a pool of melted wax. Lit from below, his face is a mask. He brings the guttering flame close to her face, but his hand's shaking so badly he tilts the candlestick and hot wax spatters over her neck and breasts. His mouth gapes as he tries to make sense of what he's seeing. Then he starts batting her away—not hitting her, it's more like somebody trying to rid himself of a stinging insect. "Go away," he's saying. "Leave me alone. Go back to where you came from. You don't belong here now."

"I belong here with you," Cassandra says.

"No." He lashes out, looks surprised when his clenched fist connects with bone.

And then he's banging on the wall, shouting for Machaon, like a small boy calling for his father in the dark.

6

I woke to the sound of hammering. It took me a moment to realize
it was coming from the passageway, rather than from inside my own
head. But then I heard Cassandra's voice, high-pitched and agitated,
followed by a disgruntled male rumble: Machaon. Grabbing my
shawl, I looked out and there they were, illuminated by the lamp
Cassandra was carrying, her face white and peaky under a mess of
tangled hair, Machaon sweaty and bleary, struggling to suppress a
yawn.

"I can't do anything with him," she was saying. "He doesn't seem
to know who I am."

I shrank back into the shadows, hoping she wouldn't notice me,
but as they walked past, she glanced over her shoulder. "Ritsa. With
me." At the dining-room door, she handed me the lamp and told
me to go round lighting other lamps, which of course I did, though
each fresh pool of light merely served to reveal the chaos. Cassandra
kicked a platter to one side. "What's all this?"

"Be the storm, I expect," Machaon said. "You know, the one we
weren't going to have?"

"Can't have been the storm."

"It did get quite rough," I said.

Cassandra sank into a chair by the table and, after a moment's
hesitation, I joined her.

"He was asleep," she said. "I thought he'd be all right . . . well, for a bit, anyway. I thought I could close my eyes. I must have nodded off because suddenly there he was, holding a candle up to my face. I think something must have startled him, because he jerked the candlestick and the hot wax . . ." She looked down at her chest, which was splattered with grey, dirty-looking discs. "And then he said, oh, I can't remember what he said, something about going back to where I came from. I thought, *Does he mean Troy?* But I can't go back, there's nothing left."

"He means Hades," Machaon said. "Don't worry, I'll deal with it."

With no more than a cursory knock, he opened the cabin door and went in. I caught a brief glimpse of a naked old man with straggly hair sitting on the edge of a bed, and then the door closed.

"He really didn't know it was you?" I asked.

"Worse than that, he thought I was somebody else."

"Who?"

Instantly, I regretted asking the question, because it seemed to bring Iphigenia closer, though Cassandra ignored me anyway so perhaps it didn't matter. Now we were alone, she unfastened her nightgown and began to examine her breasts, finding more blobs of wax and peeling them off—slowly, at first, but the search became more and more frantic until she was clawing at her skin, her nails doing far more damage than the wax had done. At last, unable to bear it any longer, I caught and held her hands.

Defeated, she said, "You know who. Everybody knows."

An exaggeration, I thought. Machaon knew, I knew, Andreas probably knew. Nobody else, or nobody who mattered. This was why Agamemnon was sailing home on a clapped-out cargo ship, attended solely by his personal physician, rather than on a warship surrounded by senior aides, priests and counsellors. Machaon was protecting his patient, his king, from those who might be tempted to use his current state of mind against him.

Cassandra was breathing normally again. Letting go of her hands, I said, "I know who he *thinks* he sees . . ."

"He doesn't *think* he sees her, he *sees* her! For god's sake, Ritsa, look at his eyes—they're focused. They're focused on something the rest of us don't see. You can say, *Yes, but she isn't real*, you can say that if you want to, but what you can't say is that he doesn't see her, because he transparently, bloody obviously does."

"So, what is it then? Guilt?"

She shrugged. "I don't think he feels guilt." She went back to peeling off discs of wax, but more calmly now, rolling each of them between her thumb and forefinger before flicking it on to the floor. "Fear, perhaps?"

As she turned her head to one side, I noticed an abrasion on her cheekbone and thought, *That's going to bruise*, but she didn't mention it, so neither did I.

There were raised voices behind the cabin door, Agamemnon insisting on another sleeping draught, Machaon advising against. There could be only one winner of that argument, and it would be bad news for all of us if Machaon's influence over Agamemnon started to wane. I made to speak, but Cassandra raised her hand, listening intently.

Agamemnon: "I know who she is, she's—"

"She's Cassandra," Machaon said, firmly. "The daughter of Priam." He might have been talking to a frightened child. "Look, she's just outside. Why don't you come and say hello? She's worried about you."

No reply, but a minute or so later the door opened and Agamemnon came out. Seeing him, my first thought was: *My god, you're a walking wreck.* He hobbled across to his chair and sat down, letting his robe fall open to reveal a sagging, thick-veined scrotum. He made no move to cover himself, but then the Greek attitude to nudity—to male nudity, at any rate—is totally different from ours. Though looking at Agamemnon's balls, I thought our attitude had a lot to recommend it. Cassandra was staring down at the backs of her hands, but Agamemnon seized her shoulders and pulled her round to face him. The question he would never let himself ask hung in the air between them. She met his gaze, steadily. "I'm Cassandra, Priam's daughter—"

He nodded. It may have been the flickering lamplight, the net of shadows it cast across his face, but I didn't think he looked at all convinced.

Machaon poured a cup of wine, added a sleeping draught and handed it to him. "Just the one now."

Agamemnon reached out a trembling hand and drank. I wondered, not for the first time, what was in the draught; I could name all the herbs and roots—the basic mixture was one I routinely made myself—and opium would be in there too, of course. And, possibly, something else? It was the something else that interested me; normally Machaon was generous in sharing his knowledge, but he hadn't shared this. Whatever it was, Agamemnon couldn't get enough of it—and Machaon was right, it wasn't working as well as it used to do. Though the immediate effects were impressive: Agamemnon sat up straighter, seemed altogether more relaxed. After a while, tentatively, he touched Cassandra's hand, but it was Machaon he spoke to.

"I did what I had to do."

"I know. I was there."

Agamemnon nodded. "Yes, you were there."

Such a short exchange, yet I felt a great deal had been said. Waning influence? Not a chance. Like everybody else who'd fought at Troy, these two were bound together by ropes of blood.

Agamemnon was still looking rather uncertain. "It'll be strange, won't it, being home?"

"Well, don't forget you're coming home in triumph. A lot of

people said Troy couldn't be taken. Do you remember? The walls of Troy, built by a god; the city, founded by a god? Nobody would take it—but *you* did."

"I did, didn't I? I didn't just take it—fucking pulverized it."

I remembered the columns of black smoke that had hung over the city for days on end. The crows circling . . .

Nudged gently by Machaon, Agamemnon began to reminisce about the war—the first of countless such conversations I've had to sit through over the years. "Do you remember when Achilles thought Odysseus hadn't invited him to a feast? God, what a storm in a pisspot that was. Achilles ranting and raving—he'd never been so insulted in all his life, first thing in the morning he was going to load his ships and go home. Oh, and Patroclus trying to calm him down—god, he was a martyr, that man. Don't know how he stood it. And after all that, it turned out he *had* been invited—he'd just been out when the heralds came. The greatest of the Greek fighters? Fuck's sake—the greatest bloody drama queen!" Belatedly, Agamemnon seemed to remember it's considered bad luck to speak ill of the dead and piously lowered his head. "May he rest in peace."

"Rest in peace?" Machaon said. "*Achilles?* That's never going to happen, is it? I'm still expecting the bugger back."

Perhaps his own reference to Achilles being universally regarded as the greatest of the Greek warriors had depressed Agamemnon, because from that moment on, his mood seemed to darken. He lapsed into silence, and pushed his chair further away from the table. As soon as his eyelids began to droop, Machaon helped him to his feet, manoeuvred him through the scattered jugs and platters to the cabin door and kicked it open. I glimpsed an unmade bed and a small lamp burning on the table beside it. Cassandra subjected me to one of her long, unblinking stares. *Don't you dare pity me.*

Moving forward, she took Agamemnon's arm, clearly intending

to help him into bed, but he wrenched himself free. "Not *her*," he shouted at Machaon. "Good god, man, have you no sense?"

Recovering at once, Machaon came towards us, holding his arms out to the sides like a shepherd herding sheep. I backed off at once, but Cassandra hesitated, looking at Agamemnon, who was sitting on the edge of the bed, his hands dangling helplessly between his thighs.

"I think you'd better go," Machaon said. "I'll take it from here."

And then, without ceremony—no leave-taking, no bow, not a scrap of consideration or respect—he slammed the door in her face.

7

The sound of that door slamming pursued us along the passage. Cassandra's shock was palpable. I had other things to think about: like not falling over, not being flung against the wall by a sudden movement of the ship. I was starting to think the *Medusa* was well named. You did get the impression of active malevolence, though that was nonsense, of course. We splashed through puddles, while the floor bucked and reared under our feet. Andreas was right: the only safe place was bed. In the end, I grabbed Cassandra and we finished the short journey hobbled together like contestants in a three-legged race. Reaching the cabin, we took it in turns to use the bucket and then, for the second time that night, I crawled under the blanket and brought my knees up to my chin. Cassandra lay stretched out like a corpse on a slab, and this irritated me so much I turned my back on her.

No hope of sleep, none. I lay and listened to her breathing, which was quiet and steady with none of the odd little whistles and groans and grunts people make in deep sleep.

Finally, I asked, "Are you awake?" A grudging movement of her head supplied the answer. "What was all that about?"

"He thought I was Iphigenia. The girl he killed."

"His daughter. It was his *daughter* he killed." Somehow it was important to say that. "And then he wakes up and he's in bed with her. Enough to drive anybody mad, I'm just surprised he didn't kill you."

"*Is* he mad?" she asked.

"You tell me."

"I don't know what madness looks like. I only know how it feels—and even that's probably just me. I mean, I'm sure it's different for everybody."

I couldn't believe she was talking as openly as this.

"How did it feel for you?"

"Amazing. To be honest. We-ell, to begin with anyway. You feel—no, sorry. *I* feel . . . I feel I can do anything—climb mountains, walk on water, kiss a god. Even the bits that must look awful, like pissing yourself—they didn't feel awful. Letting go, feeling it hot and strong cascading down your legs . . . It's not all bad."

"I wish I'd known you were enjoying it. I might have been a bit less sympathetic."

"It doesn't go on being like that. After a while, it starts shaking you to pieces, like a chariot being driven too fast, bits of it falling off." She put a hand over her mouth to keep the words in. "I know I was horrible to you."

"*Was?*"

No reply to that. "Look," I said. "We both know what's going on here. I saw things you didn't want me to see—or anybody to see—ever. And you can't forgive me for it."

"I'm grateful to you."

"No, you're not."

"No, I'm not."

I laughed. "If I disappeared down a crack in the floor, you'd be overjoyed. Wouldn't you?"

"Probably."

We lay in silence after that; the atmosphere between us had sub-tly changed, though not necessarily for the better. You can have too much honesty.

After a while, she said, "Is it my imagination or is the smell a bit better?"

"I think we've just got used to it. We probably smell like that ourselves now."

"God, what an awful thought." Cassandra was sitting with her back against the stained and mottled wall. At last, she said, "You know what just happened—it was a terrible shock."

"I'm sure."

"I mean, it makes everything . . . well, just that little bit more difficult. Do you see?"

"Of course I see. How are you going to die together when he can't bear to be in the same room as you?"

A short silence. "I wish I could make you believe me."

"I don't not believe you. I just don't understand."

"What don't you understand?"

"Well, like you see something? Right?"

"Yes."

"But what I don't understand is . . . Is what you see fixed? I mean, is it going to happen no matter what anybody does? Or is it more like a warning? You know, *Go on the way you are doing, this is what's going to happen*."

"I don't know."

"So . . . what's in the picture?"

"Two dead bodies in a courtyard. Agamemnon and me. Both with stab wounds. Oh, and I know it happens not long after we arrive, but I don't know how I know that." She made a sound that was almost a laugh. "And you don't believe a word I'm saying, do you?"

Despite the laughter in her voice, I couldn't see anything

remotely funny in her prophecy; but then again, people can become extraordinarily light-hearted when they feel the approach of death.

"What do you think I should do, Ritsa?"

"Tell him you're pregnant. He'll take care of you then."

"You sound like my mother."

"I'll take that as a compliment."

"And suppose I'm not pregnant?"

"Well, then you made a mistake. Happens all the time."

Another silence yawned open. Was the light getting thinner? I thought the humped clothes on the hooks were clearer than they'd been half an hour ago.

"He's got to die, Ritsa. If there's no justice for the children he killed, we might as well be pigs rooting around in the mud."

She waited for a reply, but I just shook my head. Eventually, she turned on to her side and a few minutes later her steady breathing suggested she'd fallen asleep. I was feeling slightly queasy because the rolling of the ship seemed to be getting worse. You're supposed to focus your eyes on a fixed point, but how can you do that when everything's simultaneously in motion? There were shouts on deck, followed by a burst of singing. Brave men to sing in this. Was it a storm? Well, obviously it was a bloody storm, what else could you possibly call it? So that was another of Cassandra's prophecies down the drain. She was convincing though; for a time there, I'd believed Agamemnon was sailing home to meet his death.

She was muttering in her sleep. Once, I thought I caught the word "mother" and listened more intently, but there were no more words, only the creaking of the ship as she shouldered her way through the raging sea.

8

I woke early from a sleep riven by dreams. A ruined house, holes in the roof that let the rain come in, rats scuttering everywhere . . . I've never lived in such a hovel, and yet, somehow, there it is in my head, a picture of utter devastation, and it's been there all my adult life. Hiding itself away, sometimes for several years, and then suddenly back. It's a dream that has the power to stain the following day, and I knew it was going to take a real conscious effort to sluice it out of my mind.

The first step was to get out of this foetid hole. Turning onto my side, I saw that Cassandra was still asleep. Given the night we'd just had, she might sleep for hours. Wrapping my shawl around me, I headed up on deck, though when I got to the top of the stairs I hung back because I could see a heavy rain was falling. Everything black or grey or silver, everything blurred, the sun itself no more than a rheumy eye peering through gaps in a bank of black cloud. Once away from the shelter of the staircase, I was startled by the ferocity of the wind, but I clung on to the rail with hands that quickly became numb. Despite the rain beating a tattoo on my scalp and a clump of wet cloth chafing between my thighs, I felt better, more alive, than I had for weeks.

Cautiously, moving hand over hand, I edged further along the rail. Below, the sea foamed and bubbled like bone broth coming to the boil, but I tried not to look down. On either side of us were warships, some still showing lights. I knew the warships were there for our protection—or *Agamemnon's* protection—but I didn't find them reassuring. For me, and thousands of other women, it's impossible to see that black, beaked silhouette and not feel terror. Intent on watching the ships, I didn't notice a figure coming up behind me, until a hand gripped my arm. "You moron. You *fucking* moron."

Andreas, of course: little blue eyes fizzing rage, his red cheeks turning a deeper shade of puce as he looked at me. I opened my mouth to speak, only to gag as the wind snatched my breath away—and just as well probably, since anything I'd said would only have angered him further. In the end, I skedaddled; I was in such a hurry to get away I slid down the stairs on my bum. Though when I stood up, wet hair dripping down the back of my neck, soaked tunic clinging to me in clammy folds, I felt wonderful. Raising my arm to my face, I smelled a mixture of rain and salt sea spray, the fug of musty blankets and stale sweat entirely blown away.

The joy didn't last long. Groping my way along the passage, I dreaded to hear Cassandra's voice calling my name, but when I peered round the door of the cabin she was still asleep—I could tell by the steady rise and fall of her breathing—so I crept in and stretched out on my bunk. I was too excited by the wind and rain to sleep, though my thoughts were not happy ones. That had been an ugly little scene just now, Andreas screaming obscenities. Pure rage. I told myself I didn't care, but the truth was I did care. But after a while, I calmed down enough to sleep. When, an indeterminate time later, I opened my eyes, Cassandra was still asleep. And I was famished.

I got up, smoothed my frizzy hair down as best I could and walked the short distance to the dining room.

The mess had been cleared up. A single oil lamp sent a wobbling light over an array of empty chairs. Nothing else: no food, no drink. If it had been me, I'd have had to put up with it—no choice—but just as I was about to leave, Machaon came in. He had a healthy regard for the pleasures of the belly, and a lot more clout than me, so off he went and hammered on the galley door. Within minutes of his return a young lad arrived bearing a tray of cooked meat and a dish of green olives. Bread appeared not long after, the loaf already cut into; I carved off the stale bit at the end and the rest, though not exactly fresh, did well enough.

Machaon was really tucking into the meat. "You're not feeling queasy at all?" I asked.

"I did a bit, last night. I'm all right now."

"How's the king?"

"*Definitely* not queasy." He was grinning. "Or if he is, it's a state secret. How's Cassandra?"

I pulled a face.

"Hmm? Might be no bad thing for them to have a bit of time apart."

No bad thing for whom? I wondered. Them—or Machaon? He did seem to see Cassandra as a rival, which was unusual, since it's rare for a royal concubine to have any real influence over a king.

At that moment, the door opened and Cassandra came in, a very much depleted Cassandra, white, bedraggled and smelling of vomit. She slumped into the chair beside me. Machaon raised his knife, offering to cut her some bread. She shook her head and, perhaps regretting even that slight movement, began massaging her temples with the forefingers of both hands.

Machaon said: "You know, you'd be better off in bed."

"How's the king?"

"Resting."

The way he said it—his whole manner, in fact—was as much a smack in the face as the slammed door had been. In the hush that followed, the whining of wind in the rigging sounded very loud.

"I hate that sound," I said—as if anybody cared whether I hated it or not.

"We'll be making good progress," Cassandra said.

"Will we?" Machaon said. "What makes you say that? For all *you* know, we've been blown off course by the storm."

"We haven't."

"Oh, no, of course not, I'm forgetting, silly me, we can't have been blown off course by the storm, can we, because there hasn't been a storm." He was absurdly angry. "So, what's the matter with you, then? Morning sickness?"

Cassandra darted a vicious glance in my direction, obviously thinking I must have told him my suspicions. Machaon noticed her annoyance, guessed what it meant and was clearly delighted to have stumbled on her secret. Cassandra sat in silence, straight-backed and tense. Probably she was hoping the cabin door would open and Agamemnon would come out; though, given the way she looked, and smelled, I thought it would be much better for her if he didn't.

The awkward silence was broken by a shout from up on deck, followed by a burst of cheering. Machaon was on his feet at once. "I'll tell—" He checked himself. "No, better be sure." And then he was out of the door, running along the passage like a boy.

Left alone, Cassandra and I stared at each other. There could be only one explanation for the cheering: they'd sighted land. Without looking at me, Cassandra got to her feet and walked stiffly to the door. People whose names and functions I didn't know peered out of cabin doors like startled rabbits. Cassandra swept past them, I followed, and we emerged into a day of mist and steady rain, calmer now. In the prow, a skinny lad with a prominent Adam's apple jerking in his throat was insisting, "I did see it." He looked around for support. "I did."

We stood looking out to sea. Nothing, not for a long time—but then a sharper gust blew a hole in the mist and there, just for a second, we saw a brown smudge. More cheers, louder now, spreading from ship to ship across the heaving water. Even the drenching rain couldn't dampen their spirits—or Cassandra's, who was as exultant as any of them. I was probably the only person on board the *Medusa* who didn't want the voyage to end.

Cassandra turned to Machaon. "There you are, you see. I told you we'd have a smooth voyage."

He was about to reply when I cut in. "Last night was anything but smooth."

I doubt if she heard me. She'd climbed to the top of the railings and was leaning far out, much further than was safe, apparently trying to touch the figurehead. Machaon looked at me, clearly expecting me to do something about it. When I didn't, he gave a *tsk* of impatience, grabbed a handful of her skirt and pulled her onto the deck. She straightened her tunic, pointedly turned her back on him and asked Andreas, "It is the Medusa, isn't it?"

"It is, yes. My grandfather carved it."

"Isn't it an odd choice for a figurehead?" Machaon asked. "A monster?"

Cassandra turned to look at him. "*Was* she a monster?"

"She turned every living thing she ever met to stone. I'd call that a monster, wouldn't you?"

"But isn't that the point? Who decides who's a monster?"

"The winner."

I could see she was taken aback by that, by the brutal cynicism of it—or the honesty. "So what you're saying is, if she'd killed Perseus—and not the other way round—*he'd* be the monster. Is that right?"

"Yes, I suppose so."

"Instead of just an objectionable little prick?"

Machaon and Andreas exchanged disapproving glances; I had no patience with either of them. Whatever the issue was here, it wasn't Cassandra's choice of words. She went on, almost dreamily, "You know, people think Medusa's her name, but it's not a name at all, it's a title. It means 'queen.'"

Machaon shrugged. "The fact is—"

"The fact is, she was a girl raped in the temple of Athene by somebody who was too powerful to be punished."

An awkward silence. I knew, and Machaon knew, that Cassandra was describing what had happened to her. When the Greek fighters were rampaging through the streets of Troy, she'd taken refuge in the temple of Athene, hiding behind a statue of the goddess. Finding her there, Ajax dragged her out of hiding but she was clinging so tight she brought the wooden image crashing to the ground beside her. And throughout everything that followed she kept her eyes on the painted face. Even when Ajax found a bloody clout between her legs and threw it away, she didn't let herself feel anything. Normally the rape of a captured Trojan woman wasn't considered an offence, but the rape of a virgin priestess in the temple of a virgin goddess was sacrilege. Nevertheless, Ajax wasn't punished. He had men, he had ships—in the end, he was just too powerful.

I don't know how Machaon's confrontation with Cassandra might have ended because, at that moment, there was a commotion behind us. We turned to see Agamemnon walking across the deck towards us. Close to, he looked not ill, exactly, but drained of energy. This was his moment of greatest triumph as king and commander-in-chief, and yet there was no joy in his face. He looked lost. But then something rather remarkable happened: the fighters on the two nearest warships caught sight of him and started to cheer. The acclamation spread from deck to deck as fighters on ships too far away to see him guessed what was happening and went wild with excitement. "Agamemnon! Agamemnon!" they shouted, dragging the name out until it became a battle cry. Raising both arms above his head, he turned a slow circle of acknowledgement, and then as the cheering ramped up, another circle, and another. The slight stoop vanished, his shoulders straightened, he seemed to grow taller as we watched, shedding belly fat, shedding years—miraculously rejuvenated by the adoration of men who could scarcely see him, and some who couldn't see him at all.

Even when the cheers finally died away, he still looked younger, fitter, full of energy and hope. He shook hands vigorously with Andreas, who said, "Don't thank me, Sir. We're not there yet."

But Agamemnon had already moved on. He walked across the deck to greet members of the crew, waved again at the surrounding warships and then, rather formally, acknowledged Cassandra. He was smiling, so evidently his fears of the night before were forgotten, at least for the present. She stood patiently beside him while he chatted to other people. Ten minutes or so later, they left the deck together.

Andreas was fuming. "Did you hear that? Thanking me for getting him there? I've never heard anything so stupid, there's another full day."

"Good!"

He looked at me. "You're in no hurry to get there, then?"

I shook my head. "No, sorry, I know you must all be longing to get back home." I looked around the deck at the sailors who'd started to drift back to work. "But I haven't got a home, not now, and I like it here."

A moment's silence. Some kind of internal struggle seemed to be going on; he seemed about to speak, but then shook his head. "I'd best be getting on."

He went off to get some repair work organized and I turned to look out to sea again. I was intensely aware of Medusa cresting the waves, the two of us bounding along at a tremendous speed with the wind in our impossible hair. At least mine didn't hiss. Normally, the endless frizz of damp weather didn't bother me, I was past caring about stuff like that—and if I was aware of it now, it was only because I'd met Andreas again and that, inevitably, made me slightly more self-conscious about the way I looked. And there in front of me, riding the waves, was Medusa, who'd presumably stopped feeling self-conscious soon after her transformation, because how else could she have lived?

Who decides who the monster is?

The winner.

I stared into the mist until my eyes began to ache, before pulling my shawl tightly round me and going below deck.

Aside from all that talk about Medusa, I was increasingly aware of the woman over there, beyond the wall of mist, who was waiting, as I was, and as Cassandra was, for this voyage to be over. The queen, Clytemnestra, who'd seen her daughter die, and must now be preparing to welcome her killer home.

She'll jump if he tells her to.

I had a feeling she might not.

9

Clytemnestra's eyes are tired with watching and today, of all days, with the coastline shrouded in mist her vigilance has seemed particularly pointless.

Distraction, that's what she needs. So, after dark, when the idiots who surround her are safely tucked up in their own or somebody else's bed, she takes two cups and a jug of wine and glides down the quiet corridor as noiselessly as a ghost. Do people notice these nocturnal excursions of hers? Perhaps; no, they must do, they notice everything else—every gesture, every movement, every fleeting change of expression—all of it commented on, speculated about. Even the regularity, or otherwise, of her periods, even the stains on her sheets—all of it is valuable information. To her certain knowledge, some counsellors bribe her maids for glimpses of her laundry. Probably they think she has a lover; Aegisthus, no doubt, since she's obliged to spend a considerable amount of time with him. Some men seem to think it's impossible that a woman might prefer to sleep alone. All that effort, and still they have no idea where she goes when she needs company, only that sometimes she leaves her rooms at night, unattended by her maids—and that, in itself, is scandalous.

At the foot of the stairs, she stops to listen. The walls are whispering together as they often do, but not of love.

The steps that lead down from the formal gardens to the wasteland at the back of the palace are in deep shadow. It's gloomy here,
and always damp. The ferns, growing thickly from crevices in the
wall, clearly love it; nowhere else in the grounds do you see such a
virulent shade of green. Below her, the ground stretches away to the
horizon. Despite its air of desolation, she's always liked this place.
It was one of her refuges when she was a young woman, newly
married and beginning to feel trapped. Tall, umbrella-shaped plants
border a small stream that flows down from the hill above, breaking into white foam around the rocks in its path. That constant
rush of water over stone clears her mind. She always feels better
here, though by any objective standard the place could hardly be
more miserable. Thirty years ago, victims of the plague were buried
here, the majority in deep communal pits. Even the few who'd got
individual graves have no real memorial. This is a place where everything's lost—identities, memories, even names.

She only has the old women's memories to go on. At the time of
the great plague she was a child in Sparta, though the plague reached
there too; she and her twin sister, Helen, had been sent up into the
mountains to keep them safe. She has a sudden flash-memory of
Helen, with a blue ribbon in her hair, skipping on ahead.

Following the narrow path beside the stream, she brushes against
wet ferns and the damp creeps up from her ankles to her knees. The
hill's steep, and the ground treacherous after recent downpours, but
straight ahead of her now, looming out of the mist, is the towering
pyramid of the watchfire. She pauses for a moment, staring at it.
Even from this distance, it's a strange mixture of dead leaves, grass,
branches, wooden boxes, storage crates, sticks of broken furniture—
there's even a purple sofa at the base, so well sheltered it stays dry
even in a storm. The sofa had been there from the beginning; she'd
once surprised Razmus curled up on it, sound asleep with his raggy
old cloak wrapped tightly around his shoulders.

"Burn a treat, this will," he'd said, when he opened his eyes and found her watching him.

"I'm sure it will—and with you on it. For god's sake! Suppose some idiot puts a torch to it while you're asleep?"

"Asleep? *Me?* When do *I* ever sleep?"

That was two months ago, when she'd first ordered the watchfires to be built. She knows him better now.

Nearing the top of the hill, she turns and looks out to sea—or rather at the place where the sea should be. A bank of mist hides everything. They're a well-known feature of this coast, these sudden, thick mists that blow in off the sea. It can be bright sunshine up here while down there in the town the sea-fret's so dense fishing boats can't leave the harbour. These sudden mists have their own distinctive, metallic smell. And they don't just smell of metal, they taste of it too, as if you'd been licking armour. She flicks her tongue round her lips and tastes it now.

"Who goes there?"

"A friend."

"Approach, friend!"

Really, how ridiculous! She knows for a fact nobody else ever visits him except the slave who brings his food, but still he insists on this rigmarole.

She climbs the last few yards to the circle of bare earth around the watchfire where a lugubrious little man with skinny legs is perched on a flat stone. In the darkness, wreathed in mist, he looks like some malignant creature from ancient myth, a creature already ancient before the gods were born. She sits down on another conveniently placed stone and raises the jug. The unspoken question has to be asked, though he's already licking his lips; as she pours the wine his eyes never leave the cup. She hands it across and then, for a moment, they sit and stare at the watchfire whose towering, silent presence dwarfs them both.

"Well, how've you been?" she asks, at last.

"Wet. Cold."

"Get that down you, you'll soon feel better."

"Oh, I'm going to, don't *you* worry." He drinks deep, wipes his mouth on the back of his hand. "I could have done with that last night."

"Did get a bit rough, didn't it? One point, I thought the roof was coming in." She hesitates. "Do you suppose it was like that out at sea?"

"Worse, I shouldn't wonder." He glances at her. "You're bound to worry. It's only natural you want your man back."

The cosiness of his tone bites deep, as it's meant to do. She doesn't bother explaining how much more complicated her feelings are than that, because he already knows. In fact, there's not much he *doesn't* know, though how—or why—he ferrets it out is a mystery. He doesn't seem to make any use of the information; she'd know if he did. Of course, a lot of inquisitive people are perfectly well intentioned; they're just endlessly fascinated by the vagaries of human nature. Not Razmus—*his* prying seems to be motivated exclusively by malice. And his carefully maintained pretence that she's a loving wife longing for her husband's safe return is—well, what is it? An exercise in power? Because knowledge *is* power, and he's perfectly well aware of that. A threat? No, he wouldn't go that far. He's one of the most consistently malign people she's ever encountered, but he's also the best nightwatchman in the business; in more normal times, he's paid good money to patrol the streets after dark, though she doubts if he's welcome in any of the houses he guards—certainly his own family chucked him out years ago.

She looks up from her cup, finds him contemplating her in his usual bright-eyed, expectant way, and thinks that his expression is—not unpleasant, exactly—but certainly knowing.

"How are the little buggers?" she asks, focusing instinctively on his weakness.

"Playing up. They don't like wet weather."

"They don't seem to like any weather."

"Heat's the worst."

The little buggers are the reason he makes such a good watch-man. He's always careful to tuck a fold of his cloak around his feet, so she has no way of knowing how bad the lesions are—if the smell's anything to go by, very bad indeed. She suspects he wel-comes night, because with darkness wrapped around him, he can remember how it felt to be a man.

Leaning forward, she refills his cup.

"Looking forward to it, then?" he asks.

That was more a jibe than a question. "What do *you* think?"

"I think there's no point arguing with the gods." His voice is exhausted, flat—the voice of a man who spends every night arguing with the gods. "Gets you nowhere fast, that." A pause, another gulp. "He did what he had to do."

"Did he?"

"He was in a difficult situation. They'd got him backed into a corner."

"So I'm not allowed to blame him for killing my daughter because he was in 'a difficult situation.' Oh dear, the poor soul."

"I'm just saying, power has limits. You've ruled Mycenae for ten years, you know that better than anybody. Perhaps he let himself be backed into a corner, perhaps there genuinely wasn't any other way out. And he'd have had the priests yakking on at him. Telling him the gods wanted sacrifice."

"Priests—I'd hang the whole bloody lot of them."

"So why don't you? You're the queen."

"Because the common people listen to them. There's no choice—you've got to keep them onside."

"There you are, then. The limits of power."

She thinks, not for the first time, though never more clearly than tonight, that this heap of stinking flesh is her only friend. Nobody would believe that, but it's true: who else is there? Dacia, perhaps—and there are many worse people to rely on than an intelligent slave. Animals, even better, because they don't know who you are, but her last dog died six months ago, and she won't get another. Poor old Mylan. He was a puppy when Iphigenia died. On the morning they set off for Aulis she kissed him good-bye, holding him up in front of her and laughing when he licked her face. Then, as the cart drew up in front of the palace, she put him down on the top step, and he stayed, edging a little forward on his belly, whimpering to see her go.

"Iphigenia," Razmus says. "A lovely girl." He waits to see what reaction that gets. "They say she went to her death willingly."

"She was bound and gagged."

But she says it without rancour because he used Iphigenia's name. Nobody else does. Oh, they talk about her: the temple to Artemis is crowded with people visiting her grave. She's loved, remembered, venerated—but nobody says her name. Sometimes, in the council chamber, when the old men have been wittering on for hours, she feels like screaming: *Somebody, please—somebody, just say her name!*

She'd dropped so deep into the well of her own thoughts that she jumps when Razmus says, "Mist's clearing."

"Is it?"

"Yes, look."

She twists round, trying to see the harbour. Is the mist a little less thick?

"Won't be long now."

"You've been saying that for weeks."

He nods to acknowledge the truth of this, but then surprises her. "I saw him the other night."

"Who?"

"Agamemnon."

"What was he doing?"

"Wasn't doing anything. He was saying: 'Not her.'"

"I expect he was picking a woman for the night."

"Don't think so. He sounded . . . frightened."

"*Frightened?*"

"Just telling you what I heard."

"You must have been dreaming. I dreamt about him last night too, I dreamt the ship went down."

"You must've been devastated."

It's there, unmistakably now: the sneer of malice. The way Razmus said that word—"devastated"—reveals exactly how much he knows about her feelings towards Agamemnon. Far, far, far too much. She should probably have him killed. He'd probably thank her if she did. But unlike Aegisthus she has no interest in killing for killing's sake. Can he do her any damage? That's the only question that matters, and for now, provisionally, the answer's no.

"Anyway"—draining her cup—"that's me done. I won't wish you a goodnight."

"Nor I you, Ma'am."

Ma'am, is it? He offers her the jug, as he does at the end of every visit, and, as on all the previous occasions, she says, "No, you keep it." She takes his cup though, knowing he'll be happy to swig from the jug the minute she leaves. They stare at each other as they often do, holding each other's eyes a second too long, and then she turns to go. No need to urge him to stay awake and watchful: the little buggers will see to that.

10

After dinner that night—the second night we'd spent on board the *Medusa* and, as it turned out, the last—I was left alone with Andreas.

Agamemnon and Cassandra had gone early to bed. Machaon decided he'd go up on deck to finish his wine—though since he took a whole jug with him, I didn't think finishing was imminent. He seemed to be expecting Andreas to accompany him, but Andreas shook his head. We chatted easily enough—about the *Medusa*, about his grandfather who'd taken up woodcarving as a pastime when he was too badly injured to go to sea—but then, realizing he was good at it, had turned it into a business. His figureheads could be seen up and down the coast. "Sometimes, you know, I'll be walking round a harbourside and suddenly I'll look up and think, *That's one of his.* And it's like meeting an old friend."

"Did you help him with it?"

"With the carving? Well, a bit, I suppose, when I was a kid, but I was never any good. The first chance I got I went to sea."

"And met my husband."

"And you."

A slightly awkward pause. I glanced round the room. "You've done well for yourself, mind." He was looking modest, almost coy. "Well, no, but you have . . . You must have led a very adventurous life."

"It's not been bad. I can't say I've ever regretted it. There've been a few tough times. Last ship I had went down—no lives lost, thank god, but the cargo was ruined. All I had left was a cartload of pissed-off customers—you don't get past that in a hurry. Fact is, I'm only just clawing my way back now. But you know—" He patted the table affectionately. "She might creak a bit, but there's a few good years left in her yet."

"Sounds a bit like me."

"Aye—and me."

The conversation moved on. We talked about Galen. After the first two years of marriage, I'd stayed at home. I was beginning to be in demand as a midwife as well as a herbalist, so I concentrated on growing that side of the business but also on establishing a proper herb garden. Small, of course, compared with the big palace physic gardens, though some of the plants in my beds you wouldn't find anywhere else. Gone, now—destroyed, like everything else. For a moment I was back in that garden, on a summer evening, waiting for Galen to come home.

"I used to envy him."

For a moment, I was lost. "Galen? Why?"

"You know why."

Whoa! He was going too fast for me, too fast for the situation we were in. Though what had he said, really? Nothing, just a slight, meaningless compliment.

Next door, Agamemnon and Cassandra were getting into bed. Whispered conversations, laughter, quickly giving way to other sounds. *I can't tell lies*, Cassandra had said. Well, not with her tongue, perhaps, but the rest of her seemed to have no problem. Meanwhile, we sipped our wine and nibbled our cheese and listened, involuntarily, to Agamemnon's protracted and noisy climax.

Silence. We again became aware of other sounds, a banging of dishes from the galley, snatches of singing from the deck, the click of each other's jaws as we chewed. I was desperate to distract Andreas because I could feel a certain tension, sexual tension, growing—and I didn't want that, I wanted this to be a nice little middle-aged flirtation, pleasant enough but not important, totally divorced from the reality of our lives.

"You know this morning on deck, when you screamed at me? I think I caught a glimpse of the real you."

He shook his head.

"Pure *anger.*"

"I wasn't angry."

"You could've fooled me."

"But I did . . . I did . . . I . . ."

He looked so stricken, I had to stop myself touching him. "I'm sorry," I said.

"Nothing for you to be sorry about." He forced a laugh. "It was just I didn't want to see you go overboard the day after I found you again." He was still half laughing, but there was no possibility of pretending now. Pushing his cup to one side, he said, "Shall we leave this?"

My mind flooded with all the many, unanswerable reasons why the only possible answer was no—and "Yes," I said. "*Yes.*"

11

Walking back from the watchfire, Clytemnestra sees how quickly the mist's clearing. There's still a misty circle round the moon, which looks full but isn't, not quite—it's slightly flattened to one side like a coin that's been tampered with. But tonight, or perhaps tomorrow night, the singing will start.

Boys and girls, come out to play, the moon doth shine as bright as day . . .

Entering the palace via the kitchen yard, she goes straight to the back stairs where she's less likely to meet anybody who matters. The walls are muttering again, louder now. A long climb in near-total darkness, feeling her way forward, brings her out into a narrow corridor, with rooms on either side. Some are bedrooms, others used for storage, a few simply stand empty. Alerted by a prickling at the back of her neck, she peers into the gloom around her.

Come with a whoop, come with a call, come with a good will or NOT AT ALL!

Always, in the songs they sing, there's this sudden burst of malice at the end. Absorbed by the voices in her head, she hears a door click open behind her, but too late. No time to turn round, there's an arm around her neck, hot fingers pressing her nose and mouth, cutting off air. Struggling, she's dragged backwards into a room and hears the door kicked shut behind her. The arm slackens its grip. Gasping, she twists round to face her assailant. Aegisthus, of course. The rush of relief does nothing to appease her anger. "What the hell are you doing here?"

"I had to see you."

"*Like this?*" She tries to bring the anger under control, because he doesn't, *can't*, understand what he's done wrong—and never will. "What about?"

"I've been thinking . . ."

"Ye-es?"

"It's got to be me. I've got to be the one to do it."

"Why? Why do you?"

"Because fighting comes more naturally to a man."

"Bollocks."

"Exactly."

By his standards that was almost clever. "But there isn't going to be a fight."

"Not going to be a fight? Really? I think you're underestimating him a bit there."

"No, Aegisthus, you're underestimating me."

"At least let me be there. He's a seasoned fighter, for god's sake, he's just fought a bloody war. There's no way you can take him on. And anyway, I've got as much reason as you to want him dead."

"Look, I'm sorry your brothers died such a horrible death, but you weren't even born when they died. You didn't know them. And it wasn't Agamemnon who killed them—it was his father. But Agamemnon did kill my daughter, and I'm sorry, I don't want to belittle your suffering, but he's *mine*."

At last, the pacing stops and he turns to face her. "And suppose I say that's not good enough?"

She laughs. "Well, yes, Aegisthus, suppose you do?" Going right up to him, in close, so they're almost touching, she says, "Don't you ever dare threaten me. And *don't* come to the palace. Do you remember, we talked about this? I can't be seen with you. I can't afford any hint of a scandal."

"*Scandal.* Do you know what they say about you in the taverns?"

"I can guess. Poor lonely woman, she's bound to want a man in her bed . . ."

"Worse than that. They say you're working your way through the palace guard."

"And do you contradict them?"

"Of course."

Liar. "Look, the time for you to appear is when he's in the palace. It's not as if you're miles away. You can be here in a couple of hours."

"I don't like leaving you alone like this."

"I'm not alone."

It's true, she isn't, any more than Razmus is alone with the little buggers laying eggs in his feet. There's a moment when she misses Razmus—misses even his smell.

"Where do you go at night?"

She'd like to say, *None of your business,* but that won't do. "Nowhere in particular. I just walk."

"You don't just walk."

He puts a hand on her arm, one of his frequent, clumsy attempts at seduction. It's all she can do not to pull away. "Look, it's not long now. He could be here tomorrow—or the day after. Fact, if he isn't here the day after, there's something wrong."

"Like what?"

"The storm?"

"No wreckage has been washed up."

She lets him embrace her, pushes him away when his grip begins to tighten. "I think you'd better be getting back."

"Right." He turns towards the door. "I'll take a look."

"No, *I'll* take a look. Nobody'll be surprised to see me."

Peering round the door, she finds the corridor empty and beck-ons to him to leave.

Minutes later, she's back in her own room. No maids waiting to undress her; she'd told them she wouldn't be needing them again tonight. But no doubt they'll be hovering about, somewhere—and if bloody Aegisthus is seen leaving they'll all think they know why she wanted to be alone. That man gives her a thudding headache every time they meet. Briefly, she wonders what he does for sex; she's fairly certain his desire for her is simply a means of getting closer to power. Men? Boys? Prostitutes? There's a candle guttering by her bed and she puts it out of its misery, pausing for a moment to sniff the coil of acrid smoke. Nothing for it now but to crawl between the sheets and attempt the difficult business of sleep.

The day after. That's what she ought to be thinking about— the day after Agamemnon's death, because Aegisthus is certainly thinking about that, and his plans for the future won't benefit her—or Orestes. With his father dead, Orestes will be in real danger, because Aegisthus won't be satisfied with anything less than the throne. At some point, she'll have to get rid of him, but not yet. He's useful now.

Drifting in the shallows, her dreams are full of screaming sailors, stricken ships, the storm in her mind raging, though outside her bed-room window there's scarcely a breath of air. A noise wakens her. She can't think what it was, can't even be sure it wasn't part of a dream, so she tries to settle down again. No use. She sits up, pushes the sheet back and reconciles herself to an hour or two without sleep.

The trouble is, her mind's buzzing from the meeting with Aegis-thus. She's known horses like him, with the same lack of respect for people's space, all of them orphaned as foals. They grow up not knowing how to be horses and—though Aegisthus would probably kill anybody who said it—he doesn't know how to be a man. He's ruthless, yes, but it's more than that. It's as if he's never heard of a world in which keeping promises, speaking the truth and being kind exist. She thinks she knows what his plan is: kill Agamemnon, marry her, claim the throne—and where does that leave her son, Orestes, eighteen years old, and with no experience of combat? Facing a man who, if he hadn't been born into the royal family, might well have become one of those men who set themselves up in the backyards of taverns, and take on any man fool enough or drunk enough to challenge them, stamping on fingers, gouging out eyes, all for the price of a bowl of stew and a jug of wine. The threat to Orestes is very real. Somehow, she's got to use Aegisthus but then as soon as possible get rid of him. And that won't be easy.

Throwing her robe round her shoulders, she walks onto the terrace, into the hour of darkness that precedes the dawn. Yawning, she notices a light growing on the horizon. Sunrise, she thinks, but no, it's not that kind of light. This is bright orange, leaping, flickering, fierce. It's obvious what it is—and yet there's a moment when her brain doesn't recognize what her eyes are seeing, followed by the slow, cool wave of shock as she realizes that in the far distance a watchfire's been lit. Of course, it may mean nothing. Gangs of lads are always setting fire to them, just for the hell of it; there've been two false alarms in the last few weeks. Her mind reserves judgement, even as her heart leaps with the flames. It's all she can do to stop herself crying out, but even as the cry dies in her throat, the gong in the hall is struck, and struck again.

She puts her robe on properly, her fingernails snagging on the silk as she fumbles with the belt. Her hands are sweaty; wiping them down her sides, she tries to steady herself. Still just the one fire, but even as she thinks that, she sees another, closer, burst of flame. *That's it.* Now it's real. She goes into the corridor, takes a torch from the sconce beside her door and, holding it high above her head, walks down the main staircase into the atrium. As she enters the throne room, the guard's drawing back the mallet for another strike so she has to wait for that noise, too, to swell and subside. There's a group of people at the far end of the hall, slaves by the look of them—obviously slaves, who else but slaves would be up at this hour? Slaves, and the queen.

"More torches," she calls, and they scatter in all directions, leaving her alone with the guard. One of Aegisthus's men: young, fresh complexion, a frank, ready smile; he'd be overfamiliar, if he dared. He doesn't dare.

"The watchfire's lit," he says.

"I know." Her voice is sharp because it's important to make it clear that she's not surprised. She was surprised once, on the morning of Iphigenia's death, believing her daughter was about to marry Achilles, seeing her sacrificed like a heifer, instead. Nothing has ever been allowed to surprise her since.

People are streaming into the hall now, buzzing with excitement, though their faces remain curiously blank. It's not just her, everybody's shocked; nobody can believe it. The world's changed, as it always does, between one breath and the next. The leader of the council, Alexandros, a decade younger and rather more vigorous than the rest, steps forward and bows. "Is it true?" he asks. "Or just another false alarm?"

The old men are muttering together. There've been so many rumours, so many false alarms, in recent weeks that they're as skittish as hens who've smelled a fox. "Do you remember, just this week gone, a couple of watchfires were lit? And that was just a pack of lads playing with torches." "Need their arses tanning." "No hope of that these days. Now, when *we* were lads . . ."

Oh my god, off they go . . .

"It's true," she says, and her voice carries round the hall, every bone in her head vibrating, as if her mouth has become the gong announcing his return. "I want fires lit on every altar, prayers, sacrifices. Today's a holiday, and tomorrow. At last, he's coming home."

She's crying now, raising her hands to cover her face, though between her fingers she notices how approvingly they nod. She's behaving exactly as a faithful wife should behave, and a large part of her is detached enough to applaud her own performance. But then, without warning, her left knee buckles underneath her and she falls to the ground.

There's a moment—almost—of peace, when she simply lies there staring at the ceiling. Only then they start clustering round her, a ring of wrinkly faces peering down. *Grey aphids*. She has a flash-memory of Iphigenia lying on the dusty path, her blood spattered over the plants behind her head. One of the drops, half hidden in the curl of a leaf, turns out not to be blood at all.

"Ladybird."

The old men look at each other.

"Bound to be a shock," somebody says. "It's been such a long time."

A long time? Up until this last moment, she'd have agreed with him. *Years* of grief, *years* of anger, followed by the urgency and secrecy of the last few weeks. And now, suddenly, it seems like no time at all. The future's hurtling towards her and, despite all the careful planning, the double-checking, the public and the private rehearsals, she still doesn't feel ready.

How can she possibly have reached this point so soon?

12

"No need for you to rush," Andreas said. He was leaning forward to fasten his sandals as he spoke, the bones of his spine jutting out of his skin like a particularly complicated snake. When I put my arms around him and pressed my face between his shoulder blades, he twisted round, pushed me back against the pillow and we lay there kissing and cuddling like a couple of kids in their teens. It all felt so easy after the spectacularly unpromising beginning of the previous evening when he'd tripped over a discarded tunic and fallen flat on the floor, emitting a string of heart-rending groans.

"Back's gone again, sorry, love, that's it. Once it's gone, it's gone."

I'd tried to help him up, but he was a dead weight—so, being more than a little drunk myself, I lay on the floor beside him and closed my eyes. I might even have drifted off to sleep, if an insistent erection hadn't persuaded him his back might last a little longer. Perhaps his falling over helped; at least it gave me something to think about other than sagging tits and stretch-marked belly and the onward march of time. None of those things seemed to matter at all now.

One last kiss and he was struggling to sit up. "I should have been on deck an hour ago!"

Despite his words, he wasn't struggling very hard. I gave him a shove. Nobody was going to tell *him* off for being late.

"What do you think Cassandra's going to say if I'm missing when she gets back? C'mon, shift your arse, I've got to get dressed even if you don't."

"She'll still be in bed. Anyway, what does it matter what she says?"

It mattered a great deal, but I didn't insist. Instead, I lay in the circle of his arms, unromantically picking a beard hair from between my teeth. I'd forgotten how good a man's body feels. I'd forgotten how good my own body felt.

"You know," I said, after a sleepy pause, "one thing bothers me."

"Hmm?"

"Why aren't they looking forward to being home?"

"They are."

"No, they're not. I don't mean the sailors, *they* are. I mean Agamemnon, I suppose. Machaon. Sometimes they seem excited, but . . ."

"No, they're not celebrating much, are they?" After a pause, he went on, "Of course, they're going back to the palace. That can't be a lot of fun."

"What's the matter with it?" I waited. "C'mon, tell me, I'm going to be living there too, you know."

"Yes, I know—and I wish you weren't."

I wasn't going to push him; in fact, if anything, I felt a slight reluctance, a hanging back. Perhaps it was better not to know.

"It's a strange place. My dad worked there for a time, he was a ship's carpenter really, but there was one year he did his back in—so he couldn't go to sea, but he couldn't afford not to work either, so he used to do odd jobs around the palace. Mainly repairing blinds, putting up sconces, that sort of thing. The whole place was run-down. Anyway, I remember looking forward to him coming home. Me mam always had a bath of hot water ready in the yard, and he used to get washed before he sat down. Well, I say *wash*, scrub more like. Top to toe, even used to stick his head underwater, and I always knew he was washing something off, and I don't mean dirt."

"Did he talk to you about it?"

"No, I was too young. I used to hear him talking to me mam sometimes. They'd sit on the terrace having a cup of wine and I'd be up at me bedroom window, listening. He used to talk a lot about the old queen, Agamemnon's mother. He was repairing the shutters in her room, and she used to lie on the bed and watch him. They'd had every healer in Greece out to her—awful bloody concoctions she had to drink. He said she spilled some once and it went straight through the rug. Even the cockroaches turned their noses up. And she just went on getting thinner and thinner—like she was fading out of life. Like somebody had got a bloody big ball of putty and they were rubbing her out."

"What did your dad think was wrong?"

"Atreus. He said being married to him would have killed any woman." For a long time, Andreas was silent. Then he said: "She was never the same after them children died."

"*Her* children?"

"No, not hers."

And then he told me the story he'd pieced together, growing up. Agamemnon's father, Atreus, had quarrelled with his brother and then, like the vicious bastard he was, arranged a "reconciliation" dinner, smiling benevolently when his brother remarked on the tenderness of the meat. Only at the end of the meal did he produce the hands and feet of two small children as a way of convincing his brother that he'd been eating his own children, whom Atreus had kidnapped, killed and cooked.

The story silenced me. When I could trust my voice, I said, "He must have been mad."

"*Mad?* He wasn't mad, he was just an evil bastard. Should have had his knackers chopped off, and there'd have been a queue of volunteers to do it, believe me."

I couldn't get the story to settle in my mind—and I'm not sure I ever have. It's not just the brutality, it's the . . . grotesquerie, which somehow detracts from the horror. It's too much like the stories old women tell on a winter's night, before sending their listeners shivering to their beds.

"It's got a nasty atmosphere," Andreas said.

"The palace? You mean it's haunted?"

"No! Oh, c'mon, surely . . . ?"

Andreas obviously didn't like the implication that he believed in ghosts. I remembered him as a boy pouring scorn on some of the more far-fetched stories the older men told, about ships that went on sailing though their crews were dead, or women with long hair and fishes' tails who sang men to their doom. He'd probably dismiss tales of hauntings in exactly the same spirit: superstitious nonsense, fit only for old women massaging their arthritic joints by the fire.

"All right," I said, teasing a little. "If the palace was empty, would you spend the night in it alone?"

A long hesitation. "I'd have to think about it. I'm not frightened of anything you can swing a sword at, but no, I don't think I would be easy doing that." He kissed me again, then hauled himself out of bed. "Anyway, it isn't empty, it's crowded. You stick with the other women, you'll be all right."

And with that he pressed both hands hard into the small of his back and began to get dressed.

The minute the door closed behind him, I was out of bed and pulling my tunic over my head, anxious to get back to the cabin before Cassandra returned and found me missing. As I was leaving, Machaon came out of his cabin. He nodded but didn't speak, and I saw as he turned to go that he was grinning. I didn't like that. I couldn't think of any reason for my being in Andreas' cabin other than the blindingly obvious, so I was going to have to live with his amusement.

Pushing open our cabin door, I found the room empty and Cassandra's bed not slept in. Quickly, I pulled back the blanket on mine and dented the pillow. Me, at my age, hiding the signs of illicit sexual activity from a girl. But she was my owner, and this body that had taken and given so much pleasure belonged to her, not me.

She came back a few minutes later, lay down on her bunk and hid her face in her hands. I waited.

"Well," she said, pulling her hands down so the insides of her lower lids showed red. "I told him."

"Was he pleased?"

"Yes, I think so."

"Then it was the right thing to do."

"Not that I had much choice. Apparently, Machaon's been dropping hints. Thanks to you."

"*I* didn't say anything."

"Didn't you?" Staring straight at me. "Honestly?"

"Not one word."

She scanned my face, nodded.

"Don't make an enemy of Machaon," I said. "I know you don't like him, but he's powerful. And there's not a lot he misses. Healing starts with observation—you know? And he's very, *very* good at it. Agamemnon trusts him, more than he trusts anybody else, certainly more than he trusts you. He's lost Odysseus, Nestor, Calchas—all the people he used to rely on. There's only Machaon left."

No response to that. Perhaps she just couldn't bear to hear Machaon praised, though every word was no more than his due. *Bastard.* I'd started brushing the tangled mess of her hair, holding every strand near the root, so the tugging wouldn't hurt. Then I noticed she was crying, and that was sufficiently unusual to make me put the brush down.

She wiped her nose on the side of her hand. "Sorry."

"What's wrong?"

"Nothing, it's just I get so sore. You can pretend about everything else, but you can't pretend about that. Not that he ever notices. Bit of spit, in he goes."

Her hair was near enough done, so I fastened it in a simple knot at the nape of her neck. I didn't want to pull her about any more than I had to.

"You know what we could do with?" She twisted round to look at me. "Your goose-fat jar."

I laughed at the memory. It had made many a poor woman's life marginally easier, that jar. "Not a lot I can do about that."

"No jar?"

"Worse, no goose."

She laughed. We hadn't got on this well, since . . .

Well, since for ever.

I was shaking out her blue tunic when a knock came at the door. Andreas, looking suddenly red-veined and unfamiliar.

"Summat you might like to see."

Cassandra was already reaching for her shawl. We followed him along the passage and up the stairs, where I stood beside her in the prow, breathing cool, moist air. A light mist transformed the sails into spectral shapes above our heads. We could make out lights on board the two ships nearest us, but further away the fleet had disappeared behind a grey wall. Creaking of joists and rigging, lapping water—altogether a peaceful scene, though the sailors crowding round us were tense. At first, it wasn't obvious what we'd been brought up on deck to see, but then Cassandra clutched my arm and pointed. Deep in the mist, a flicker of fire. "You see?" Andreas said, touching my back, then snatching his hand away. "They've spotted us."

Soon that fire was joined by another, and another, tongues of

flame passing the news along faster than rumour, faster than fear.
A mizzling rain was making the fires burn black; the smoke didn't
disperse but merged into the milky air. To me, there was something
ominous about those black columns that seemed to rise out of the
earth like a row of leafless, branchless trees. But the Greeks were
happy, deliriously happy, because they were only hours away from
home.

After a few minutes, there was a stir behind us—and Agamemnon, attended by Machaon, came on deck. Immediately the atmosphere, no, more than that, the emotional weather, changed. His gaze
swept from face to face and all of us, with the possible exception of
Andreas, tried to make ourselves look smaller. It was extraordinary,
the effect he had: the way articulate people suddenly stuttered and
groped for words, confident people hesitated and took a step back.
After acknowledging the cheers, he joined Andreas in the prow.

"How long now?"

"Hard to say, Sir. The wind's dropping."

"Today, though?"

"Oh yes, as long as the wind doesn't die down altogether. Probably late afternoon."

Suddenly, Cassandra tightened her grip on my arm. I couldn't
work out where she wanted me to look, but then I noticed a building on the headland, its columns gleaming bone-white against the
grey sky. At first, I thought it must be a temple to Poseidon, lord
of the sea; every port has one, so sailors can pray before setting out
on a voyage or give thanks for a safe return. But this, though it did
look like a temple, was too far away from the harbour to be easily
visited. And it would be a very steep climb. Glancing sideways, I
saw that Agamemnon had noticed it too.

"That's new," he said. "What is it?"

Andreas coughed. "Iphigenia's tomb."

Every bit of colour drained from Agamemnon's face. At first, he went on standing there, his knuckles white as he gripped the rail, but then he made a curious choking sound and, followed by Machaon, went rapidly below. There was silence after he left; people glanced at each other, but furtively, as if nobody wanted to be the first to speak.

She could have buried Iphigenia anywhere, most obviously in the family mausoleum—the palace would have one, every Greek palace had a place where the kings and their immediate family could be buried with ceremony and with honour. But to bury her there, where her tomb would always be the first thing returning travellers saw . . . where it would be the first thing Agamemnon saw . . .

Think you can turn your back on her? Pretend it never happened? Think again. She's right here, in front of you. This is the future, not the past.

The voice was so strong I found it hard to believe it was just coming from inside my own head.

Cassandra glanced at me. "She's clever." She turned and stared through trailing mist at the tomb again. "Oh my god, yes, she's clever."

13

A great feast's been prepared, fire pits dug, extra spits installed, animals tethered in the kitchen yard, waiting to be slaughtered. Every helmet, sword and shield on the walls has been taken down and polished. She's spent the whole day walking from room to room, supervising the preparations, taking decisions, giving orders, immersed in every pernickety little detail. Amidst the bustle and excitement, she notices the sad faces, people whose gaiety is forced because their husband or son or brother won't be coming home. Tomorrow, when Agamemnon rides in triumph through the Lion Gate, there'll be some who hide themselves away or stride across the hills like lunatics, shouting out their grief and pain.

She'd be one of them, if she could.

Can't, of course. Can't shout, can't curse, can't howl like a wolf that's seen her cub killed, though her grief's every bit as raw as theirs. She keeps Iphigenia's nightdress in a linen case beside her bed and sometimes—not every night, she's careful to ration herself—takes it out and buries her face in its greying folds. She knows there's nothing of Iphigenia left—can't be, after all this time—but some-times, on a good night, she thinks she catches a trace of her scent or, better, the smell of her skin.

Agamemnon won't reach the palace tonight. She's spoken to experienced sailors and their forecast, based on the current position of the ships, is that he'll reach the harbour late afternoon. Since nobody wants to hold a triumphal procession in the dark, the earliest he will be here is around midday tomorrow—and that's pushing it; they'll have to be up polishing armour, grooming horses and unloading chariots all night. Their problem, mercifully, not hers. So: animals slaughtered, spits in place, vegetables, fruit, cheese, bread, olives, wine—gallons of it—all the food in stock or due to be delivered. She's thinking like a housewife because she doesn't dare let herself think in any other way. If this elaborate pretence, this warm, joyful welcome home, is going to work, then, at some level, she's got to mean it. Be the blossoming flower—*and* the snake beneath.

It's a relief, in the hottest part of the day, to retire to her room and lie on the bed. This is the first minute she's had to herself since the gong sounded to announce that one of the watchfires had been lit. Ever since, she's been wearing a mask and behind it her face is crumbling. The exhaustion—if that's what it is—was overwhelming at this morning's brief rehearsal. It's been agreed that the ceremony should start with the Lion Gate closed, simply because there's no other way to prevent the crowd from stampeding down the road to meet him. But, seeing the gate slowly open, she'd started to imagine the moment when he'd drive into the court and she'd see him, face to face, for the first time since he killed Iphigenia. There'll be hundreds of people there, watching that moment, alert for any change of expression on his face or hers. Standing at the top of the steps, looking across the white desert of the courtyard, she'd thought: *I can't do it.* She's got to see him in private first, to meet him for the first time unobserved.

It's easily arranged: he can stay overnight at the Sea House, where they'd spent so many happy times when the children were young. If that doesn't make his brain boil, nothing will. Within minutes of taking the decision, she's dispatched heralds to await his arrival and another, more discreet, messenger to the Sea House telling Dacia to prepare a meal.

She's finding it difficult to rest even in these few moments she has to herself. After lying with her eyes closed for what seems an interminable length of time, she gives up and goes to stand in front of the bronze mirror, wondering whether she can be bothered to try on her robes for tomorrow, though really what *is* the point? Like everything else, her dress was decided on weeks ago; it's too late for second thoughts. Meeting her gaze in the shining metal, she turns her head from side to side, tries on a smile . . . Now this really is mad; this is where she loses all patience with herself. On board ship, at this very moment, Agamemnon will be shouting at his aides to polish his armour, check that his tunic's properly aired and pressed, wash any remaining blood off his chariot wheels—oh yes, good luck with that! But one thing he absolutely will not be doing is peering anxiously at his own reflection, trying to convince himself that his crow's feet are really laughter lines, or that the blurring of his jawline will be less noticeable if he holds his head in a certain way.

Who is she? This woman staring back at her, with that nervous, placatory smile? Iphigenia's mother, Agamemnon's wife, the Queen of Mycenae?

No. She's—

Oh, you know . . . Not Helen. The other one.

Clytemnestra?

What?

Cly-tem-nest-ra?

Oh yeah, that's right, that's her. They were always dressed alike, do you remember? Same dress, same ribbons, same sandals . . .

Well, you know, they were twins.

And Helen was always the one in front. I used to feel a bit sorry for her.

Who, Helen?

No, the other one.

That's who she is: *the other one.* Helen of Troy's plain sister. What a burden to carry through life. But once, she was the mother of Iphigenia—*and she still is.* Not even death can change that.

Restless, bloated, she wanders out onto the terrace where the late, full-blown roses seem to be storing the day's heat. Everything feels breathless, the air so hot it scorches the back of her throat. What she'd really like to do now is visit Iphigenia's grave, then have a simple meal, sitting in the garden under the trees, somewhere nobody will pester her. But it's no use, she can't leave the palace just yet, she'll have to wait an hour or two. Sitting down, she kicks off her sandals, lifts both feet off the ground and looks at them in disgust. Talk about suet puddings; her sandal straps have left grooves in the puffy skin. What are they going to look like by this time tomorrow, when she'll have been standing for hours in the midday heat, singing the praises of that murderous, blood-sucking bastard? *Welcome home, great king.* The marble terrace feels blissfully cool against her bare skin, and on top of the water jug there's a square of white linen weighted down by blue beads. It's such a small thing, that cloth, but looking at it gives her enormous pleasure. Simple, beautiful—and useful too, keeping the flies off the drinking water—the flies that are zooming all round her as if drunk on the smell of her sweat.

Their buzzing takes her back to the journey home from Aulis, Iphigenia a tightly wrapped mummy at her feet. Closing her eyes, she experiences another of the flashes that have plagued her day and night for the last ten years. Iphigenia's head cradled in her arms, she's staring blankly at a clump of green plants beside the path when she notices a patch of red on one of the leaves. At first, she thinks it's blood—there's blood everywhere, drenching her tunic, spiking her hair—but then she sees that it's a ladybird, doing nothing in particular, simply being there. *Ladybird, ladybird, fly away home, your house is on fire, your children are gone.* Words breaking the surface of a mind which, without them, would have been as empty as the sky.

She hears her bedroom door open and somebody come into the room, but she can't see into the dark interior. Nobody disturbs her here, not her maids, not the priests, not the loquacious old counsellors—not even Aegisthus, on the rare occasions when she allows him into the palace. Leaning forward, she sees a girl's slim shape flit across the room and, just for a second, feels a stupid flare of hope. Then she says, flatly, "Electra?" because really who else can it possibly be?

"I couldn't find you."

The voice is plaintive, but in a well-practised way. Electra comes out onto the terrace and tries to curl up beside her, but the chair's not big enough for the two of them. "Come on," she says, the patience in her voice resolutely maintained. "Let's go inside."

As if to underline the reasonableness of this suggestion, a flurry of cockchafers arrives, huge, flapping insects blundering into everything. Fleetingly, she remembers an evening before the war when an absolute plague of them had descended. *Chaos*—women screaming, men jumping about, jostling each other as they squashed insects between their hands, Agamemnon and Menelaus competing against each other, as they always did. Agamemnon won, or claimed he'd won—nobody was likely to contradict him, after all—and accepted a celebratory drink, only to spit the wine out as he saw his hands. Menelaus held out his own hands, which like his brother's were gloved in dead and dying insects. "Look at them," Helen said, her voice glacial. "How old are they? Ten?"

Clytemnestra draws the blinds, shutting out the blue sky and the smell of roses. When she turns back into the room, Electra's setting a lamp on a low table by the couch. As she leans forward, the cracked and oozing patches on her face are mercilessly lit. As always, she feels the state of Electra's skin is a reproach, though she's not sure what she did to bring it about—*if* she did anything—still less how to put it right. She sits on the couch and Electra curls up beside her;

within minutes the patch of skin where their bodies touch is slick
with sweat, but Electra's making little contented mewing sounds so
it's difficult to pull away. After a while, she throws her leg across her
mother's thighs, pinning her down.

Carefully casual, Clytemnestra asks: "Where's Iras?"

"Dunno, I gave her the slip." Electra giggles, fully aware she's getting Iras into trouble. "She wanted me to have a stupid bath."

"Well, it might make you feel better."

"No, it won't. And anyway, she's a slave, she's not allowed to tell
me what to do."

Electra's almost sitting on her knee now, they're so entwined.
And she's pinching Clytemnestra's arms, as she often does; her
skin's covered in small, circular bruises, every shade from black to
purple to yellow to green. Sometimes, in the council chamber, she
sees the old men looking at them, speculatively—and it bothers her
so much she's taken to wearing shawls or long sleeves in public even
on the hottest days.

"When's Daddy coming back?"

Daddy. It's what Iphigenia said as Agamemnon raised the sword.
She'd been calling him "Dad" or "Father" for two or three years
before her death. Only right at the end, piss streaming down her
legs, had she reverted to the baby word: *Daddy.*

A final plea for mercy.

Ignored.

She pushes Electra's leg off her knees. "Tomorrow."

"But the watchfires are all lit."

"You'll see him tomorrow. He'll stay at the Sea House tonight."

"Why?"

"Because he's got a lot of soldiers with him and they've all got to
get up very early in the morning and march into the city. And—"

"Why?"

Electra's constant "whys" aren't requests for information, they're demands for attention. But they do have the unfortunate effect of making her sound stupid (which she is not) and babyish as well. "Because people want to celebrate, they want to cheer and throw flowers and . . . and they can't do any of that in the dark." *Please, please, don't ask why.* "Look, tomorrow night there'll be a big party in the hall and—"

"Can I come?"

"Yes, of course you can."

No, she can't. *Face that when I come to it.*

"And can I wear my dress?"

"Yes."

They've been through all this so many times. Like every other conversation with Electra, it's repetitive, maddening—and, fundamentally, false. This is the way you'd talk to a small, overexcited child, and Electra isn't a child, she's nearly fifteen. The same age Iphigenia was when she died. Young girls are powerful presences. Is that why everything—the singing, the running footsteps, the handprints on the wall—seems to be getting worse?

"Can I wear my dress when he arrives?"

"I don't know, I'll have to think about it."

Part of her likes the idea of the dark-haired girl standing in front of the rows of grey-haired counsellors, her dress an unignorable splash of ox-blood red against the white of their tunics. But that might be a bit too soon.

Electra yawns. It's a relief, that glimpse of healthy normal skin on the inside of her mouth. "You're tired, aren't you? Why don't you go to bed a bit early? You won't enjoy tomorrow if you're tired."

"I can't sleep."

"Well, then, perhaps Iras is right? A bath might help you sleep."

"No, it won't."

Fretful now, accusing. Is she aware of the constant stab of accusation in her voice? *Is it there, or do I imagine it?* She hasn't been a good mother to Electra. For the first two years after Iphigenia's death, Electra had been abandoned to the care of slaves. Orestes too, for that matter, but he was older, and already spending much of his time in the training yards, absorbed into the world of men. Perhaps because of that he'd suffered less—or learned to hide the hurt better?

Now, when she tries to reach out to this living daughter, she just feels jets of anger, because here she is: breastless, hipless Electra, covered in sores she won't stop scratching—except when she's pinching her mother's arms. Skin *hurts*—that seems to be the one constant in Electra's world. Even now she's clawing at the scaly patches on her feet. "Try not to," Clytemnestra says, hopelessly.

"I can't help it. It's *them*."

That's another thing: she's got it into her head she's got jiggers. It's not clear how she even knows about jiggers unless she's heard some of the slaves talking about Razmus. There's no other way she could know. Another puddle of sweat is forming between her body and Electra's, who's now dumped both feet onto Clytemnestra's lap. Doesn't the sweat sting? It must do: look at the cracks in her skin. She starts to ease herself away but instantly Electra's grip tightens. She tries to make herself relax, to accept and even welcome the unwanted closeness, but then, suddenly—

Enough! She pushes Electra away. "C'mon, you need a bath. It does help, and even if it doesn't you've still got to be clean."

"The water stings."

"You're going to be awfully tired tomorrow, if you go on like this. And you want to be able to enjoy it, don't you? Seeing Da—" No, no use, her tongue would rot if she said it. "Seeing your father again."

"Hmm."

"Now what?"

"Suppose I don't recognize him?"

"You will. He's the king. Everybody's going to be looking at him."

"Suppose he doesn't like me?"

Wearily, she strokes the long, black hair. "Of course he'll like you."

He'll be utterly repelled by her. Agamemnon, in all the time she'd known him, had never showed a scrap of sympathy for sick or disabled people; in fact, he did everything he could to avoid them. Even his own mother when she was dying. What's odd is that he doesn't seem to feel disgust, it's more like fear, as if somehow their weakness might be contagious, putting him at risk of catching it. She's seen him kick beggars in the street. Illness in his own family he finds especially difficult; she'd learned early in her marriage never to be ill. The same applied to the children; they weren't allowed to have weaknesses, because they had to reflect well on him. And nobody did that better than Iphigenia: beautiful, charming, intelligent, glowing with health and vitality—no wonder he adored her—though he was blind to the fierce, uncomfortable integrity that had been her most distinctive quality.

This is the hardest thing of all for her to acknowledge: that Agamemnon loved Iphigenia.

Another painful tweak to her skin. "Mummy?"

"What's wrong, baby?"

"I don't know. I want Daddy."

"He'll be here soon."

Gradually, Electra falls asleep in her arms. Clytemnestra sits watching a cockchafer dancing around the lamp, its big, clumsy shadow flickering over the walls. Tonight, as soon as Electra's settled, she'll go to the Sea House and meet Agamemnon there—*if* he's willing; he may not be. Though she can't imagine he'll want their first meeting to take place in public any more than she does. She eases Electra off her knee and onto the couch. She jerks her arms and legs—the way a drowsy baby does when you try to put it down—then slips into sleep again. After waiting a few moments to be sure, Clytemnestra goes to the door, intending to summon Iras and impress on her yet again the need for Electra to be carefully supervised—and particularly tomorrow.

The door open, she pauses for a second to look back into the room. Steady, quiet breathing: good. At first, the palace seems equally peaceful, but then she catches the sound of footsteps on the stairs. It's more than one person: there's a lot of conspiratorial giggling going on. Earlier, she thought she heard the children singing, though it's rare for them to sing by day. Now, stepping out into the corridor, she's met by whispering and laughter and a pattering of feet as they run towards her, closer, and then closer, hurtling towards her, though there's nothing to see. The laughter reaches a peak as they rush past her, running, always running, down long, twisting corridors, starved of light.

14

By mid-afternoon, the mist was closing in again. I still hung over the railings, though with every passing minute there was less to see, the land reduced to a brown blur and the shoreline visible only as a sprinkling of white foam where the sea broke over half-submerged rocks. We were making progress, but slower than before, until at last, in a frenzy of shouted orders and rattling chains, the sails were furled and men took their places on the rowing benches again. Rows of muscular, sweaty backs bent to the oars—a novelty, at first, though it wasn't long before the *thud, thud, thud* of the staff beating time became indistinguishable from the pulse of blood in my head.

Cassandra was leaning forward, like a second figurehead, urging the ship on. I thought of the women who'd spent the entire voyage crammed into the holds of other ships; what were they feeling? Perhaps the prospect of release from that stinking darkness might be enough to make them welcome arrival on a foreign shore. I could more easily imagine *their* feelings than Cassandra's. After a while, I felt a sprinkling of rain on my bare arms; Cassandra must have felt it too, but even then she was reluctant to go below. It took a sudden sharp downpour to make her move.

I'd already done most of the packing. As we sat on the edge of our bunks, we heard the boxes being taken away, but I still had charge of the "special" clothes bag and the jewellery case.

Sitting there, listening to the rhythmic beating of the staff, I realized I had no idea what was going to happen next. "Are we going to the palace tonight?"

"No, it'll be too late for that."

"So, are we staying on board?"

"I don't know, I don't know any more than you do. Agamemnon thinks he might stay at the Sea House—apparently, they used to spend their summers there when the children were small." As she spoke, her fingers were hard at work smoothing out the creases in her tunic. Perhaps she'd begun to understand that Agamemnon's marriage, like all long marriages, had a complex history: nooks and crannies, holes and corners, blossoming orchards and abandoned barricades, the varied landscapes of a shared life; and now, suddenly, she was feeling like an interloper, treading on ground she'd thought was solid but was crumbling fast beneath her feet. "I know he wants to get an early start. They all do—nobody fancies marching in the heat."

We sat in silence for a while. Heavy footsteps tramped along the passage outside our door.

Cassandra stood up. "You know, I think we'd be better up on deck."

"You'll get soaked."

"Better that than sit here. Have you got the bag?"

I nodded at the back of the door.

"Whatever you do, hang on to that."

We went up on deck and stood around, shivering. An hour passed. As the ship drew closer to land, Agamemnon appeared, wrapped in a long, dark cloak with only a gold circlet round his head to indicate his rank. The sailors were busy with ropes and chains, their sharp eyes estimating distances; one slip between the ship and the dock wall could be fatal. I was looking over the rail at slabs of phlegm-green water slapping against the side. Seagulls skimmed the water, squabbling over scraps. There was a powerful smell of fish. We were told to stand well back as ropes were passed from deck to land, looped around bollards and fastened in complicated knots. At last, the ship was subdued, though never entirely still; only a constant creaking and straining of ropes bound it to the harbour wall.

A brief wait, before Agamemnon stepped onto dry land. A moment in history, I suppose. A group of men in ceremonial robes, waiting to greet him, cheered. Raising a hand in acknowledgement, he started climbing the steps and—still attended only by Machaon—took his place under a richly embroidered canopy. Andreas came up to us and indicated to Cassandra that she should follow the king. Instantly, she grabbed me—one of those moments of childish dependence that filled me with exasperation, and pity. For once, she managed the transfer from deck to land as nimbly as a boy. I can't claim to have been equally agile, but at least I managed not to trip and fall flat on my face. Though the relief was short-lived: the minute I tried to walk, I realized my legs had turned to jelly.

"Don't worry, love," one of the sailors said. "Soon get your land legs back."

If anything, Cassandra was worse than me, pale, sweating, barely able to stand up. We clung to each other, two women taking their first steps on foreign ground—in effect, learning to walk again.

Perhaps Agamemnon was having the same problem; he did seem a bit unsteady on his feet, though he disguised it well. Even under the canopy, he was surrounded by people eager to touch him. Any bit of him they could reach was clutched, stroked, pawed, fondled . . . It was extraordinary, like one of the phalluses you see standing outside temples, their carved wood worn smooth by countless thousands of rubbing hands. Finally, a squad of guards appeared and began pushing the crowds back, clearing a space around him. There he stood, a great king—arguably, at that moment, the most powerful man in the world—setting foot on his native soil for the first time in ten years, having won the greatest military victory in history.

I didn't give a toss for any of that. Glancing back at the ship, I saw Andreas leaning over the rail and thought, perhaps foolishly, that he was looking for me. There'd been no time to say a proper goodbye; somehow, in the last busy hours, this parting had crept up on us. Now, it was too late, though keeping my hand half-hidden in the folds of my shawl I did give a discreet little wave.

Whether he saw it or not, I don't know.

Cassandra loosened her hold on me and, together, we took a few independent steps, though we gave up almost immediately and clung to the sea wall. On the steps below us, a crowd of women were mending nets: laughing, talking, obviously fascinated by what was going on above their heads. They never paused in their work, and hard graft it was too, by the looks of their hands. They were calloused—particularly, I noticed, in the triangle between thumb and forefinger. Some of the younger women had patches of raw skin there. It helped to focus on small details, because the ground was swaying beneath my feet and the rows of houses lining the road ahead rose and fell like waves.

Agamemnon was speaking to a herald, a grey-haired man in early middle age who'd have been tall even without the magnificent horsehair plumes nodding above his helmet. After taking leave of the king, he came up to Cassandra and bowed—to my eyes that bow looked skimped, even a tad sarcastic—and told her she was to get into the cart that had just pulled up at the end of the jetty. From where we stood, that looked a long way off, but my balance was improving all the time and even Cassandra was moving better. All the same, it was a relief to climb into the cart and know that all we had to do now was sit there and let the driver take us to the Sea House, if that was where we were going.

With no more than a casual glance behind him, the driver clicked his tongue and the bullocks walked on. Cassandra leaned forward to ask where he was taking us. "The Sea House," he replied. His manner was civil enough, though I thought I detected the same subtle lack of respect I'd noticed in the herald. There'll always be people who label captive women "whores" because they lack the basic empathy to imagine what it's like to have no say in what's done to your body.

Once we'd left the harbour, there was nothing much to look at except the back of the driver's head, which was completely bald, with one deep fold of fat in his neck that looked disturbingly like a mouth. Like I say, it helps to notice the details. After a while, since Cassandra asked no further questions, the driver started to talk, apparently eager to show off his knowledge, though how he knew was a mystery. He told us that Agamemnon and the queen virtually lived in the Sea House during the summer months when the palace became stiflingly hot. "People think it's cool, up there in the hills, but it bloody isn't. Back end of summer, it's like a frying pan. Whereas down on the coast you always get a bit of a breeze. And they could lead a normal life—away from the palace. All that pomp and ceremony, they don't like it, you know. The king always used to say, 'Why do they keep giving me beef? I'd just as soon have a nice bit of fish.' Freshly caught, mind you, straight off the boats. Oh, and barley porridge—he's *very* fond of that. Underneath, you know, they're just like you and me."

"Agamemnon's just like you?" I said.

"Why, aye, you could have a drink with him, bit of a laugh . . ."

Best mates with Agamemnon. Oh my god. Over the years, I must have learned the medicinal uses of . . . oh, I don't know, *hundreds* of plants, and never yet found one to cure stupidity.

We'd left the town behind us now. To our right, you could see all the way down to the beach where a pool of water, left behind by the retreating tide, had trapped the moon. The air smelled of salt and something sharper: sea lavender, perhaps. We were jerking from side to side, and I was holding tight to the edge of the cart. I was starting to feel sore, but then we turned a corner and saw the villa straight ahead of us. And it *was* a villa—I mean, a family home, not a palace.

"What's that building over there?" I asked. "You know, the one you can see from the harbour?"

Of course, I already knew the answer, but I was curious to know what he'd say.

"Ah." Despite the ruts in the road, he turned to look at us. "That's where Iphigenia's buried. Bless her holy name."

Cassandra, clear and cool: "Agamemnon sacrificed her, didn't he? To get a wind for Troy."

"He had no choice. The gods required it."

Cassandra laughed. "The gods must have broad backs, don't you think? Anything anybody does gets blamed on them."

An affronted silence. Even the back of his head exuded offence. Meanwhile, the cart lurched onwards; we were going up the steepest part of the hill, the bullocks making an odd barking sound as they took the strain. I put both arms behind me, bracing myself against the side. My back was complaining bitterly, not just about the lurching of the cart, but about the horsehair mattress I'd slept on for the last two nights.

Gradually, the ground began to level off and we started to feel a cool breeze.

"Why's she buried here?" Cassandra asked.

"It's where she was happiest, I suppose. The queen likes to come here. She spends a fair bit of time by the grave."

Craning my neck, I saw hundreds of thousands of stars, so bright they looked like swarms of fireflies. I nudged Cassandra to look up. "Amazing," she said, but I could tell her mind was on other things. We lapsed into silence after that, partly because the track veered close to the edge of a sheer drop and neither of us wanted to distract the driver. He'd started singing tunelessly under his breath, a song about a man who had a rabbit. That was it, no rhyme or reason to it, just that, on and on and on. It helped him concentrate, I suppose—or at least I was hoping it did.

At last, we pulled up in front of the villa. A short flight of steps led to an imposing entrance with skilfully carved stone lions on either side. The lions of Mycenae. Cassandra stretched her legs and waited for the driver to hand her down. Bugger all point *me* waiting, so I slid off the tailgate and took a few experimental steps. The jelly legs had gone. Realizing that no assistance would be forthcoming, Cassandra scrambled down after me, took a deep breath and strode towards the steps. At that moment, the door opened to reveal a spare, angular figure, chest as flat as a boy's, though judging by the length of the tunic it had to be a woman. Since she was silhouetted against the light, her face wasn't visible until she came a little way out of the house and looked down at the driver.

"No king?"

"Got waylaid. Couldn't swear to it, but I think a jug or two might be involved."

"Huh, that's him set up for the night, then. I don't know, first he's coming, then he isn't. What am I supposed to do? Give him a fry-up if he walks through the door?" She was peering past him into the darkness. "Who's this, then?"

"She's the latest . . . you know."

"Well, I'm certainly not cooking for *her*."

"The king sent us," Cassandra said.

Sharp, chestnut-brown eyes raked her from head to toe. "Did he now? I suppose you'd better come in, then. And you—" She nodded at the driver. "There's a meal for you in the kitchen." She saw him start to climb the steps. "Oh no you don't—*that* way."

Crestfallen, he slouched along the gravel path and disappeared round the side of the house, the crunch of his footsteps fading slowly into silence. By this time, Cassandra was inside the hall. Despite her apparent confidence, I could tell she was uncertain. An overnight stay in a house she hadn't even known existed, till Agamemnon mentioned it, didn't fit into the rigid parameters of her prophecy. She and Agamemnon were meant to die in the palace within hours of their arrival. Now, unexpectedly, here was another night of life, and I could see she didn't know what to do with it. Terrible to be so young and so wedded to death. Me, I was just looking forward to some food, perhaps a walk round the gardens and then a good night's sleep in a halfway decent bed. But I was looking forward to it—that's the point.

Meanwhile, I followed her into the hall, where the woman who seemed to be the housekeeper—almost certainly a slave, but a slave with some status—was still looking her up and down. Cassandra's hair was straggly, her skin flushed from the hours she'd spent on deck. I thought the woman looked contemptuous but perhaps slightly relieved. Nothing for the mistress to worry about there. That's the impression I was getting, anyway.

"I daresay you'll be wanting your bed."

We followed her up the stairs to a room on the first floor sparsely furnished but with a blue coverlet on the bed and a good tapestry on the wall. From the woman's attitude, I'd been expecting a broom cupboard. She set the lamp down on a table by the bed and took her leave, having scarcely said a word to either of us. As soon as the door closed behind her, Cassandra fell onto the bed, every bit of energy draining out of her, though only an hour or so ago, I'd been thinking what a good colour she had. But that's early pregnancy for you.

"I'm going to see if I can get us a proper meal," I said.

That was me taking charge, taking decisions, a return to her first days in the camp when madness had left her incapable of deciding anything for herself. At the door, I hesitated. "Are you all right?"

She considered for a moment. "Yes, I think so."

"I'll not be long."

The kitchen, I knew, would be tucked away at the back of the house, but even without that knowledge my nose would have led me to it. Roasting meat, herbs, spices . . . I opened the door and a blast of hot air met me. The woman who'd taken us to our room came towards me, wiping her hands on her apron. I said something conciliatory about the delicious smell.

"Nice joint you've got there."

"He's very fond of lamb," she barked.

"Me 'n' all," the driver said. He was sitting at a table by the far wall, wiping grease from his mouth on the sleeve of his tunic.

"Oh, you—you'd eat anything."

But she was smiling as she said it. Apart from that: well, poor woman. She'd been right at the back of the queue when looks were dished out. Teeth, they were the first thing you noticed, very white, healthy looking, but leaning every which way like tombstones in an ancient graveyard. She was one of those slaves who spend their entire lives in the kitchen, scouring pots, turning spits, red-faced, sweating, hair stringy with grease, and the one thing you can guarantee about those women is that they hate concubines: women who lie flat on their backs, legs wide open, leading comfortable lives and doing bugger all to earn it, or so it must seem to a kitchen slave. I knew every woman Agamemnon had slept with in the past year, and it was no joyride, believe me.

"Well?" she said, in a marginally less hostile tone. "What do you want? Room's all right, isn't it?"

She had a big brown mole on her chin, with a single spiky black hair growing out of it. Perhaps I was looking a bit too closely because she started fingering the hair.

"Room's lovely, I love that tapestry," I said. "I was just wondering if my mistress could have something to eat?"

"*Mistress?* She's a free woman, then?"

I nodded, cautiously. Cassandra was a free woman, *if* her "marriage" to Agamemnon was valid, *if* he ever bothered to remember it had taken place.

"That looks delicious," I said, pointing at the simmering pot. "Do you think you could spare us a bit?"

"Don't see why not. No bugger else is here to eat it."

"Excuse *me*," said the driver.

"Shurrup, you. You've been fed." She turned to me. "I'll make you up a tray. Go on, sit yourself down."

I climbed onto a high stool. "I'm Ritsa, by the way."

"Dacia."

"Pretty name."

"Mistress likes it." She took the wine jug and poured me a generous cup. "It was her picked it."

"Oh. So what was your real name?"

"Can't remember. I was only two when we came here, me mam died not long after, so I don't know what she called me. She must've called me something, mustn't she?"

I raised my cup. "Aren't you having one?"

She looked around and was obliged to acknowledge that nothing required her immediate attention. "Aye, all right."

I watched her pour a cup for herself. "Must be quiet when the family's not here."

"It is, but I'm used to it. There's not been a proper family gathering here for—oh, I don't know how long."

"Ten years?"

"Not as long as that. Fact, the queen used to bring the children here a lot during the war. There was the tomb being built, and she needed to keep an eye on that." Mentioning the tomb produced a momentary hoarseness, quickly flushed away by a gulp of wine. Surfacing, she wiped her upper lip. "This is home, you know—far more than the palace is."

"It feels like a home."

That pleased her. Another longer gulp; the wine was good, but she wasn't drinking it for pleasure, she was drinking to numb pain. I know the signs.

"The tomb's that building further up?"

"That's right. It's a temple to Artemis really. The grave's inside the temple."

"Her mother brought her back? Because she didn't die here, did she?"

"No, she died at Aulis." The silence after she finished speaking went on so long I thought she wasn't going to say any more, but then she said, "The queen brought her all the way home in a cart. She wasn't going to leave her there on her own."

"No, well, you wouldn't, would you? I lost a daughter the same age as Iphigenia. She died at home, but if she'd died anywhere else, I'd have stopped at nothing to get her back."

"Oh, I'm sorry," she said. "It's awful to lose a child at that age. Well, at any age . . ."

"What was she like?"

"Lovely. She was lovely. Always hanging round the kitchen, especially if it was baking day. *Can I lick the bowl?* I always used to leave a little bit extra because I knew how much she liked it." A deep sigh. "And now people pray at her grave."

"Do they blame the king?"

She looked over her shoulder at the driver, but he seemed to have nodded off. "Some do."

His eyes opened. "No, they don't. Nobody blames the king."

"I suppose most people think he was just doing the best he could." She finished her wine. "Anyway, I'd best be getting on. I'll just cut you a couple of slices off that." She cut two generous portions of lamb and added bread, cheese, olives, two cups and what was left of the wine. By the time she'd finished, we had a substantial meal.

"Can you manage that? I can easy send a maid."

"No, it's all right, I can manage. Thanks."

Cassandra was sitting up in bed when I got back. Lowering the tray onto a table, I said, "Here, get some of this down you. Do you good."

We ate in silence for a while. Then I said, "I got talking to the cook." She showed no interest; in Cassandra's world, the gossip of kitchen slaves had no possible significance. "I think the queen comes here a lot."

"At the moment, I'm more interested in the whereabouts of the king. Where is he?"

"Oh, he'll have been given a bed for the night. And a girl to go with it, I should think."

"What else did you find out?"

"People pray at Iphigenia's grave."

"Do they blame the king?"

"I doubt it. People don't turn against a king in wartime, no matter how big a bastard he is."

"Yes, but the war's over. Don't you think they're going to start asking questions?"

I shook my head. "No, they'll move on. Be years before anybody looks back and says, 'What the fuck was all that about?' We'll be long gone."

"I will."

I sighed, a protracted, deep, audible, intended-to-be-irritating sigh. We finished the meal in silence after that.

Then she handed me the tray. "I think I might try to sleep."

She slid down the bed and, within minutes, her breathing had steadied, leaving me to contemplate the night ahead. Sleep wouldn't come easily, I knew that, so I decided to go out, have a look at the temple, pay my respects at Iphigenia's grave; remember how it felt to queue for hot bread and cinnamon buns on a bright, windy morning in Lyrnessus; remember how it felt to have a daughter waiting for me to come home.

15

I slipped through the house, carrying a candle that threw a quivering light over the tapestries on the walls. Good tapestries too, mainly depicting scenes from the stories surrounding Artemis, the lady of animals.

Me, twelve years old, on my way to her temple in Lyrnessus. Like every other girl when her bleeding starts, I'd been told I had to take my dolls to the temple and leave them there. I'd never been one of those girls who were devoted to their dolls, though there was one I'd quite liked, perhaps because my father had made her for me; I'd been reluctant to let *her* go. At the same time, I hadn't wanted to seem childish, so I'd swung her carelessly by her woollen hair as I'd walked to the temple with my mother and left her there before the altar. Not once had I looked back, though I'd thought I could hear her crying for me.

My mother had brushed my hair back from my forehead. "There's a good girl." I'd just looked straight ahead.

Dolls are supposed to prepare you for motherhood, but that doll wasn't a pretend baby, she was *me*, or a version of me, and I hadn't been anywhere near ready to give her up.

Leaving the house by the main entrance, I paused on the top step. There was light enough to see by, so I set off along the side of the house, my feet crunching gravel as I went. As soon as I rounded the corner, I saw the temple straight ahead of me and walked towards it over an expanse of silver grass. An owl hooted in the trees; seconds later, another owl replied.

A high wall with an iron gate set into it divided the temple grounds from the garden of the house. I half expected to find the gate locked, but it swung open the moment I touched it. Well oiled, well used. Closing it quietly behind me, I found myself in a court-yard paved with slabs of white stone. There were beds of flowers and shrubs around the edges, but my first impression was of scouring white light. The moon shone mercilessly down, so bright that every leaf—every vein on every leaf—was distinctly present. It reminded me of a rhyme we used to sing when I was a child. *Boys and girls, come out to play, the moon doth shine as bright as day.* A happy rhyme—or so it had seemed to me at the time. It's only when you get a bit older you begin to see the weirdness of it.

Everything here was so quiet. Nothing moved. Not a breath of air, though a heavy scent hung over the flower beds that lined the surrounding wall. Night-scented stocks, a flower I love, and have no luck with whatsoever, though other people find them easy enough to grow. Instinctively, feeling as exposed as a black beetle in that harsh glare, I made for the shadow of the tomb. Halfway along the facing wall was a dark slit barred by an iron gate, wide enough for one person to enter, though only just. That surprised me, even disappointed me, a little, for surely a building as imposing as this required an equally impressive entrance? Not a secretive aperture that seemed designed to discourage visitors rather than invite them in. Beside the cleft stood a full-length carving of Artemis, one hand resting on the neck of a young hind. Usually, statues of the gods are merely bland images of divine beauty, blank eyes, braided hair, a smile that barely curves the lips, but this face was startlingly indi-vidual: thick eyebrows, deep-set eyes, a squarish jaw—unmistakably the portrait of a real person.

Piled up on the ground around her feet was the usual collection of dolls: some with brightly painted eyes and clean, white tunics; others, patched, dirty, mottled, threadbare; a few hardly more than sticks with bits of wool stuck on to resemble hair. As always, I found the sight moving but disturbing too. Dolls are powerful; they shouldn't be, but they are. I was glad to turn away.

Peering between the railings, I saw a short passage leading to an inner courtyard where an oblong of flickering lights marked out a grave. No elaborate tomb; this whole edifice had been built to contain a much simpler memorial to the dead girl. I felt uncomfortable, as if I'd stumbled upon a place of private grief. Memories of my own lost daughter began to slide over each other, forming, re-forming, endlessly intersecting like those planes of clear water you see at low tide. Somewhere close at hand, a horse whinnied, a sufficiently surprising sound to send me scurrying across the dazzling white flags to the shadows at the other side, where a fringe of oily, black leaves provided shelter from the glare of moonlight. I found a bench and sat down, squeezing my lids tight shut, as tears began to smart and burn.

When I opened them again, she was there. Plainly dressed, no obvious signs of rank, though I guessed who it was immediately: something about her easy familiarity with the place. She was looking through the gate at the grave, so I couldn't see her face. Her shoulders were broad, her arms white and muscular, and I wondered, in passing, how she'd developed that physical strength, since this was a woman who would never in her life have needed to lift a comb to her own hair. She was chafing her arms, as if she were cold, though I didn't see how anybody could be cold in this heat. As I watched, she began walking up and down, stopping now and then to look towards the road, obviously waiting for somebody. Terrified she might turn round and see me, I edged along the flower beds until I stumbled through an archway leading into a walled garden beyond. Keeping to the grass verges, I managed to reach a bench on the other side without making any noise at all. Sitting down, I noticed that I could see straight through the archway directly to the tomb. I could see the flickering of small lights. *She sits here*, I thought. *This is her bench.*

The thought was enough to move me on. Cautiously, I began to walk along the paths between the beds. There were roses—masses of them—and lilies, with their raw, swooning scent. Other plants, particularly at the edges of the garden, were more surprising: yarrow, fennel, dill, angelica, sweet alyssum. Marigolds, everywhere. All the plants that ladybirds love; no wonder her roses were aphid-free. An eccentric garden, I thought, in many ways—much more so than appeared at first sight. I loved it—and just as well, since I seemed to be trapped in it. There was no way out except through the archway, I would have to wait for her to go; but when I returned to the bench, I saw that she was still pacing up and down. More arm-chafing: that had to be some sort of nervous tic. Perhaps she was getting tired of waiting? With any luck, she'd give up and go, and I'd be free to go too. Meanwhile, I sat back and enjoyed a rare moment of peace.

16

He isn't coming. It's perfectly clear by now that he's not coming, and yet still she lingers. It's humiliating, hanging about like this, waiting for him—or at least, she's starting to feel it is. One more walk up and down the terrace and then she'll go, *definitely*. She's even beginning to wonder if it was a good idea to arrange to meet him here: the last thing she wants is for this place, of all places, to be contaminated by his presence.

From where she's standing, she can't quite make out the horses, though she can hear them, cropping grass. Right at the end of the terrace, and then a little further, she can just see Apollodorus sitting on the grass, absent-mindedly stroking his horse's neck. Now, if she were "working her way through the palace guard," that's where she'd start, Apollodorus, no question—and having started with him, would she even bother to move on? Anyway, no possibility of that. So much of her life over the last ten years has been spent in the service of death. A waste? Some would say so. The majority, perhaps.

One more turn and then that's it, she's leaving. At the exact moment she turns to go, he steps out of the shadows. She hears herself give an involuntary gasp, the sound a very young girl might make on unexpectedly encountering a lover. Decades out of place. Would she ever have made that sound for him? Doubtful. He stands there, not moving. Does he expect her to go to him? Deep, steadying breath—and then, in a clear, cold voice, she says: "I was just about to go. I didn't think you were coming."

"Clytemnestra."

The way he says it, it sounds more like a label than a name. She sees him assessing her, inspecting her for changes, and his scrutiny makes her self-conscious, too aware of her own face and body to be able to identify changes in him. She has a confused sense that he's bigger than she remembers, taller, broader across the shoulders, stronger perhaps, but that's just a vague, chaotic impression. And meanwhile, she's being appraised, scanned—almost, it seems, catalogued.

"It was a good excuse to get away. The last thing I need is a heavy night. We've got to be on our way before dawn."

"It just seemed the obvious thing to do—to meet in private first. There'll be no time to talk tomorrow."

A brief silence, then he clears his throat. "What's happening tomorrow evening?"

"There'll be a feast. Quite small." She sounds breathless now. "I thought for the first night we'd keep it quite intimate, just a few of your . . . well, your most loyal supporters. And they have been loyal, they never wavered, even when—"

"Even when?"

"The casualty figures were high."

"A lost generation. That's what they're saying, isn't it?"

"Is it? I—"

"A generation of young men sacrificed to give my brother back his whore. It's not pleasant, you know, hearing that." He wipes a hand across his mouth. "But then I don't suppose it's pleasant hearing your sister called a whore."

"Oh, I'm well used to that. It's all the old men ever talk about: Helen, the whore. I'm not even sure it's about Helen, I think it's a way of getting at me."

"But there's been no resistance?"

"No, of course not, they wouldn't—"

Dare, she had been going to say, but she doesn't want to sound too ruthless—or, for that matter, too competent, though she has been both. She moves further away from him, closer to the slit in the side of the tomb. "I'm afraid there's one person who won't be there tomorrow . . ."

She pauses, and there it is, the first crack in his façade—his jaw, neck and shoulders tensing up as he waits for her to say the name.

"Orestes, I'm afraid he won't be there."

"Why, what's the matter with him? Is he ill?"

"Oh, no, don't worry, he's fine, it's just he's been staying with a friend. The messenger's already left. He'll be back home in a couple of days."

"He should be here."

"Yes, I know, I'm sorry." She hesitates. "It hasn't always been easy, you know. He blamed me when he wasn't allowed to go to Troy."

"He's my only son. I couldn't risk losing him."

"Achilles' son fought at Troy; he was an only child. As soon as Orestes knew Pyrrhus was there, he thought everybody was laughing at him, sniggering behind his back. *Proper little mummy's boy, Orestes, can't fight, daren't fight*, that sort of thing. I couldn't get through to him after that, so when he asked if he could go and stay with his friend, it just seemed better to let him go." She waits for him to speak, but he is looking around the courtyard. After letting the silence go on for a while, she says, "I notice you don't ask about Electra."

"Electra?"

"Your daughter?"

"How is she?"

"Unhappy."

"What about?"

She laughs. "I can think of one or two things, can't you?"

He shakes his head, not in denial, more like somebody trying to shake off a wasp. "Sometimes you've just got to get on with it."

"*Get on with it?*"

"Well, isn't that what ordinary people do?"

Ordinary people. She'd forgotten how often he uses that phrase, always with the same . . . well, what is it, exactly? Curiosity? Fascination? As if "ordinary people" were some kind of exotic species you'd be lucky to spot twice in a lifetime. That's what being the son of Atreus did to you. He's moved closer to her now, even reaching out as if to touch her arm, though his fingertips fall short. That aborted touch, or appeal, or even—god help us—caress, brings everything to a stillness. Even the flowers seem to hold their breath. She wants to move her arm but forces herself to stay still. The tension crackles in the space between her skin and his.

Finally, she says: "You won't even look at her."

"Who?"

"Your daughter."

He glances haplessly from side to side as if he expects to see Electra, the dumpy little girl he only half remembers, racing across the court to greet him.

But Clytemnestra's pointing to the carving. "Look at her. Go on, *look*."

He flicks his eyes to the statue, and away.

"What was I supposed to do? Sweating sickness, no drinking water, food running out, latrines overflowing . . . Nestor—he's an old man, for god's sake, you can't expect him to live like that."

"Oh, so you're telling me you sacrificed our daughter so Nestor could have a comfortable shite? Is that it?"

"Every priest in the camp was saying the same thing. We'd offended the gods, *I'd* offended the gods, there had to be a sacrifice, and not just a cow or a sheep either. It had to be something that mattered, something that was going to hurt. The gods demanded it."

"Like you ever cared about the gods!"

"I did care. I was made to care." He stops and looks around him, taking in this huge building and the gardens that had not been there when he left. "I'm not going to apologize for what I did."

"*Apologize?*"

"It was either that or the whole fucking coalition would have fallen apart."

"Oh, yes—and you wanted your war."

He throws up his hands. "What's done can't be undone. The only thing worth talking about now is how we get through the next few days. After that . . . I don't know. You can live separately, if that's what you want. You could live here."

"That'd suit you, wouldn't it?"

"Why d'you say that?"

"I know what went on, you and your women . . ."

"How do you know?"

"I had spies."

"Do you think I didn't? You can talk all you like about my women, what about Aegisthus?"

"What about him?"

"He's been sniffing round you for years."

"Is *that* what they told you?"

"Yes."

"That's just pathetic. I was a woman governing alone, I needed somebody to bash heads together now and then."

"And you chose him?"

"Why not him? He can fight."

"Oh, yes, he can fight all right, vicious little bastard. But he's no friend of mine, and you chose him knowing that."

"There wasn't a lot of choice. Virtually every man of fighting age was in Troy."

"No, well, I had no choice either. The women were awarded to me by the army, I couldn't refuse."

"Oh, poor you. Anyway, what do you mean, you couldn't refuse? You had the power!"

"*You've* had power for the last ten years. How easy have you found it?" He sees her look away. "No, you see? It doesn't solve everything, does it? In fact, it's bloody amazing how many things you can't do *with* power."

"All right, I give you that."

"You know, to a very great extent, *you* decide what happens next. You might find you want to step away from the palace. It's not as if you've ever been happy there!"

"Is anybody?"

"And you've always liked it here."

"Still do."

He turns towards her with fresh hope. "So, we agree then?"

"I'll do whatever you think is best. I don't intend to make trouble."

He lets out an audible breath. "Has it helped, meeting in private like this?"

"Has it helped *you?*"

"Do you know, I think it has . . ."

An awkward pause, or perhaps just a recognition that they've reached the end of the road. "You'd better get some sleep," she says. "Long day, tomorrow."

"Yes."

Though not as long as you think.

17

The clop of horses' hooves faded into the distance, leaving a wash of silence in their wake.

I was sheltering in the shadow of the archway, praying for Agamemnon to go, but he seemed in no hurry to leave. He looked around, his tall figure dwarfed by the immensity of the tomb. After a while he walked up to the slit and peered through the gate, seeing, as I'd seen earlier, an oblong of small lamps burning round a grave—nightlights, perhaps, for a child who might once have been afraid of the dark. What was he thinking? I couldn't imagine and was afraid to try. After a while, he straightened up, squared his shoulders and set off towards the house. I listened to the scuffle and crunch of his footsteps moving from stone to gravel; then, nothing. Even the owls were silent. Only when he'd turned the corner did I breathe easily again, though many minutes passed before I felt confident enough to follow him.

Inside the house, I picked up the candle I'd left burning on the hallstand and started retracing my steps through the quiet house. I remembered my way by the tapestries, particularly the one of Acteon being torn to pieces by his own hounds because he'd accidently seen Artemis naked, bathing in a stream. A good tapestry, powerful. How vengeful the gods are, and how fiercely that vengeance was being celebrated here. A little further along I came to the door of our room and was about to enter when I caught a murmur of voices: Agamemnon's, deep, persuasive; Cassandra's, blurry, only half awake.

Shrugging, I set off to find myself somewhere to sleep, walking along corridors and opening doors at random until I found a bedroom that looked unoccupied. For several minutes after I crawled under the coverlet, I didn't think or feel anything, but then in flashes began to revisit the scene I'd just witnessed: Clytemnestra's mouth, which I remembered as a scarlet gash while knowing that it hadn't been like that at all; Agamemnon's hand frozen an inch away from her arm. Her skin had twitched like a horse's when it's being plagued by flies. I hadn't seen that—I couldn't have done, I was too far away—but there it was in my mind's eye. So much anger, most of it directed from her to him. At times, he'd seemed indifferent, even bored. Oh, he'd dissimulated, he'd said whatever he needed to say to get what he wanted—and what he wanted was to get this woman out of his life. To have her settled in the Sea House tending her daughter's grave, far enough away for him never to have to think about her again. About either of them. Only a few minutes after parting from his wife, he'd been in bed with Cassandra. No hesitation, no pause for thought, but then he was the king; when it came to the women in his life, he could do as he liked.

Almost. There were some things he could neither change nor ignore: for ten years, Clytemnestra had governed Mycenae, in his absence; and she was the mother of the future king.

————

Next morning, raising my head from the pillow, I realized I'd been sleeping in a child's room, sparsely furnished, really just a place to wake up and race down to the beach from. Dust motes seethed in a shaft of sunlight. I lay sleepily looking around. Nothing had been tidied up, nothing put away or thrown away. On a table by the window was a collection of shells, arranged in concentric circles, with a mermaid's purse—evidently a real treasure—at the centre. I picked it up, caught a trace of the salty tang it must have had on the day a child discovered it and brought it home. Iphigenia? Or was this Orestes' room? Iphigenia's, I decided. His room would have changed, evolved, as he grew from childhood to manhood, whereas this was frozen in time.

It was past dawn. How far past I couldn't tell. I looked out of the window, but shadows mean nothing if you're not familiar with the place, so I set off to Cassandra's room. I half expected to be met by the sound of Agamemnon snoring, but there was no sound. No sound and no Cassandra. I felt a tweak of anxiety, though I knew where she'd be: Iphigenia's grave—she wouldn't leave here without seeing that. So I ran downstairs and set off for the temple. The barred entrance was open; looking along the passage, I saw Cassandra on her knees but didn't go to join her.

When she came out, she bowed to the statue of Artemis, bent down to look at the dolls and only in rising caught sight of me. Raising her veil, she came towards me.

"Has the king left?" I asked.

"Oh yes, he was up and off before dawn. *We* don't need to rush though." She looked around. "It's a beautiful place. I'm not surprised they loved it."

"The queen still does. She was here last night."

"Was she?"

"Yes, they had quite a long talk. He didn't mention it?"

"No." She walked on, perhaps more thoughtfully now. "I was looking at the offerings. You know, it's not just dolls, there's lots of toys, even a baby's first sandals." She held up her forefingers. "This big." Another few paces and she turned to look back at the tomb. "They worship her, don't they?"

"I think it's a cult, and the queen encourages it. I mean, look at the carving. It's supposed to be Artemis, but it's a very individual face. Whoever carved it, he knew that girl."

"Do you know she *wanted* to die? She went to her death willingly because the gods required it."

"Not what I've heard."

"Why, what have you heard?"

"That she fought them to her last breath."

"This is from Machaon?"

"Well. He was there."

"Yes, he was there—he was part of it. They all were."

"Look, you want to believe she was a martyr. She wasn't. She was just a young girl who had her life snatched away from her. This is Agamemnon, isn't it? Saying she was a martyr. I'm surprised you prefer his version of events. Next thing you know, the Trojan children will be throwing themselves off the battlements."

She opened her mouth to speak but checked herself.

I wasn't surprised by any of this. I thought she was in love with the idea of Iphigenia, a princess who'd sacrificed her life for her people, and was still being honoured for it, years after her death. Perhaps she found comfort in that, but if so it was a false comfort because one thing was certain: there'd be nobody praying at Cassandra's grave. She'd be lucky if they didn't put her out with the rubbish.

We walked on in silence, and as we approached the house, I dropped back a little, still keeping that one, crucial, catch-fart step behind.

Climbing the steps to the front door, she said, "You know, you pay far too much attention to Machaon. There may come a time when you have to choose." She retreated into silence again after that, and I certainly wasn't going to break it. Choose? *Me?* Chance would have been a fine thing.

Back in the bedroom, she glanced round the room. "Where's the bag?"

I fetched it from the corner and set it down beside her, expecting her to pull out a dress, but what she produced was a priest's robes and staff of office. No wonder the bag was so heavy; the staff alone must have weighed a ton. I wondered how she'd got her hands on those garments, because her own robes—the ones she was wearing when she arrived in the camp—had been ripped beyond repair.

"Calchas," she said, answering the unspoken question. "One priest to another. I'd have done the same for him."

Calchas, though Trojan by birth, had been the chief priest of Apollo in the Greek camp. After witnessing the destruction and carnage that had followed Agamemnon's victory, he'd taken off his priestly robes and walked, alone, across the battlefield into the ruined and still-smouldering city. Nobody and nothing was left alive, except for crows and feral dogs competing over the rotting remains. He'd been—and perhaps still was; I mean, he could still be alive—an immensely tall man, but if he'd given her his own robes, anyone of a hundred women in the weaving sheds could have altered them to fit.

And they did fit. After shaking out creases in the skirt, I stood back and was once again astonished by her, as I had been the first time we met. She was a different person, her youth and beauty subsumed in the dignity of her office.

"Well?" she said.

"You'll do."

We went downstairs, where we found the driver waiting. The previous night, his manner had been casual, bordering on insolent, but this morning, once he'd got over the shock of seeing her, he fell over himself to help her into the cart. Once she was settled, I slipped back into the house to say goodbye to Dacia, who seemed to appreciate the gesture. She was a woman I could have made a friend of if things had been different. It's one of the worst aspects of being a slave, the way you can't form any bonds that last, because you're always at the mercy of somebody else deciding it's time to move on.

Going downhill, the journey was faster, though no less alarming where the track veered closer to the edge. We found the little town in turmoil, its narrow streets clogged with chariots and horses. We sat on a low stone wall by the harbour, waiting to be told where to go. I looked over my shoulder, trying to locate the *Medusa*, and eventually found her but there was nobody on deck. Crowds of people milled all around us: young men of the elite guard glittering like gods, slave women blinking in the bright light after their confinement in the darkness of the holds. Those women compelled my attention then as they crowd my memory now. Did they even know what country they were in?

Close to where we were sitting, two chariots met head on, both drivers shouting and waving their whips, refusing to back down, until an obviously superior figure appeared and order was restored. Apart from that, nothing much seemed to be happening and, although we were in the open air, within a hundred yards of the sea, a stale smell hung over everything, as if yesterday's heat, trapped inside walls and withered grass, was slowly being released.

When, finally, the procession got started, I found myself unexpectedly near the front, walking behind the chariot in which Agamemnon rode with Cassandra by his side. I was surprised—shocked, really—that he chose to put her so conspicuously on display, but then, she was King Priam's daughter, once a princess, now Agamemnon's concubine, obliged to lie in his bed and bear his children. What better symbol could there be of Troy's defeat? In war, men carve messages on women's bodies, messages intended to be read by other men. But Cassandra was refusing to play the part. She held her head high, her priest's staff of office prominently displayed. You can be a princess in Troy one day and a bed-girl in Mycenae the next, but once a priest you are never not a priest. She was the voice of Apollo, and his scarlet bands were wound around her head. I felt proud of her; simply as a Trojan woman, a slave, trudging along behind Agamemnon's chariot, I saluted her. She disrupted the story they were telling about us, and that did, and does, matter.

As far as I could see, there was only one road leading out of the town. Halfway up a steep hill, I spotted a chandler's shop and remembered Andreas saying his brother-in-law was a chandler. This might be his shop—must be, in fact, because the town wasn't big enough to support two. I tried to see through the window, but in no time at all we were past, shops and houses thinning to a straggle and then disappearing altogether behind clouds of roiling dust. A long, straight road lay ahead of us, running between fields of pale stubble. Harvest was almost over. Even on the one farm where work was still going on, they were down to the last stand of corn, a ring of scrawny men and scrawnier dogs waiting for the hares and rabbits trapped inside to break cover and flee. Some of the men turned to stare, before turning back to the quivering grain. Agamemnon and his victory meant less than having something to put in the pot that night.

Looking down, watching the red dust inch up from my feet to my knees, I lost all sense of time. Dimly, I was aware of the long procession behind us, the chariots in pride of place behind Agamemnon, columns of marching men even further behind and, bringing up the rear, the Trojan women, some almost too weak to go on walking but managing somehow to limp on, the luckier among them clinging to the tailgate of a cart. By now, I'd given up even praying for the march to end, so it was a shock when, suddenly, the drumbeats stopped. Dazed, I looked around, remembering the existence of a world beyond sore feet and a dust-caked tongue. Charioteers jumped down to stretch their legs; goatskins sloshing with water were passed from hand to hand. When my turn came, I glugged eagerly, though the water smelled and even tasted of goat.

When we started marching again, I found I'd stiffened up quite badly. Every muscle in my legs ached and I was starting to shiver, though the sun was nearing its full height and there was no shade. Mouth open, thinking of nothing, I watched my feet appear and disappear from under the hem of my tunic, which like everything else was caked in red dust. At last, a buzz of excitement from the columns behind made me look up, and I saw a building that could only be the palace, shimmering in the heat. The pace quickened after that. Within half an hour, we were waiting outside a gate that was flanked by two carved lions towering above our heads. It was cooler here, beneath the high walls. I rested one sweaty hand against the stone and concentrated on getting my breath back.

Agamemnon had put on a mask of beaten gold, in shape rather like the face guards of a fighter's helmet, though the thin metal wouldn't have offered much protection on a battlefield. But then, it wasn't meant to. This was a purely ceremonial object, designed to inspire fear and awe. It succeeded. You caught a glimpse now and then of the eyes behind the mask, but otherwise the face was as inscrutable as a god's. Cassandra leaned over the edge of the chariot and passed a goatskin down to me. Our eyes met and she raised her eyebrows—an expression that could've meant anything or nothing, though it was obviously a comment of some sort on the mask. But I had no idea what she was thinking.

At last, after a few minutes filled with the uneasy stamping of horses' hooves, there was a great blaring of battle horns and the huge doors swung slowly open. A roar went up from the crowd as they caught their first sight of Agamemnon's chariot. I was pushed to one side, flattened against the wall by the press of fighters surging past. As soon as I could, I scrambled along the marching columns until I reached the front again, as close to Agamemnon's chariot wheels as I could get. The crowds had broken through the cordon; a forest of outstretched hands reached out to touch his robes, his skin, his hair. I watched the movements of that god-like mask as he turned his head from side to side, talking to the crowd, trying to calm them down. Even when I grasped the danger we were in— horses screaming, chariot rocking—I still didn't feel afraid. None of it seemed real until somebody's elbow jabbed me painfully in the breast—that was real! Soldiers of the elite guard quickly formed a ring around the chariot and began pushing people back. At last, order was restored, with the guards facing out into the crowd, swords drawn and shields raised.

Now, for the first time, I was able to take in my surroundings. The chariot had stopped at the foot of a vast stone staircase lead-ing up to the palace. At the top of the steps, wearing a dark blue robe, stood Clytemnestra, with two rows of grey-bearded counsel-lors lined up on her left, and priests in ceremonial robes bearing their staffs of office on her right. There was a moment of silence, broken only by a jingle of harness as horses tossed their heads. The sun's heat seemed to have narrowed to a single sharp point that was boring a hole in my skull. I desperately needed a drink of water and that made me realize I'd lost sight of the goatskin. When had that happened? I tried to imagine lemons being cut and squeezed, pic-tured the tart juice dripping into a blue bowl, but none of it helped. I couldn't even swallow, my mouth was so parched.

Finally, Clytemnestra began to speak. "Great king," she said. "Great king, welcome home!"

That was it: the crowd erupted. I mean, to be honest, she didn't need to say anything else after that, though of course she did. A lot of it passed me by; I was too busy dreaming about cold water and rubbing my sore breast. One thing did stand out, though: she didn't once look at him. She kept her eyes fixed on the crowd, almost as if she were addressing a court of law, putting a case. And when, finally, she did turn to face him, she started talking about a person who should have been there to welcome him home, a glaring gap in the rows of people lined up in front of him, and how baffling and painful that absence must be . . .

Everybody waited for the name.

"Orestes," she said. Orestes wasn't here to greet his father, but he'd been sent for and would be home in days.

She'd played exactly the same trick yesterday, but today was different: public, impersonal, an indictment.

She was sorry she'd had to send Orestes away, but really life in the palace had become intolerable. Messenger after messenger bringing news of Troy, and never good news. Agamemnon wounded, slightly wounded, badly wounded, hovering between life and death. If he'd been wounded half as many times as the messengers claimed he had, he'd be standing there in front of them with as many holes as a fishing net.

A ripple of amusement from the crowd, but only a ripple. She was dragging it out a bit, I thought, though by this time my bladder was bursting and any speech would have been too long. Fortunately, Agamemnon kept his short. He thanked the gods for granting him victory; if there was glory and honour in that victory, it belonged entirely to the gods. Though that turned out to be a bit debatable, since he went on to boast about the part he'd played in it. He hadn't just beaten Troy, he said, he'd *pulverized* it. One of the last things he'd done before leaving for home had been to walk around the ruined city and he'd seen with delight—yes, with delight!—how many areas had been completely flattened, not one building left above knee height. These, of course, were the poorer parts of the city where houses and workshops were made of wattle and daub and easily burned. It wasn't a gracious speech; a cock crowing on a dunghill could have managed more generosity of spirit. He even managed to get in a concluding jab at Clytemnestra, whose speech had been, he said, "like my absence, far too long."

After he'd finished speaking, there was a pause in which nobody seemed to know what was happening. Out of the corner of my eye, I saw Clytemnestra coming down the steps towards us, her dark blue robe billowing around her. She came to a halt in front of Agamemnon's chariot, her face inches away from the horses' tossing heads. Shading her eyes, she looked up at the golden mask and spoke, though what she said was drowned out when one of the horses trumpeted a greeting to its stable mate several rows behind. Agamemnon lifted the gold mask an inch away from his face—it must have been torture wearing that thing in the heat—and he and the queen spoke briefly. Judging from his tone, he seemed to be protesting about something, but Clytemnestra turned her back on him and waved to a woman at the top of the steps.

A row of white pillars formed the lower portion of the palace façade: very impressive, though to my mind they looked disturbingly like teeth. Well, imagine several glossy red tongues emerging from between the teeth, tongues that were getting longer by the second. That's what I saw, though my brain struggled to make sense of it. More women appeared, their arms full of red cloth, what looked like the garments that clothe the statues of the gods, and tapestries, coverings for altars, some plain, some richly embroidered in silver and gold, like the standards you see carried in procession on the feast days of the gods. Sacred things. They scattered them, moving from step to step until all the whiteness of marble became red.

"What's this?"

Agamemnon sounded almost frightened.

"Red cloths—a carpet for you to walk on."

"But they belong to the gods."

Clytemnestra pointed to the crowds, who were jumping up and down and cheering now because they'd worked out what was about to happen. "Look at them," she said. "As far as they're concerned, you *are* a god." She lifted her arms, urging the crowd on, and they responded with even louder cheers. "You're the closest thing to a god *they'll* ever see."

"I *can't.*"

She was holding on to the side of the chariot, looking up at him, smiling, persuasive. "If you won't do it for yourself, do it for them. They've had ten years of war. And yes, I know it was hard at Troy, but it was pretty bloody hard here too. Twice, the harvest failed, *twice*—and we still had to find money for the war. The war bled them dry, *and* they lost sons, grandsons, brothers, husbands . . . Let them at least share in your triumph. Go on, do it for them."

Behind the expressionless mask, you could sense the struggle going on. Despite his words—and I do think he was genuinely shocked—he wanted to walk on those cloths. He'd conquered the city of Troy, pulverized it, torn down its walls, walls so strong they were said to have been built by a god. He'd done that. *He'd* done the impossible, *he'd* done what nobody else thought could be done. So? He deserved this, didn't he?

"At least let me wash my feet."

Instantly, as if she'd been expecting this, Clytemnestra raised her arm to summon one of the maids, who knelt before Agamemnon, offering him a golden bowl full of clear water with rose petals floating on the surface. Climbing down from the chariot, he waited impatiently while his feet were washed and dried. Only then, bracing himself as if for an ordeal, did he turn to face the steps.

He was about to step into the red stream when a gasp from Clytemnestra stopped him.

"Who's this?"

Cassandra, who'd been sitting in the well of the chariot, had stood up to see what was happening. Agamemnon shrugged. "She was awarded to me by the army, I couldn't refuse."

"Who is she?"

"Priam's daughter."

Clytemnestra looked from Agamemnon's mask to Cassandra's face and back again. How strange people are. I was convinced she hated her husband with every fibre of her being, and yet . . . There was a flicker just then of something that wasn't hatred. Jealousy, perhaps?

Exercising his authority over the women in his household, Agamemnon said, "Be kind to this foreign woman."

"*Kind?*"

"Yes, *kind*. Nobody chooses the life of a slave."

And then he turned his back on her and took the first step, and the next, and the next. Since he couldn't see the edges of the treads, his progress was slow, even a little unsteady; but still he climbed, cloth by cloth, sacrilege by sacrilege, until he reached the top. There, he stood, the gold mask flashing in the sunlight as he turned his head from side to side. Then, raising both arms above his head, he started laughing—we could hear his laughter even above the roars of the crowd. At that moment, he didn't just feel like a god, he *was* a god. You could see it in the way his clenched fist fucked the air.

The people went mad, waving their arms, jumping up and down, cheering loud enough to wake the dead—a risky thing to do in the Lion Court, though I didn't know that then. There were doubters; one or two people made the sign against the evil eye. I noticed them, but only because I was looking for them. Not everybody had enjoyed seeing his bare, podgy, curiously shocking feet tread on material that had been woven to honour the gods. And all that redness was cumulatively disturbing; there was so much of it. After a while, it started to hurt the eyes.

I don't think I'm the only person who remembers seeing Agamemnon wade into his palace through a river of blood.

18

There was silence after Agamemnon disappeared between the white pillars, followed by a subdued murmur of voices. Nobody seemed to know what it was they'd just witnessed, though the temple-like hush testified to its importance. People looked to the queen, but Clytemnestra was already climbing the steps—though I noticed she was careful not to tread on the red cloths. Before going into the building, she gestured to her maids to start gathering them up. Instantly, a dozen or more women swarmed down the steps and began folding the cloth, lining up edges, smoothing down creases, a constant flow of movement towards each other and away, as graceful as the courtship dance of cranes and done by women from time immemorial.

By now I was bursting for a pee. Not even the thought of naked gods and goddesses shivering in their temples could keep my mind off my bladder for long. I was tempted just to let go. I mean, really, who cares if a fat, middle-aged slave pisses herself?

"I'm going to find some water."

Cassandra didn't so much as glance at me.

"I'M GOING TO FIND SOME WATER."

At last, she nodded, and I took that as permission to leave. Though finding water would be easier said than done. I remembered seeing a pile of goatskins in one of the carts; there might be a few drops left in some of them. Weaving my way through the dispersing crowd, I walked back to the gate and found dozens of bullock carts lined up outside. Five carts along, I found the one with the skins. A burly red-faced driver was leaning over the side, talking to his mate. Addressing the back of his neck, I asked, "Can I have one of these for my mistress?"

No reply. He was getting to the punchline of a joke and evidently thought it too good to interrupt, so I tried several of the skins and picked two that had water sloshing around inside. Just then, as luck would have it, one of the bullocks spread its legs and released a hot, steaming jet of piss that cascaded down on to the red dirt, splashing my feet and the hem of my tunic. Well, that did it. I wriggled underneath the cart, hitched up my tunic and had far and away the most enjoyable pee of my entire life. I emerged from the shadow of the cart and, pretending the flood-tide sweeping across the cobbles was nothing to do with me, walked away. I felt like a new woman, ready to take on the world.

I found Cassandra crouched in the well of the chariot with her head in her hands.

"Cassandra?"

I gave her the goatskin. She gulped water down so fast she choked, but her colour improved. I poured water into my cupped hand and rubbed some around the back of her neck and then did the same for myself. Almost immediately, I started to feel better.

The crowd was dispersing more rapidly now. People walking past paused to peer into the chariot: we might have been exotic animals in a cage.

"She's a priestess, is she?" one woman asked.

"Yes," I said.

She looked doubtful. "Are you sure?"

Obviously "slave" and "priestess" were mutually exclusive terms in her world.

The women were the worst. They would keep trying to make her talk; I think they'd have poked her in the ribs, if they could. At last, in desperation, I said, "She can't talk."

A babble of response:

"Well, that's no good, is it? What's the point of a priest who can't talk?"

"She's not a priest, she's a concubine."

"Well, she won't need to talk then, will she?"

"No, just lie flat on her back with her legs apart and wait for them to bring the next meal."

"Nice work if you can get it, it was never my luck."

Eventually, they got bored and drifted away. Not long afterwards, a married couple stopped by the chariot, too busy arguing to pay us much attention. They were on their way to choose a slave; apparently, some of the Trojan women were being sold off cheap. Or free, for tenant farmers. "Mind," the woman was saying, "I don't want a fancy piece with big tits, I want a good strong girl who's not afraid of a bit of hard work." Her husband, who was quite a bit older than her, with a slack mouth and receding chin, kept saying, "Yeah, yeah, right." Meaning: *Shurrup, woman, for god's sake, I know what I'm doing.* I watched them set off towards the gate, the old man sprinting on ahead, his angry wife puffing along behind.

Turning to Cassandra, I said, "Shouldn't we be going in? We need to get out of the sun."

No reaction. Ever since we left Troy, I'd been watching Cassandra for signs of the agitation that had been such a problem when she arrived in the camp, forgetting all the other times when she'd been so low she could hardly speak. I was just about to repeat the question when I saw a man in priest's robes with the scarlet bands of Apollo wound around his head coming towards us down the steps.

He stopped in front of the chariot. "Praise the lord and giver of light!" Automatically, Cassandra's lips framed the ritual response:

"Now and for ever, may his name be praised." And then, to my surprise, she hauled herself to her feet, and stood there, swaying a little but resolute. The priest was a portly young man, full of his own importance. Keeping a safe distance from the horses' heads, he launched into what was virtually a sermon, assuring her of Apollo's continuing love and care. "The lord of prophecy will help you."

Cassandra hooted with laughter. "When has Apollo ever helped me? All my life I've seen people I love, my own father, make fatal mistakes, because they didn't believe me. Have you any idea at all what that feels like? You know what Apollo told me? That I'd never be believed until I prophesied my own death. Well, now I do prophesy my death—mine, and Agamemnon's. And does anybody believe me? No. So, that's another lie. Apollo always tells the truth—well, yes, perhaps he does, but he never means what you mean. You say, 'Praise the lord of light!' But there's a dreadful darkness in Apollo—and people just can't see it. You have to be close enough to feel his breath on your face—*then* you see it. I'm going to die—and very soon, hours, not days. And your king is going to die with me, because what he did at Troy was so horrific, so totally devoid of humanity, that even the gods were sickened. So, go on, celebrate, sacrifice the best bull in the herd, sing your piddling little hymns of praise, drink yourself stupid, but it won't save me—and it won't save your precious king either."

Even before she'd finished, he was backing off, falling over his feet in his eagerness to get away. Merely listening to talk of a king's death is treason. I was shaken, not by the change in her mood, which was dramatic, but by a change in myself. Up to that moment, I'd scarcely believed any of her stories, it was all too far away from my experience. But now, suddenly, I sensed a relationship. I believed that when she prayed, she spoke to Apollo and he answered her. When she spoke about the darkness of Apollo, I sensed she was telling the truth, or at least a version of the truth. This was Apollo *as she knew him.*

I couldn't afford to think like this; I had to focus on the practical-
ities of our situation, because if I didn't, nobody would. "C'mon," I
said. "We're going inside."

Cassandra was looking over my head. Turning, I saw Clytemnestra,
who'd come silently down the steps and was standing in front of
the chariot. For what seemed like an age, neither of them spoke,
but then Clytemnestra's eyes seemed to focus on Cassandra's staff
of office.

Not bothering to disguise the sarcasm, she said, "Praise the lord
and giver of light."

"Now and for ever, may his name be praised."

"You're fucking my husband."

"I'm a slave, I do as I'm told."

"He said, 'Be kind to this foreign woman.'"

"I heard what he said. And you always do what he says?"

"Of course."

"Oh, all right, I can go along with that. I'm a slave, you're an obe-
dient wife. Do you think we'll ever be able to talk to each other—
properly, I mean?"

"I haven't got time for this." Clytemnestra raised a hand to wipe
sweat from her forehead and as she did so her sleeve fell back to
reveal an arm covered in small, circular bruises; every stage of
bruise development on show from black, through purple, to red,
to yellowish-green. Quickly, she pulled the sleeve down. "Look,"
she said. "You're welcome to come inside, you'll be given food and
water and a clean bed to sleep in, but if you want to stay out here
and fry your brains, feel free. It really doesn't matter to me either
way."

As she turned to go, her eye fell on the horses standing patiently
between the shafts, sweating in the heat. "Fuck's sake!" For the first
time, there was an explosion of rage, though her anger had been
simmering just below the surface right from the start. "What do I

pay grooms for?" Raising her fingers to her mouth, she produced a whistle that would have done credit to an overseer on a building site. An aide came running and she sent him off to the stable yard. "Tell them to come here, now, at the double. And if they want to know what it feels like to be tied up without water on a day like this, it can be arranged."

I liked her. I liked her practicality; I liked the way she cared about the horses; I liked her whistle. *A whistling woman and a crowing hen, no bloody use to gods or men.* I remember my mother telling me that when I was eight years old I was desperate to whistle like my brothers could. I used to practise in the backyard—out of earshot of the house—finally producing a sound that was respectable at least. My poor mother, she'd have been mortified.

I watched the queen walk away. She'd just begun climbing the steps when a streak of red appeared and a black-haired girl threw herself into her arms.

"Electra! Where's Iras?"

"Asleep. Where's Daddy?"

"Inside."

"Can I show him my dress?"

"Not now, baby, perhaps a bit later. Remember, we talked about this? He's got people with him at the moment."

"I could go in just for a minute . . ."

"*No*, he's too busy. Come on, let's find Iras."

"You'll have to wake her up."

"Oh, don't you worry, I'll wake her up all right."

She'd forgotten about us, didn't even glance in our direction as she seized the child's hand and half dragged her up the steps. Only, she wasn't a child. Cassandra flared her eyes at me, asking without words: *What the hell was that?*

That was a young girl, possibly even old enough for marriage, but pitifully thin, no breasts, no hips, her face disfigured by silvery scales. Perhaps I'm not getting across how disturbing she was, because it wasn't just her emaciation or the state of her skin; it was the way she behaved towards her mother, like a demanding small child. Or worse than that, perhaps: some kind of malevolent sprite.

We watched them reach the top of the steps and disappear between the pillared teeth.

Cassandra was looking up at the roof. I felt her cool fingers close around my arm. "Do you see them?"

"Who?"

"The Furies."

I knew who the Furies were: goddesses who punish crimes within the family; they are the most terrible, the most relentless, of the gods. But when I looked up, all I could see were birds, squabbling and jockeying for position on the roof ridge.

Cassandra's grip tightened. "You do see them?"

Dumbly, I shook my head. "C'mon, let's go in."

I felt like shouting: *For once in your bloody stupid life, can't you just do the simple, natural thing?* But then I suddenly gave up. Whatever was going to happen, let it happen. I turned my back on her, looking instead at the milling crowds. The couple I'd seen earlier were coming back from the slave market, the wife tight-lipped, the husband slyly triumphant; behind them, a young woman with a grizzling baby in her arms. She was using her veil to try to shield its eyes from the sun; when that didn't stop the crying, she pulled out a huge, blue-veined breast and plugged the nipple into its voracious, sea-anemone mouth. What future did they have, that young woman and her child? Seeing them made me—perhaps unfairly— even more exasperated with Cassandra. I was very close to the limit of my endurance. I'm sure it was no pleasure rattling along in Agamemnon's chariot, but I'd walked, for god's sake—I'd *walked*. So, I simply went across to the steps and sat down, not abandoning her but not helping either.

As I looked around, something caught my eye: a scrap of red cloth snagged on the rough edge of a stone. Reaching over, I worked it free, then let it lie on the palm of my hand. It was amazingly beautiful: dark ox-blood red with a single leaf embroidered in gold thread. I was tempted to close my hand, to keep it, but even as the thought formed, a freshening breeze snatched it up and carried it away. A trifle—I've never told anybody about it till now, because really, what was there to tell? But I've always remembered it. I watched it drift across the steps until the wind whirled it aloft and carried it out of sight.

When I looked back into the Lion Court again, I saw Cassandra walking towards me, and stood up to meet her. I let her lean on me and, preceded by our four-legged, two-headed shadow, we supported each other up the steps and into the cool darkness of the atrium beyond.

19

"You're hurting my hand."

The usual accusatory whine. "Sorry," she says, letting go. Surreptitiously, she wipes her fingers on the skirt of her tunic. They turn the corner, and there's Iras, flat-footed, breathless, running towards them.

"I thought I told—" Clytemnestra stops, because she knows there's no point. "Look, I need you to make sure she stays in her room, just for the next few hours. For god's sake, Iras, you've only got one job—just *do it.*"

She senses Electra behind her, smirking, no doubt. It's great fun getting slaves into trouble when you're basically a rather nasty little girl. Turning round, she grabs Electra's arm only to release it a second later when Electra winces. Guilt, not love, gives her patience. "It's only for a couple of hours. Daddy's talking to his counsellors now. As soon as they go, you'll be able to see him. The best thing you can do is lie down and have a rest. You won't enjoy the party if you're too tired." She looks at Iras. "And get that dress off her, look at it, it's creased. And see what you can do with her hair."

Standing at the corner of the passage, she watches until Iras and Electra are safely inside the room. Though that won't last. Electra's bursting with nervous energy and yes, sometimes it does result in complete exhaustion, but not before she's been running round the palace like somebody demented for hours on end. But what's to be done about it? You can't keep her permanently locked up. Agamemnon hasn't even mentioned her, not today—and not last night either, until she prompted him; it's as if Electra doesn't exist, though only just now, in the council chamber, he'd been telling anybody who cared to listen how surprised and disappointed he was that Orestes hadn't been there to greet him. He can't possibly have been surprised: she'd told him Orestes wouldn't be there. But perhaps he senses that Orestes' absence is a sore point, a weakness, something he can pick away at?

There'll be plenty of people in the council chamber only too eager to pass on rumours and gossip. They can't tell him the truth, because they don't know it; she's not even sure she knows it herself. The official version is that Orestes has been traumatized by the constant, exaggerated reports of his father's wounds. True—though that had been going on for years. More recently, he felt humiliated by not being allowed to go to Troy to fight beside his father. Did he blame her for that? Probably. A mother's place is permanently in the wrong. But she doesn't think either of those things really accounts for his absence. About nine months ago, there was a series of incidents in the training yards, fights breaking out, Orestes limping back to the palace with a black eye or a split lip. He'd always seemed to get on well with the other lads, so this succession of minor injuries was a bit of a puzzle. At last, she sent an aide to find out what was going on. "Do some training, hang about, listen." A few days later, the man had returned, blushing and stammering, to tell her Orestes was being teased.

"Teased? What about?"

"Aegisthus."

"What about him?"

"They seem to think he's at the palace quite a lot."

"Well, of course, he's at the palace—" And then she realized what he was finding so hard to spit out. She couldn't deny it to Orestes, because even denying it admitted the possibility that it might be true. So, when he asked to leave the palace and stay with his friend Pylades, she let him go without argument, though she hadn't expected him to stay away as long as this.

His absence does strike people as odd. Only this morning, some of the counsellors had wondered why he wasn't waiting on the steps to welcome his father. Her mind, like a dragnet, had scooped up their mutterings: "How old will he be now?" "Eighteen." "Well, he's a man then. It should have been him giving that speech, not his mother." "Ah, but if he's a man, why wasn't he at Troy with his father?" "The queen wouldn't let him go." "I don't think it was that." "Where is he, anyway?" "Visiting a friend." "Bloody long visit . . ."

No doubt there'll be plenty of questions once she and Agamemnon are alone, and not just about Orestes either. He'll want to talk again about the future, *their* future, and this time he won't just be testing the ground. He'll come with a list of demands, and he'll want firm decisions that he can start implementing. To her, it's an obscenity even to think of such a future, but she'll have to comment, make suggestions, agree—oh, yes, agree! Disagreement won't be tolerated now. Probably, he'll want her to retire from the court, and from his point of view that makes perfect sense. He'll want her out of the way and unavailable to complaining underlings. There'll have to be negotiations, of course. She'll have to compromise on every important point but without seeming to be too much of a pushover. None of this really matters—he has no future—but nevertheless, he's got to believe that she intends to live in the Sea House, tend the gardens and the grave, spend the rest of her life praying to the gods as cast-off women are supposed to do. She can easily make him believe that; he wants to believe it, so he's more than halfway there already.

Her feet are taking her back to the atrium through a labyrinth of corridors she navigates without thinking, though as a young woman, newly married, she'd spent most of her life getting lost. "Oh, I'm sure you'll soon get used to it," Agamemnon's sister had said, packing her bags, or rather throwing stuff into them, she was in such a hurry to leave. And she had got used to it, though nobody helped her settle in; nobody explained anything. Agamemnon's mother, far from being the all-powerful mother-in-law so many young brides dread, was a bloodless wisp of a woman, her skin as dry and transparent as a sloughed-off chrysalis. She remembers bumping into her one day when, heavily pregnant with Iphigenia, she'd come to a halt on one of the second-floor corridors. "Oh, don't worry, my dear," the queen had said, rather breathlessly—she was always breathless. "Everybody gets lost here."

Not long after that, she died, or faded away—it was impossible to imagine her doing anything as decisive as dying—and a month later Iphigenia was born, a girl so vibrantly alive you could warm your hands at her. A total contrast to those other children whose presence could never be mentioned.

Are the corridors usually as dark as this? The lamps do seem to be burning dim, though she doesn't need light to find her way around, in fact she's better off without it. She knows how to negotiate the labyrinth and not get lost. Don't think too much, don't try to remember the route, look at your feet, move quickly, leave sights and sounds and whispers behind you. And above all, pretend you're walking through a complicated building, rather than following the convolutions of a diseased brain. Ignore the singing. Not that she's ever managed to do that. They're singing now, though so softly it might be the wind rustling blinds in empty rooms. *There was an old woman who swallowed a fly. I don't know why she swallowed a fly, perhaps she'll DIE.*

The last word's shouted in her face. She feels flecks of spit hit her skin and raises a hand to wipe them away, but there's nothing there. Hurrying on, she reaches the top of the main staircase where the palace begins once more to make sense. A long, slow descent, trailing her hand along the banister. Entering the throne room, she sees Agamemnon standing underneath one of the tall windows, surrounded by his counsellors, who until this morning had been *her* counsellors. He's holding forth in that rather plummy, I'm-speaking-in-public kind of voice that irritates the hell out of her, though she contrives to fix an approving smile on her face.

A slave notices her standing by the door and comes over carrying a tray with cups of wine. *One*, she tells herself; she can't afford to have her judgement impaired, not when she has such a challenging evening ahead of her. There's no hope of an afternoon nap, not for her, though Agamemnon's certainly going to need one, the rate he's knocking it back. Several of the counsellors are red-faced, sweaty and slurry, but even the sober ones are a problem. None of them ever wants to be the first to leave, because they don't trust the others not to stab them in the back. How many meetings has she presided over in the last ten years, coddling these men whose backs now form a solid wall against her? A day ago, they were hanging on her every word; that's gone now. She'd felt their restlessness during her speech, noticed the way they turned towards Agamemnon, as naturally as sunflowers following the sun. She's nobody now. *Well*, she thinks, looking at the row of backs. *Enjoy it while you can.*

It's odd. She hadn't expected to mind the draining away of power, but she does mind. And if she hasn't managed to foresee her own reactions to this situation, what else might she have missed? Already, unexpected things have begun to happen, the girl with the yellow eyes for one—and yes, she minds about her too. Not a great deal, it has to be said, but she does mind, a little. It's the same feeling, really: the sense of being relegated to the sidelines of life, the ebbing away, not so much of power, as of significance. Agamemnon too. She's hated him for so long that she's turned him into a caricature of himself. He was never a clever man: though he managed to appear so sometimes, particularly if he happened to be standing next to his idiot brother, Menelaus, but no, not a clever man. After only a few weeks of marriage, she'd known that, but somehow during his long absence at Troy she's forgotten the strength of his political instincts, his dominating physical presence, his ability to sway a crowd. He's more intimidating than she remembered, more persuasive too. Even now, standing underneath the big window, his eyes darting from face to face, he's taking them with him every step of the way. She'd have liked to shout out, to wake them all up, remind them that this war, this victory they're so proud of, has bankrupted the country. At some level they must know this, and yet still they cheer.

She notices that another line of handprints has appeared behind the throne. Normally furniture's moved to hide them, but you can scarcely move the throne. No amount of scrubbing gets them off, though they do fade with time, to be replaced by other handprints, in other places. This has been going on for years. It bothered her enormously when she was a young wife, though Agamemnon always brushed her concerns aside. If the house was disturbed, he seemed to think that that was her problem, not his. *And what did she mean anyway, no amount of scrubbing gets them off? Any stain could be removed if you scrubbed hard enough. Flog one of the slaves, you'd soon have the rest of them scrubbing harder.*

She looks across the throne room at her husband, taking in the changes in his appearance, the grey hairs, the mound of his belly that the looseness of his robes doesn't quite hide. Does he still believe any stain can be removed by scrubbing or flogging or war? Probably. Almost certainly, in fact. *But you're wrong.* Her words, swift and silent as arrows, fly across the room. *Nothing gets it off.*

The knee she hurt when a half-broken horse threw her is starting to ache; sometimes, without warning, it buckles underneath her, producing embarrassing collapses in public places, though normally she's careful to make sure there's a chair available. No chair here, except the throne, and she'd certainly cause a stir if she sat down on that. So, she sinks instead on to one of the steps leading up to it, resting her sweaty hands on the marble floor, feeling the cold strike up through her robes. The nausea she'd felt under the glaring sun in the Lion Court briefly intensifies, then clears.

Agamemnon's giving what he obviously hopes is the final summing-up of this no-agenda meeting. He'll take on board and carefully consider everything they've said; some things will remain the same, others may have to be modified—a few decisions, perhaps, reversed. He takes the point about the state of public buildings, but we can't solve everything in one day, can we? Meanwhile, he hopes to welcome them all again this evening at the feast—the feast which has been organized by his excellent wife. Scattered rumbles of approval. *Back in your kennel, woman,* she takes that to mean. A few of the old men are breaking away from the circle, though slowly, with frequent pauses to chat.

This thinning of the group enables her to see somebody or something flitting about behind Agamemnon. A flash of red. Always, whenever she sees that colour, there's a surge of hope. She's not dead; it's all been a mistake, a nightmare, a dream from the pit, though the hope quickly dies. It's Electra, of course, it's always Electra; somehow, she's managed to give Iras the slip again. She starts to call "Elec—" but checks herself, because this could be the right moment, or as good a moment as any. Not when he's alone in his private apartments, but here, where the most powerful men in the kingdom are gathered, when they can witness the confrontation.

She doesn't have long to wait. Turning to acknowledge a departing counsellor's good wishes, Agamemnon glimpses, out of the corner of his eye, a thin-armed, black-haired girl in a red dress creeping towards him, and he lashes out, not intending to hit her, not consciously intending anything. But he's a fighter, he's been at war for ten years: he doesn't miss. He doesn't know how to miss. His clenched fist lands squarely at the centre of her chest and sends her flying across the floor.

There's a moment's shocked silence. Near the door, a departing group go on talking for a moment until they register the stillness and their words dribble away into nothing.

Agamemnon stands at the centre of everything. Alone. He looks down at his hands, seems surprised by the size of them. Watching, Clytemnestra sees the enormity of what he's done begin to sink in. Though he still can't grasp what's happened, only that in trying to ward off a ghost he's somehow connected with living flesh and bone. Something, some feeling, is struggling for possession of his face. And then he's on his knees beside the screaming girl—only she isn't screaming, not this one, not this time, she doesn't shout *Daddy* like the other one did . . . She looks as if she'll never speak again. He crouches down beside her, lifts her up and holds her, whispering, "Electra, my little girl, my baby girl, I'm sorry, I'm sorry," while all around him the dumbfounded counsellors gape, and Electra, lying motionless inside the circle of his arms, gazes vacantly into space.

20

"Tonight," Cassandra said. "It's got to be tonight."

We'd been sitting on a bench in the atrium for some time now, watching the life of the palace go on around us. Nobody spared us a glance. A few minutes ago, there'd been some kind of commotion in the room opposite. A herald appeared, legging it across the atrium and down the steps, returning almost immediately with Machaon, who had half-moons of sweat in his armpits and a blood vessel throbbing in his forehead. I knew that white worm well. Only fear for Agamemnon's life could have made it swell like that.

"Well, you say 'tonight'—I've a feeling the gods might be a bit ahead of you there."

We waited to see what would happen. There was no sound of weeping and lamentation coming from behind the closed door, so evidently Agamemnon was still alive. At last, an aide appeared carrying a girl in a red dress: Electra. The queen and Machaon followed, and the little procession set off up the stairs. The knots of gossiping old men who'd emerged from the throne room went back inside. Not long afterwards, the queen and Machaon returned and stood talking together. Once, they turned and looked in our direction, though I couldn't think why we would be a source of interest, particularly as they seemed to be looking at me, rather than her. It was a relief when they went back into the hall.

Water. I was parched, Cassandra was parched. There had to be water somewhere. Cautiously, I opened one of the doors that led off the atrium and found myself in a room with a big horseshoe-shaped table. There was a smaller table opposite on which various cups and jugs had been assembled. Quickly, I sorted through the jugs. Most of them contained wine, good wine too, judging by the smell. I diluted two cups and returned to Cassandra, who pulled a face at first but then gulped the wine down so fast some of it came back up. I averted my gaze from the red dribbles on her chin.

The atmosphere all around us was tense, with that undertow of malicious excitement you get when people contemplate the misfortunes of the better-off. I was just glad we weren't involved. Once Cassandra had finished her wine, I got up to take the cups back and spotted a capable-looking woman, a slave by her dress, but one with some responsibility in the household. "Oh yes," she said, dismissively. "I'll show you where to go." She pointed to a flight of stairs, told me to turn right at the top and walk down a corridor until I came to another flight of stairs. "You want the servants' rooms, second floor." She looked at me and saw, for the first time I think, a woman of her own age, doing her best, as I'm sure she was doing hers. Her expression softened a little. "Don't worry if you get lost. Everybody gets lost here."

She was right about that. One floor up, another woman, less friendly, directed us to the back stairs, which were obviously intended for slaves going about the business of the palace. Scarcely any light. Brushing sticky cobwebs away from our faces, we felt our way from step to step, coming out eventually on the top floor. Cassandra said she needed to rest, so we stopped for a moment; I avoided looking at her. As we walked along the corridor, I pushed open doors and peered in. The rooms were clean, at least, though some of them contained three or four straw mattresses. Others were used as storage. At last, we came to the door at the far end and, slowly, I pushed it open. A fusty smell met me, as if the room hadn't been occupied for a long time, but the bed was made up, so evidently the room was intended for use. I couldn't be certain it was meant for us, but I was so exhausted I claimed it anyway. Crossing to the window, I opened the blinds and looked around. Not bad: a washstand and a wooden chest, two chairs, a table near the bed. "Well," I said, dumping the bag I was carrying on the floor. "This'll do."

"*This'll do?*"

She was panting and, for a moment, I wondered whether she was ill. To be honest, I rather hoped she was, because then I could put her to bed, hint at the possibility of something infectious and with any luck they'd all keep well away. Though I didn't know who "they" were; we weren't exactly in demand.

"Are you all right?"

She nodded, then abruptly sat on the bed.

"You could have a lie-down."

"I need to get this stuff off first." She was tugging at her robes, pulling the scarlet bands out of her hair. Before getting into bed, she kicked them violently away, then lay staring up at the ceiling. "God, this place. Don't tell me you can't hear it?"

I could hear it: a constant murmur like the susurration of wind in trees, but these were human voices, though pitched too low for the words to be audible. But I'd no desire to indulge her morbid fantasies, so I simply picked up the robes and folded them neatly. "You'll need to decide what you want to wear tonight."

"What have we got?"

"There's the yellow dress."

"That'll do."

Looking down at her, I saw lines of weariness round her eyes. "I'll hang it in the window, then. Get the creases out."

As I pulled the clothes out, I got a whiff of the awful stench there'd been in the cabin and my mind flooded with memories: seasickness, damp blankets, but also, and more importantly, Andreas's kindness; his awkwardness on the one night we'd spent together, and how in the end it hadn't mattered at all. It was a real ache in my mind that I hadn't had the chance to say a proper goodbye. Shaking the dress out, I went to the window to see if there was anything to hang it from. There was a rail which must have had a cloth blind suspended from it at some point, though there was only a wooden blind there now. I threaded the dress over the rail, straightening out the creases as I went. The breeze I'd first noticed on the steps was freshening, blowing the dress towards me, wrapping my face in damp cloth and the smell of the ship.

"Did you hear what he said?" Cassandra had raised herself up on one elbow, pale but sounding more like her usual self. "He called me 'this foreign woman.'"

"Yes, well, we are, aren't we? Foreign."

"He didn't even say my name." She took a deep breath, steadying herself. "He said: 'Nobody chooses the life of a slave.'"

"He did tell her to be kind to you."

"*Ye-es*—be kind to her new slave!"

"He could hardly introduce you as his new concubine, could he? He was just trying to—"

Cover his arse.

"I am not his concubine."

I stared at her.

"He married me. You were there, you know he did."

"Yes, he married you."

She nodded, drawing her knees up to her chin. Her lids were drooping—with any luck she might sleep.

I busied myself with the dress, running my hands over the cloth, smoothing out creases. Anything to postpone the moment when I'd have to talk about the wedding. More and more, that awful morning came to seem important, because it was true: he had married her, or gone through a form of marriage, at least. Nothing lacking in the ceremony at all that I could see; there was a priest, vows, everything—except he was already married to the queen. A queen who'd given him a son, ruled Mycenae in his absence and came from a powerful family who'd avenge any insult offered to her . . . Oh, but he was the conqueror of Troy, equal to the gods, he could do anything he liked. And he was a man past his prime, needing firm, young flesh to get him going, dreaming no doubt of a new beginning, a new life. In other words, a lethal mixture of arrogance and insecurity. Drinkers' droop too, probably—perhaps not all the time, but now and then. Not something victorious kings are meant to suffer from, but hey—time lies in wait for us all.

And then, this morning, lined up in rows like the waves of the sea, his counsellors, his elderly relatives, tribal chiefs, the priests of every god on Mount Olympus and, in front of them all, Clytemnestra, his wife, whose thickening waist and blurring jaw summed up the whole dead weight of what confronted him—and there was no way he could escape. He was swaddled like a fly in a web, and so he said: *Be kind to this foreign woman. Nobody chooses the life of a slave.* And, after all, he could still sleep with Cassandra, for as long as she held his interest, still acknowledge her child as his. Nothing Clytemnestra could do about any of that. He'd brought a concubine back from the war, as men do. As they've always done.

I needed air. The yellow dress was swaying in the breeze, almost as if it were alive, a third person in the room. Pushing it to one side, I looked out. My nose had been telling me what to expect, so it was no surprise. We were at the back of the palace, overlooking the kitchen yard, where animals had been slaughtered ready for the feast tonight. Piles of intestines stinking in the heat and, gathered in a circle round them, jabbing and darting and squabbling, were the black birds I'd seen earlier on the roof. *There's your Furies*, I thought, obscurely pleased by how craven and squalid they seemed, how utterly devoid of the meaning Cassandra had attached to them. A farm slave carrying boxes of vegetables and fruit for the feast walked across the yard, and a girl came out to take them from him, one of the kitchen maids, solidly built with greasy hair straggling into her eyes and a small baby strapped to her chest. She tried to take the trays from him, but couldn't—they were too heavy and the baby got in the way—so she ushered him into the kitchen. The minute they disappeared, the birds advanced again, snatching at gobs of meat.

When I turned back into the room, I saw that Cassandra was sleeping. It didn't seem right to leave her alone with the swaying dress—though immediately I told myself: *For god's sake, it's only a dress.* The susurration of voices was getting to me. If I didn't get a grip, I was going to end up jumping at shadows. *Think.* We were going to need water for washing and drinking, so the best thing I could do was to get that sorted out. I ran a comb through my hair and then, quietly, crept out of the room and closed the door behind me.

The staircase was worse going down. I clung to the rope banister, remembering a story I'd heard told around the fire in Lyrnessus about a staircase that went down all the way to Hades, though it seemed quite normal when you were going up. But I came out safely on the floor below and immediately got lost—and I mean really lost, passing and re-passing the same tables, the same chairs, the same faded tapestries hanging despondently from the same walls. The corridors were poorly lit—and, considering the spacious rooms on either side, they were also surprisingly narrow. Eventually, I reached the main staircase, a great sweep of marble obviously not intended for the use of slaves, but I ran down it anyway. I could always plead first-day ignorance if somebody challenged me. In the atrium, I skidded to a halt before walking quickly and casually into the open air.

A blast of heat hit me, rising from the hot, white stones. There was a burnt smell—I don't mean a smell of something burning, it was more as if the air itself were scorched. Even here in the gardens nothing smelled fresh. Following my nose, I located the kitchen and looked through the open door, hoping to find someone who could give me directions, but like all kitchens on a feast day it was full of shouting, sweating, screaming, desperate women and I was glad to back away. In a covered walkway just off the yard, I found a row of jugs—all shapes and sizes—and selecting two of the largest, I set off in search of the well.

After a while, I stopped to ask a woman for directions. She was kneeling beside a basket of teased wool, and as she looked round at me, I recognized her as somebody I'd known in Lyrnessus. I hadn't known her particularly well, though the way we greeted each other you'd have thought we were long-lost twins. After hugging and crying, we stood back and looked at each other. "I'm sorry to see you here," she said.

"You and me both." I wiped my nose on the side of my hand. "What's it like?"

"Oh, you know . . . Not bad, they feed you all right." She was struggling to speak, as if something was squeezing the breath out of her. "Just don't let it get to you."

I could see she didn't really want to talk, so after another hug and a promise to watch out for each other, I let her get back to work and set off to follow her directions to the well. Now that I'd been pointed in the right direction, it was easy enough to find: an imposing structure right at the centre of a formal garden. Soaring above it was a statue of Poseidon wielding his trident, skewering some kind of sea monster, I thought, though as I got closer, I could see it was merely a huge fish. There were puddles leading up to the well where slaves carrying buckets had let water slop over the sides onto the path.

As I walked towards the well, the heat seemed to intensify, I felt clammy all over, hot air scorching my throat. The sooner I was out of this furnace the better. I seized the handle and started winding the bucket down, but it descended slowly, clanking from side to side, and I leaned over the rim to check its progress. A dark, dank smell; clumps of wet ferns, a toxic, virulent green, grew out of the walls. I waited for the splash, which was a long time coming, then put my back into rewinding. After what felt like ages, the bucket reappeared, bringing with it a smell of long-buried things. A knock as it hit the side sent a shudder up the chain into my arms, but finally I had it balanced on the rim of the well. I was breathless, glad of a moment's rest, but then something made me turn and look back the way I'd come.

A line of wet footprints was coming along the path towards me. Nothing remarkable about that, except that nobody was making them. Step by step, they came, not stopping till they reached the side of the well close to my feet. I looked down; next to my own left foot, there was a perfect print, so small it could only be a child's. There, for a moment, wet and gleaming—then gone. Nobody in sight. "I'm sorry," I said, dropping words like stones into the vacancy surrounding me.

My voice provoked a moment's listening stillness. And then, slowly, I became aware of the speckled throats of foxgloves, bees fumbling from one flower to the next, men's laughter in the distance—and of the intolerable heat. There were cups chained to the rim of the well; I dipped one into the bucket and drank deep. Then, refusing to think about the footprints or what they might mean, I filled the jugs and set off to the palace. I had no desire to get there. I didn't want to go inside and have to listen to the murmuring walls. If people keep silent, the walls will speak . . .

On the way, I passed a door set in a high stone wall and knew at once this was the entrance to the herb garden. I tried the latch, thinking it would be locked, but it opened at once and I stepped inside—though cautiously, expecting at any moment to be challenged. I stood just inside the door and looked around. Apricots glowing red and gold on the opposite wall, further along the tall, black railings of a poison garden, but otherwise the entire space given over to beds of herbs. Some effort had been made to contain the real spreaders, but most had been allowed to grow and seed themselves freely. The whole hot, enclosed area was loud with the buzzing of bees. I started walking round, kneeling occasionally to take in the smells or examine a particular plant in more detail. Close to, you could see the sacs on the bees' legs crammed full of pollen, but still they worked as if knowing this late-summer heat was a delusion and the year was already spiralling down into the dark.

Looking around for somewhere to sit, I saw a bench under an apple tree and settled down on that—an unfortunate choice in some ways because windfalls lay all around, brown, rotting, patched here and there with white fungus and irresistible to wasps. If you keep still, they will ignore you, and so I concentrated on keeping very still indeed. Slowly, an inch at a time, I turned my head from side to side. As I say, not the best-kept herb garden I'd ever seen, nor the most extensive, but still a greater collection of plants than you'll ever see outside the grounds of a palace. Normally, I'd have been happy to spend hours wandering from bed to bed, greeting old friends, alert for the presence of strangers, though these days, there were very few plants I didn't know. But the morning's long walk had exhausted me and now the cidery smell of rotting apples, the furious buzzing of wasps and the net of shadows that covered my arms combined to make me so drowsy I seemed to be sinking into the garden, becoming part of it.

I closed my eyes. A long moment of peace, and then a darkening on my lids made me look up and there was Machaon, smiling broadly, though the smile didn't reach his eyes. "I thought I might find you here," he said, sitting on the bench beside me. Always, whenever Machaon and I were alone, I remembered that night in the storeroom, how I'd been on the verge of sleep when I opened my eyes and saw him standing there. "Do you know what happened?" he went on. The question sprang so naturally—and so nastily— from my memories that it took me a second to realize he was talking about the present. "No?" I said, thinking this was the safest response.

"Agamemnon was with his counsellors—quite an informal meeting, more a getting-back-in-touch sort of thing. Anyway, towards the end, Electra came in. She crept up behind him, wanting to surprise him, I suppose . . . and she was wearing a red dress, like the one Iphigenia was wearing on the day she died. Not just similar—identical. He caught sight of her out of the corner of his eye and thought— well, I don't know what he thought. Same age, same dress . . . He just lashed out, punched her in the chest, sent her flying. She's only a little scrap of a thing." He looked sideways at me. "He could easily have killed her."

"Is she badly hurt?"

"Nothing much. Couple of cracked ribs . . . Very shaken, though. She wouldn't have anything to do with me, wouldn't let me examine her. All I could get out of her was: 'Daddy didn't like my dress.'"

He wasn't meant to like it. In my mind's eye, I saw a woman working late at night, alone, because she didn't want anybody to see what she was doing. No sound inside the room except for the constant rattle of the shuttle; no sound outside either, just the breathless hush of the sleeping palace in which nothing living stirred.

I couldn't think why Machaon was telling me this, unless he was so horrified by what he'd seen that he simply had to tell somebody, but no, I didn't believe that. Ten years of Troy? His mind had been crammed full of horrors, and he'd never needed to talk about them.

"The queen did that on purpose," he said. "No way was that dress just coincidence. She turned her own child into a weapon."

"She's not a child, though, is she?"

"No, she isn't." He glanced at the branches above our heads, and said, a little too casually, "I mentioned you to the queen."

"Me? Why?"

"Somebody's got to keep an eye on the girl."

"But you'll be here?"

"Well, that's just it, you see. I'm rather hoping I won't be. My father's got a farm not far away . . ." He nodded to the hills behind the palace. "And, you know, he's an old man now, he can't be managing very well on his own, and I think he's only got one slave. I'd like to make sure he's all right."

"When will you go?"

"First thing tomorrow. I was hoping to go tonight, but the king says he needs me here."

It wasn't often I detected resentment of Agamemnon, but it was certainly there now. "You'll enjoy the feast," I said.

"I'd just as soon give it a miss, to be honest. Anyway . . ." He slapped his knees, cutting off an unwelcome train of thought. "Can I show you my workshop?"

I got to my feet and followed him along a narrow path between the herb beds until we reached a long, low building on the right. "Gardeners this end," he said. "Not that they seem to be doing a lot, do they? Me the other end." He came to a door shrouded in cobwebs and clawed them away. "Do you know, when I left, I thought I'd be gone two months? Two months. God knows what state it's in."

After the bright heat of the garden, the interior was cool and dark. I had to stand for a moment, blinking, before I managed to see anything. A workbench ran the length of the far wall and Machaon went straight over to it, delighted to be back but horrified by the layers of dust and dirt. A jug of wine stood beside the chopping board—a stirrup cup before he'd climbed into his chariot, perhaps? The wine would be vinegar, if it hadn't dried up altogether. "Ten years," he said, sounding stupefied. There were handprints everywhere; I saw Machaon frowning down at them and couldn't understand why, until I saw how small they were. Perhaps one of the gardeners had children and they'd been allowed in here to play? The thought made me realize I hadn't seen many children in the palace. Machaon was recovering himself now, picking up the jug as if intending to rinse it out and put it away.

"Why doesn't anybody talk about it?"

He looked at me. Surprised. Defensive. "About?"

"The handprints, footprints. Voices. Are they too frightened?"

"They are frightened, but it's not just that. Everybody sees or hears something different. Some people don't hear anything."

"Has anybody ever seen them?"

"Some people have." A dragging pause. "Me, for one."

"*You?*" He was the last person I'd have expected to see something like that, or to admit it if he had. I don't think I've ever known a more sceptical man.

"I was walking across the Lion Court, and I'd had a few. We were all of us getting ready to leave and there were flashes of lightning. Not a storm, just the flickers you get on a hot night. There was a full moon, they were singing—something about chopping off heads. It's a song children sing round here . . . And suddenly there they were, in front of me, very close." He raised a hand to his face, flinching and snapping his head back. "In life they were innocent victims, but that's not what they are now."

"But they're harmless, surely?"

"No." He smiled. "They mean harm all right. Be careful on staircases. Watch where you're putting your feet."

I didn't know if he was teasing or not. With Machaon it was often hard to tell.

"Anyway," he said, pointing at the bench in front of him. "You can see where everything is."

I could. Under the layer of dirt, everything was well thought out. Jugs, knives, chopping blocks, pestles and mortars: all lined up neatly on the shelves. Candles, several lamps. He walked back across the room to the window, swept aside a curtain of cobwebs and let bright sunlight stream across the floor, as the spiders whose world he'd just destroyed raced for the shadows.

"That's better, we can see what we're doing now. And here—" he threw the door of the storeroom open. "Well, come and see." Reluctantly, I did as he said. Big, deep shelves crowded with baskets; on the floor, a row of hessian sacks containing roots and tubers, rotted now or crumbling into dust. "I don't suppose there'll be a lot we can still use."

He pushed the door further open and indicated I should go inside. I made myself step over the threshold, though the dry-earth smell was making me feel queasy. Empty sacks were stacked up against one of the walls. Involuntarily stepping back, I saw a makeshift bed, stubs of candles ranged around it as a gossamer-thin defence against the dark. Suddenly my mouth was full of bile and I had to turn aside to spit it out. Machaon handed me a cloth to wipe my mouth, and with shaking hands I used it, even though that, too, smelled of soil.

"Are you all right?"

"Yes." *Yes*, I thought, though this time answering myself. "I think I've had a bit too much sun."

"That march was brutal."

There was such an expression of ignorant goodwill on his face, I didn't know whether to laugh or burst into tears. Of course, I did neither, just looked around at the sacks and the candle—and then picked up a pestle and mortar from the shelf. Always cool, a marble pestle, no matter how hot the weather or sweaty the hand.

"Better?"

"Yes, better."

"Do you think you can walk?"

"Oh, heavens, yes, I'm all right now."

He held out his hand and after a moment's hesitation I took it, not because I was in any way reconciled, but because not taking it would have been a problem. He helped me out of the storeroom and a few minutes after that, we left.

The one good thing that stayed with me as I began climbing the back stairs—*be careful on staircases, watch where you're putting your feet*—was the feel of the pestle in the palm of my hand. That touch, though fleeting, had sent a fizz of excitement running along my veins, something I hadn't felt for a long time. I knew if I could just get back to that, to the work that defined me, I'd be all right, I'd be myself again—oh, no doubt with a few bits lopped off here and there, but still, identifiably, *me*. And if that meant dealing with the queen and her desperately unhappy child, then that's what I would have to do.

Twenty-eight steps and counting, but was it twenty-eight? I realized I'd lost count. The rope banister was burning my hand, I kept stumbling, and when, finally, I reached the top of the stairs I came out on to a corridor I didn't recognize. Slowly, I walked along it, but right up to the last moment, when my hand was already pushing the door open, I wasn't sure that this was the room where I'd left Cassandra.

21

Cassandra lies blinking at the ceiling, knowing she'd been woken by a loud noise but unable to remember what the noise had been. Perhaps she'd heard it in a dream, because her dreams had been dark, running down endless corridors hearing a child scream, knowing however hard and fast she runs she won't get there in time. She's totally awake now; no hope of more sleep and no desire for it either. With so little time remaining, why would she want to sleep?

Throwing back the coverlet, she goes across to the window and looks down at the kitchen yard. One of the kitchen maids, with big beefy arms under her breasts, is standing talking to a young man who's about to climb into his cart and drive away. At the last minute, when he's settled and holding the whip, she reaches up and touches his hand. Her son? He clicks his tongue for the bullocks to walk on and she stands there watching till he's out of sight.

It's strange how merely by looking out of a window you can catch glimpses of another life. As a young girl in the temple, she'd watched the ravens stalk around the inner courtyard, their wings clipped so they couldn't fly, seeing how tame they were when people threw them scraps, though for a long time she'd been afraid to do it herself. And, later, the whores who'd taken their clients into the alley beneath her bedroom window—another glimpse of clipped wings and desperate lives, and yet even those lives were lived more vividly than her own. When she thinks of what happened to her, she feels angry and cheated—and at first doesn't notice that the congested feeling in her neck is accompanied by the return of voices in the walls. That's interesting. It might be just coincidence, of course, but the change in her mood does seem to produce a reaction, anger feeding off anger. Deliberately, she stokes her rage, remembering times when she was locked up in the palace and punished for things she couldn't even recall doing. As her rage rises, the voices become high and pure and shrill until at last she can hear the words clearly: *Now wasn't that a dainty dish to set BEFORE THE KING?* An extraordinary burst of aggression right at the end, followed by scampering footsteps disappearing into darkness.

Enough of windows. Get dressed, go out. She hesitates, then chooses a plain tunic from the bag and ties her hair in a simple knot at the nape of her neck. Down the back stairs, tripping frequently and grabbing the rope, then onto the main staircase, which she walks down automatically, without thinking, simply because she's been walking down staircases like this one all her life. Crossing the atrium, she comes out onto the top steps. This is a house of stairs. Stairs, stairs everywhere. At ground level, she stops and looks around. Right, or left? Left, she suspects, might bring her to the kitchen yard with the vegetable garden and the well close at hand. Right, then. Turning the corner, she finds herself walking past a long, low room that extends the full length of the building and is full of clacking looms. That sound beats time to everything else that happens here, births, marriages, deaths, war, peace—murder.

She stops to watch the women hurrying up and down the looms, servicing them, like worker ants feeding grubs, every day the same, on and on: the life of most women, the life she's only ever seen from outside. Coming towards her along the terrace is a young woman carrying a laundry basket full of teased and washed wool, and she knows the face because the woman's very pale and very pretty, with long, slightly curly red hair. One of the slaves who used to be employed in the temple. The woman hesitates, obviously not knowing whether to speak or not; she doesn't bow and her gaze, raking Cassandra from head to toe and taking in a tunic as plain as her own, is little short of insolent. She won't have been in the Lion Court to see Cassandra arrive in a chariot by Agamemnon's side. She's thinking: *Oh yes, you're going to find out what it's like now, you with your pride, the way you used to look straight through me when I knelt at your feet holding a golden bowl for you to wash your hands.*

"Sarai," she says. "How are you?"

The woman flushes a dull, ugly red, pleased to be remembered and angry with herself for being pleased. "All right."

Cassandra notices she's pregnant, not far on but showing, and wonders how she'd managed to escape the spear that ended the lives of so many pregnant women in Troy, in the belly or between the thighs. That's just one of many sights in the fallen city that Cassandra can't forget.

"I ran away," Sarai says, in response to the unspoken question. "I went back to my parents' house. They hid me in the loft and I just stayed there under a mattress when the fighters came. They killed my father and my brothers. I don't know what happened to my mother. I searched for her everywhere, but she'd gone."

"They killed my father and my brothers too. And my nephew. Threw him off the battlements."

"I don't suppose he was the only one."

"No, he wasn't. There were hundreds of them."

Tears brim like acid. The young woman, who's also crying, brushes her tears angrily away. "Well, I'd best be getting on."

They stare at each other.

"Good luck," Cassandra says.

Sarai mutters, "And you."

Then, lowering her head, she pushes past Cassandra and disappears into the weaving room.

Cassandra goes on walking and comes eventually to the altars of the gods with their attendant priests, wilting garlands, tinkling bells, and the smell of incense and of blood that hangs over it all. She stops and breathes in the smell, remembering sunny days spent learning to interpret the stinking entrails of sacrificed animals. These smells, these sounds, the coolness of marble, the candles adding to the heat though they burn dim in the light of the sun.

What a world to condemn a child to. And yet her footsteps have led her here, almost as if they're confirming the decision her mother made. Not good enough for men. Give her to the gods—or rather, to one god. She walks along the row of altars through air that bends in the heat. All the other gods have had their red robes restored; only Apollo's statue is nude. Apollo doesn't need clothes; he's got perfection instead. She sits on the ground looking up at him, and Apollo looks down on her, a quiver full of plague arrows slung elegantly across one shoulder, his right hand carrying the silver bow. The same unearthly smile, the same blank eyes. She doesn't know why she's here. What is she doing, bringing her grief to Apollo? He doesn't want anything to do with pain. Revenge, perhaps? He's a good god to petition if you want revenge. She closes her eyes and calls to mind the vision that's at the heart of her prophecy: her body and Agamemnon's naked in a courtyard, naked and dead. Flies everywhere—buzzing, zigzagging, frantic to break through the smoothness of skin and turn smell into meat. Somewhere close at hand, though out of sight, a man and a woman are arguing. She's certain the woman's voice is Clytemnestra's, though she doesn't recognize the man's.

Is all that set in stone—or can it be changed? And if it can be changed, would she want to change it? She knows what Ritsa would say, what Hecuba would say: *You're young, you're pregnant, you've got your whole life ahead of you—and even if he tires of you, or rather when he tires of you, you'll still have the child, and a house and slaves to take care of everything.* All true, but suppose that's just not possible? Suppose those two corpses in the courtyard *are* the future? Well, then, she has to make her peace with it, not just once either, every day, sometimes several times a day. When she was young, one of the priests in the temple at Troy had told her: "You can't cherry-pick a prophecy. It's fulfilled in its entirety or not at all." She hadn't grasped the importance of what he was saying at the time, but she certainly does now. Suppose she *can* choose to live, but in choosing life for herself she chooses it for Agamemnon as well? Are their fates as inextricably linked as the closeness of their bodies in her vision implies? If that's true, then of course she has to choose death, because the one thing she's never wavered on is Agamemnon's death. She saw Hector's baby son, her nephew, thrown from the battlements of Troy, admittedly not by Agamemnon himself, but by the son of Achilles, acting on his orders. And then all the other little boys hurled to their deaths, the babies tossed into the air and caught on spears while their mothers were made to watch. She knew, from that moment, that Agamemnon couldn't be allowed to live.

Death, then? She's crying now without restraint, rocking backwards and forwards, deaf and blind to everything around her, until she feels a cool hand descend on her arm. Looking round, she sees a priest with scarlet bands—not the self-important young man she'd spoken to in the Lion Court, this one's old, frail, cadaverous, the hand on her shoulder cold even in the blistering heat. "Praise the lord and giver of light."

"Now and for ever may his name be praised."

"I'm sorry for your grief," he says. "But you're bringing it to the wrong place. Apollo's not interested in pain."

"No, I know," she says. "I'm sorry."

He helps her to her feet and she turns to face him, half expecting him to recognize her from the morning, but when she looks into his eyes, she sees they're milky with cataract. He has no more reason to praise the lord of light than she has. So she just squeezes his hand gently, and slips away.

22

I entered the room gasping and put the jugs straight down on the floor. "I'm sorry, I—"

No need to apologize. In fact, nobody to apologize to: the room was empty. Stupidly, I wandered round, checking: there was a dent in the pillow where her head had rested and the yellow dress still hung in the window, swaying gently in the breeze, but no other trace of Cassandra and no indication of where she might have gone.

I sat on the edge of the bed and tried to talk sense into myself. I was overreacting because of all those nights in the hut when I'd lived in dread of her getting out, finding a torch and setting the place alight. Which might be exactly what she was doing now. In the end, I just sat by the window and waited, looking down into the yard where yet another cart was delivering goods to the kitchen door. I liked the fact that our room overlooked the yard, because that seemed to be the one area of the palace where normal life carried on. Good food, hot water, wine—people working their arses off supplying it. That was real. Yes—but so were the handprints on Machaon's workbench and the footprints by the well.

After a while, I heard quick, light footsteps and Cassandra came in.

"Where have you *been?*" I asked. It was such a reversal of our normal roles that for a moment I found it funny.

"The temple."

This was said in a *where else would I have been?* tone of voice that discouraged further enquiries. She'd been crying, I could see that. "Why don't you get washed?" I said, indicating the jugs.

As she splashed her face and neck, I was careful to stand ready with the towel. She'd just been forced to explain her actions to her maid; that wouldn't fit with her sense of the natural order of things, and might suggest a change in our relationship that she'd struggle to accept.

She was shaking out the yellow dress, clearly getting ready to put it on. "I want to go out."

"You've just been out. It might be a good idea to have a little rest. Whatever happens, it's going to be a long night."

"No, Ritsa," she said, sounding half irritated, half amused. "It is *not* going to be a long night."

I helped fasten the ties at the back of the dress, then brushed her hair—it had gone frizzy in the heat and needed a lot of work. All the while, as I teased out cotters and tangles, I was thinking back to my meeting with Machaon. Why had he recommended me to the queen? I was Cassandra's slave; nobody else had any say in how my time was spent. Unless, in Machaon's mind, I wasn't her maid at all but still, potentially at least, a nurse—or even a keeper? Right from the beginning, she'd treated me as her slave, but then, nothing she'd said or done in those early weeks bore much relation to reality. I suppose the real mystery was why I'd gone along with it, why *I'd* believed it? I've never thought of myself as a weak person—quite the opposite, in fact—but perhaps I was, at least in comparison with Cassandra? She could change the atmosphere in a room merely by walking into it.

I was turning to put the brush down when there was a knock on the door. We exchanged glances—who could it be? Who even knew we were here? I went to answer it. Clytemnestra, her presence simultaneously shocking and the most natural thing in the world.

Looking over her shoulder, I expected to see a couple of maids at least—but there was nobody. She was alone. Why? Why here, why now—and why alone? It could only be curiosity, a desire to get a closer look at her husband's new concubine. She raised her eyebrows, which made me realize I'd been gawping when I should have been standing aside to let her in. I took a step back. Out of the corner of my eye I saw Cassandra bow, a much more graceful bow than the sketchy little bob I'd just managed, but then Cassandra didn't seem surprised. She seemed to have been expecting this.

They looked at each other, like wrestlers in a ring, searching for signs of weakness before the bout starts.

Clytemnestra made the first move. "My husband told me to be kind to you. He said: 'Be kind to this foreign woman. Nobody chooses the life of a slave.'"

"I heard what he said."

"Somehow or other—I daresay it slipped his mind—he didn't get around to mentioning your name."

"Cassandra, daughter of Priam."

"King Priam's daughter, a slave?"

"You know as well as I do what happens to women in war."

Clytemnestra was looking around the room. "Do you have everything you need?"

"For the moment. I'd like a bath before the feast."

"I'm sure you would." There was a kindling of amusement in the queen's eyes. "Remember, you're not there as a guest. You'll just be serving food and wine like the other slaves."

No response from Cassandra, but in the silence that followed the atmosphere subtly changed.

"I had a daughter once," Clytemnestra said. "Bit like you—pig-headed little madam. She'd be your age now, if she'd lived."

At that moment, I felt . . . Well, what did I feel? Humbled, I suppose. Everything I'd been attributing to her—curiosity, malice, envy of a younger woman's slim waist and glowing skin—had been wide of the mark. When she looked at Cassandra, she saw Iphigenia. Grief for her lost daughter overrode everything else.

"So," Clytemnestra went on. "How do you come to be here?"

Cassandra flinched, the impossibility of answering stark on her face. Burning towers, columns of black smoke rising into the still air, the stench of decay coming from the rubble of ruined houses, children's bodies piled high at the foot of the battlements . . .

"My husband says you were awarded to him by the army."

And suddenly Cassandra's released into speech. "*Awarded* . . . Is that what he says? Not true, I'm afraid. The *other* kings were awarded prizes of honour: women, weapons, suits of armour— mainly women. Not Agamemnon. Whenever a city was taken, he always got first choice."

"And chose *you?*"

Cassandra shrugged.

"I don't mean to be rude, but people do say you're mad. So, it's a perfectly reasonable question—why you?"

"I'm Priam's daughter."

"Priam had a lot of daughters. Some of them younger than you. And prettier."

"But I'm the eldest unmarried daughter—he wants to unite the two houses. He wants a son."

"He's got a son."

"And as we both know, one son's not enough. Two hours of the sweating sickness and he's gone. You should ask Agamemnon about it because you'll see it in his eyes. The dream. Trojan history, Mycenaean gold."

"You don't seem to realize how totally the Greeks despise Trojans. Priam was a barbarian king."

"Barbarian? I don't remember my ancestors killing and eating children." She looked around the room. "Honestly, how can you live in this place? Stinks of blood."

"Does it? I've never noticed."

"Oh, don't lie." Cassandra had begun pacing up and down. I was afraid she was going to embark on one of her long, gabbling, hand-waving, spit-flying rants, but when she spoke again her tone was measured. "There's no point talking to each other at all if we're going to tell lies."

They were silent for a while after that. The walls were murmuring again, but I couldn't tell if Clytemnestra heard them; I know Cassandra did.

"Is there any point anyway?" Clytemnestra asked.

"I don't know, but I'm ready to go on trying if you are."

"All right."

Though this was followed by another long silence, as Cassandra felt her way forward. "You've got it all planned, haven't you? You must have been planning it for months."

"*Months?* Years." Clytemnestra raised a hand to her mouth. "If you mean the celebrations, well, yes, of course they've been planned. Rehearsed. We've done nothing else for weeks."

"Right down to the last detail."

"You seem to think you know everything."

"No, there's a lot I don't know—I mean, one example. He's a strong man, he's used to killing—he's done nothing else for years. He could wring your neck with one hand, so *how* are you going to do it? Get him drunk? Well, good luck with that! He could down a barrel and still be on his feet. Or have you got somebody lined up to do it? A man . . . ?"

"Do you really think I'd let anybody else do it?"

"No, I don't suppose you would." Cassandra had stopped pacing up and down and was looking into Clytemnestra's eyes, their faces only an inch or so apart. It was far too close for two people who didn't know each other well, but then hatred generates its own intimacy. "And *yet* . . . right at the last minute, when it's nearly within your grasp, you're having doubts. You are, aren't you? Can you go through with it? Do you *want* to go through with it? It won't bring her back. Nothing's going to do that. So why not live out the rest of your life in peace? You don't have to live here. You could go to the Sea House, she was happy there, wasn't she? There's the grave, there's the gardens . . . And so, you lie awake, thinking: *Why risk everything? Let him live, let him suffer—*"

"He doesn't suffer!"

"Besides, there are so many other ways of getting revenge. Turn the other children against him. I'm sure you're well on the way with that."

"No. No, you're wrong there. Electra adores her father—though she has no idea who he really is. Until this morning, she'd have walked past him in the street. Knows him now, of course, he's the man who punched her in the chest, but it won't make a scrap of difference, she'll still adore him. *And* Orestes. He's just the same: 'I don't care what he's done—he's still my father.' If they blame anybody, they'll blame me."

Cassandra didn't respond. She seemed to be pursuing a train of thought that had nothing to do with the woman standing in front of her.

"But perhaps you're just thinking you should wait. He's popular with the people now, but it'll soon wear off. I was looking at everything on the way here. Some of the farmhouses are derelict, the buildings in the harbour, the walls . . . It's all a bit run-down, isn't it? All that wealth squandered—so a red-faced sweaty baboon can climb on top of your sister. Poor woman, she must be so bored."

"I wouldn't waste too much sympathy on Helen. It's all turned out rather well for her. She's Queen of Argos again."

"I thought he was going to kill her."

"Oh, that's all forgotten about now." Clytemnestra smiled. "Don't look so shocked. Do you really expect me to leap to my sister's defence?"

"No. It can't have been easy, all those years, no matter how hard you tried—always *the other one*."

Such an innocuous little phrase, but it had an extraordinary effect on Clytemnestra. "I . . ." She blinked. "I've never told anybody that."

"Helen of Troy's *plain* sister. What a fate. Do you ever look at Electra and think she's the other one now? Because she is, isn't she? She can't compete either. No matter how hard she tries. Every day of her life, trailing along behind her beautiful, brilliant, *dead* sister."

Clytemnestra was swaying on her feet. I stepped forward and helped her to a chair. "I'm all right," she said. "It's just my knee."

"It's not your *knee*," Cassandra said.

"Would you like me to have a look at it?" I asked.

"You can, if you like, but there's nothing to see."

Clytemnestra raised the skirt of her tunic. There was no redness but a certain amount of swelling when compared with the other knee, and when I put my hands on the skin it felt hot. I asked her to bend the joint a little and could hear grating. "I could make you something for that," I said.

She looked at me. "You must be the woman Machaon mentioned. Poor Machaon, I don't think he can be bothered with moaning women. I certainly wouldn't want to go to him with my knee."

"No, well, it's not his thing, is it? Now, if you had an axe-head sticking out of it . . ."

Cassandra, who'd resumed her pacing up and down, came to a halt in front of us.

"Have you finished?" Her anger was directed at me, though she turned immediately to the queen. "I'm not surprised the Sea House seems attractive. I mean, you wouldn't need to see him more than once a year. He could have his girls—notice the plural, I'm under no illusions here—and you'd get the respect due to you as queen. So why not? Why not enjoy what remains of your life?" Cassandra looked down at her. Not a compassionate glance, though it did contain a certain amount of respect. "But it's all nonsense. All that—gardening, looking after the grave. Pottering about. You know you've got to kill him."

"Do I? Why?"

"The gods require it."

"You think I give a fuck what the gods require? The gods required my daughter's death—if you believe the priests."

"Then do it for *her*. Or even better, do it for yourself."

Clytemnestra's eyes narrowed. "I know a lot about you. To be honest, I've always thought you were a fraud. *I* don't think you can foretell the future; I don't think anybody can. I think what you're really good at is worming your way into other people's minds. Just now you told me something I've never told anybody else, and I have to admit I don't know how you did it. But you're completely wrong about the rest of it."

"Am I?"

"Yes."

"Go on, then, tell me. What would make you do it?"

"Guilt. Not his guilt, he doesn't feel any, but I do. I should have protected her, I shouldn't have been so . . . gullible. So insanely fucking *stupid*."

"You couldn't have guessed what they were planning."

Their faces were so close together, so pale in the deepening shadows of the room, that they looked like conspirators. They'd even started to resemble each other. This had an extraordinary effect on me. I was beginning to doubt the evidence of my senses, as if I'd looked up into the night sky and seen two moons.

"I've never had a child," Cassandra said. "When I was thirteen I was sent off to be a priestess, a virgin priestess, so when my brother Hector had a son I got very attached to him, and Andromache, my sister-in-law, was generous and she let me . . . share him, I suppose, to some extent . . . And then, when the palace was taken and the men were all dead, they started on the boys. And he was thrown off the battlements."

"Did you see it?"

"Yes."

"I saw my daughter die."

"I made up my mind there and then. Agamemnon had to die."

I felt Clytemnestra start to pull away from this melding of minds. "Look, Cassandra," she said, very much the queen now. "I've got nothing against you. None of this is your fault, you didn't choose any of it, any more than I did. What I'm trying to say is: you don't have to be involved."

"I *am* involved."

"Why? Because you sleep with him?"

"Not by choice."

"I'm not *jealous.*"

"You mean, you don't mind?"

Clytemnestra blinked. "Well, to be honest, this morning I did mind a bit. The way he flaunted you. There was no need for that. But then I thought: Well, if it hadn't been you, it would have been somebody else. His girls have never lasted long. After a couple of months, Achilles would sack another city and there would be another crop of girls to choose from. Sometimes the previous girl just got thrown out. You know? *It's winter, there's no fighting, the men deserve a bit of fun . . .* At least, you've been spared that. Though I suppose there's always the stable yard."

"The stable yard?"

Clytemnestra shrugged. "It happens."

"It won't happen to me."

"Because you're Priam's daughter?"

"No, because I'm Agamemnon's wife." She looked directly into Clytemnestra's eyes. "He married me. I bet your spies didn't tell you that, did they?"

"No, because it's not true."

"Oh, I think you'll find it is. Machaon was there."

"*Machaon?*"

"Yes. Why don't you ask him?"

"Agamemnon's not nearly as committed to you as you seem to think. Only just now, he was saying: 'She doesn't matter.' He did say that. Those words. He said, 'If she's a problem I'll get rid of her.'"

"I don't believe you."

Clytemnestra shrugged again. "Suit yourself." Then, casually, as if the answer were of no importance: "Who else was there?"

"Odysseus. Calchas. He performed the ceremony."

Clytemnestra gave a curious yelp. "That bastard. Where is he, anyway?"

"Last seen walking into Troy."

"You're not doing very well, are you? Who else?"

"Ritsa, here."

They turned to stare at me. At that moment, I knew how a woodlouse feels when the stone's lifted and all that scouring white light floods in. I'd been so sure nobody would ever ask *me* about the marriage. The unsupported evidence of a woman counts for nothing. Except, possibly, to another woman.

"You were there?" Clytemnestra asked.

"Yes."

"We-ell?"

"Everything was done that should have been done. Their hands were fastened together, he said—Calchas said—the binding prayer and then they exchanged vows . . . I can't think of anything that was left out. There was a cake . . ."

"A *cake*? You think that's what makes a marriage valid?"

I remembered the clag on the roof of my mouth, how difficult it had been to swallow. "No, but he did make the vows."

"Vows! He'll forget it ever happened."

"He won't," Cassandra said. "I'm pregnant."

There was a buzzing all around me as if a swarm of flies had got in through the window, though I couldn't see any. They must be outside in the yard, feasting on the blood of animals that had been butchered for the feast.

"He needs another son," Cassandra said. "And he's not going to get one from you, is he? You're too old."

Clytemnestra grunted. The flabby skin on her cheeks puckered like boiling porridge as she jumped up from her chair. Raising her arm, she brought her hand slashing down across Cassandra's face— not a slap, more a chopping movement, using her rings as a weapon. A weal, seeded with blood from eye to lip, sprang out on Cassandra's cheek.

Clytemnestra took a step, made a few ineffectual erasing movements with both hands, then turned on her heel and left the room.

23

"God, I hate this place."

Cassandra was touching her lip as she spoke, feeling the puffy outer corner of her mouth, so the words were barely intelligible. Taking her by the arm I led her across to the window, where I could get a better look at her face. Not too bad—typical, in fact, of the injuries you get in spats between women.

"It won't scar," I said. She'd been lucky though—another inch, it would have caught her eye. "At least we've got some water." I set to work: dabbing, lifting the cloth, waiting for fresh beads of blood to appear, dabbing again. I could see it was painful but, to be honest, a small part of me wanted it to be. "There," I said, throwing the cloth down. "It won't be too obvious. You'll just have to pull your veil forward."

"I'm not wearing a veil."

"Up to you. If it was me, I'd hide it."

"Well, yes, of course *you* would."

I was tired of being the always-available object of Cassandra's contempt. "Try it," I said, throwing a thin veil over her hair. Immediately, she looked older, more dignified—regal, even—and the folds cast just enough shadow to obscure the injury. "I think it works."

We had no mirror so she couldn't judge for herself, but she

decided to leave the veil in place "for now." I put the jug down on the floor, wrung out the blood-speckled cloth and spread it over the window ledge to dry. All this, without speaking. Behind me, I heard her sigh.

When I still didn't turn round, she said, "Go on, then. What?"

"Could you have said *anything* more to antagonize her?"

She pretended to consider. "I suppose I could have said Agamemnon's a marvellous lover, I'm having a wonderful time in bed—but unfortunately, thanks to Apollo, I'm stuck with telling the truth."

"You heard her say it: 'You don't have to be involved.' She's got nothing against you."

Clicking her tongue, she pointed to her cheek.

"You provoked her."

"Oh, so this is my fault?"

"I think she meant what she said. It's not about you."

"She meant *this*." She jabbed at the cut and winced. "As for justice for Iphigenia, I don't trust her; I think she's on the verge of backing out."

"I don't agree."

"You don't agree?"

"I think you're underestimating her. And you know, Cassandra, you do that quite a lot."

"Do what?"

"Underestimate people."

"Who?"

"Machaon. Your mother. The queen."

"Oh, and you too, I suppose?"

"I don't matter. But it might be very dangerous to underestimate the queen."

"She's wavering."

"I don't think she is. You're a clever woman, Cassandra, and you may be right. I'm just saying, I don't see it."

"Underneath the front she puts on, she's got just the same weaknesses as everybody else."

"Cassandra, she's held power in a man's world for the last ten years. Supreme power—over a load of heavily armed, obstreperous men. A woman like that isn't necessarily hiding her weaknesses, she's just as likely to be hiding her strengths."

"I don't know, we seem to have met two completely different people! I saw somebody on the verge of collapse."

"Physically? Well, I suppose the knee is a bit of a concern—"

"*A bit of a concern?* Listen to yourself! This is Agamemnon's wife we're talking about. It shouldn't worry you if her knees drop off. Anyway, there's nothing wrong with her knee, she's just losing her nerve." She was fiddling with her veil. "Are you sure this is all right?"

"Yes, you look good." (Said sincerely, by the way—despite her rapidly swelling lip, she did look good.)

"What do you think, necklace as well?"

"No, the embroidery fights it."

I didn't, I have to admit, like to see her wearing the opal necklace which belonged by rights to Briseis.

"All right," she said, patting the front of her dress, though she didn't look convinced. "Now, what about you?"

"*Me?*"

"Yes, I can't have you traipsing round after me looking like a scarecrow." She tipped the clothes bag out on to the bed, selected a tunic, plain, but good quality, and threw it at me. "There, try that."

It made an enormous difference, not so much to the way I looked, but to the way I felt. There was nothing much to be done about my sandals, but I wiped them clean with the same cloth I'd used on her face and then sat on the edge of the bed. I expected her to hand me the brush, but no, she started struggling to get it through my frizzy hair. "This is impossible!" she said, and I was reminded painfully of my poor mother, who'd said those exact same words every morning of my childhood. "Well, that's the best I can do," Cassandra said, stepping back—once again, same words. I was crying, and trying not to let her see. So, there we were: me, on the bed, snivelling; Cassandra standing over me, brush in hand. A click as she put the brush down on the table brought me back to the present day.

"Come on, let's go," she said.

"Isn't it a bit early to go down?"

"No, I want to look around. I haven't seen the gardens yet."

As soon as we left the room, I started walking the regulation catch-fart pace behind her, but she slowed down, forcing me to drop still further back, whereupon she slowed down again. We spent an hour strolling round the formal gardens and then I said I'd like to go to the herb garden. I was thinking about Electra's skin, but also wanting something better than tepid water to bathe Cassandra's cut. Once there, I knelt and started putting small bunches of herbs into a basket. Meanwhile, Cassandra walked across to the poison garden. When I went to join her, I saw that she was gripping the black iron railings that enclosed it, peering at the luxuriant plants inside.

"Isn't that belladonna?" she asked.

I looked. "Yes."

"So, it is poisonous?"

"Very, especially the eye drops. Women blinding themselves to look beautiful. I shouldn't worry though, your eyes are bright enough without them."

"Do you remember my mother plotting to kill Helen? She wanted Briseis to give her a poisoned cake because she knew they were friends and Helen would trust her."

I did have a vague memory of Briseis saying something of the sort. "You must miss your mother," I said, thinking of my own mother, trying to establish some common ground.

"No."

So, no love there at all? Thinking back, I realized I'd only ever heard Cassandra express love for her father. She was Priam's daughter through and through, like the goddess Athena, who'd sprung fully armed from the head of Zeus. No female mess and pain accompanied her birth. Women didn't really count with Cassandra; their views and opinions had no possible relevance to her—except for now, when she was confronted by a woman whom she couldn't ignore.

She turned away from the bars and I followed, glad to leave the glossy, green plants in their deep, moist shade. I've never liked poison plants, they always make me feel uneasy, though I do work with them, of course. They're the source of the most powerful medicines we have. As we walked along the path, I noticed how our shadows had grown even in the short time we'd been there. At the gate she turned and looked back. The sun was well past its height, blue shadows gathering under the trees.

"It's getting late," she said.

"Not *too* late. You could still have a life."

She stared at me, obviously shocked that I'd answered the unspoken thought. She was allowed to do that; I wasn't.

"Suppose you just don't go to the feast? Nobody's going to cancel because you're not there. And she'll still do whatever it is she's planning to do."

"You can't cherry-pick a prophecy. It's fulfilled in its entirety or not at all."

I thought she was repeating something she'd been told, perhaps when she was still a child. "So, what does that mean? If you save yourself, you may be saving him as well?"

"Yes."

"Are you sure?"

"No, I'm not sure, but I don't feel like taking the risk. He's got to die, Ritsa. You can't murder a people and walk away scot-free."

Outside the herb garden, we stopped. Neither of us wanted to go back into the palace. "We haven't seen the lions," I said, "not properly."

So, like a couple of casual visitors killing time, we went to the main gate to see its huge carvings: the lions of Mycenae. It was cool in the shadow of the gate, but still, we didn't linger. The lions were impressive—the longer you looked, the more impressive they became—but our lives had been ripped apart by their claws and no amount of aesthetic appreciation can survive that. As we toiled across the vast, windswept, gritty desert of the Lion Court, we were treading on our own shadows, which seemed to flee towards the palace, though god help anything that sought safety there. At the foot of the steps, I paused to get my breath back, remembering how the bales of red cloth had rolled towards us like so many lolling tongues.

Cassandra was staring at a small figure on the top step. I say small, though anybody would appear minuscule against that towering façade. She stopped, but immediately recovered and walked steadily on. Agamemnon caught sight of her and began coming down the steps to meet her. Cassandra waved at me to go on ahead, and I ran the rest of the way, turning to look back only when I'd reached the safety of the atrium.

They stood together, halfway up the steps, the freshening breeze lifting her veil and the hem of the yellow dress. Everybody was watching them. I don't mean there were crowds of people in the courtyard—in fact, it was almost empty—though the guards at the gate turned to look, and a driver, on his way to the kitchen, let his bullocks stand idle while he openly stared. But the real pressure of scrutiny was behind me. The darkness of the atrium blossomed with eyes, all focused on the couple who'd met in the full glare of sunlight and now, even as I watched, openly embraced. Agamemnon raised his hand to brush aside her veil and with one finger traced the cut from her eye to her swollen lip; then he withdrew his hand and placed it on her belly. Cassandra brought her own hand up and covered his hand, and there they stood, as motionless as flies in amber, a man and a woman, together, celebrating and protecting their unborn child.

Glancing to my left, I saw Clytemnestra standing in the shadows, watching. Everybody must have seen her, but nobody approached, or greeted her, or even bowed in acknowledgement of her presence.

In all that crowd of silent watchers, she was utterly alone.

24

Running up the steps towards me, Cassandra tore off her veil and thrust it into my hands. "I can't wear this, I look like a poky old woman. Anyway, let them see what she did, I don't care."

"She was watching you." I patted my belly (which looked a good deal more pregnant than hers). "The queen." I nodded to the place where the queen had been standing. I hadn't seen her go.

"Good." She looked at me. "*What?* She didn't see anything she didn't already know."

She was back to being brisk, determined, distant. I folded the veil. "Shall I see about a bath, then?"

"No, there's no time. What you could do is go and fetch the opals." She was clawing at her chest as she spoke. "I just think it needs something. It feels a bit *bare.*"

She sounded frenetic, though I daresay people who didn't know her as well as I did might not have noticed the difference. I took the main staircase, which I knew was forbidden to slaves, but with everybody busy getting ready for the feast, I thought I could probably get away with it. Walking rapidly, head down, I prayed that Cassandra would get to the end of the evening without some embarrassing public display. I could see her only too clearly, pacing the dining hall, arms jerking, spit flying, telling the assembled Greeks that Agamemnon deserved to die. She'd be lucky to survive to the end of the meal. Oh, and she'd get herself into such a state—puking, stuttering, pissing—I didn't want the Greeks to see her like that.

Plodding on, eyes on the floor, I became aware of someone blocking the way ahead and looked up to see the queen, leaning heavily on the balustrade. I stopped and waited. As I watched, she put her foot on the next step only to cry out in pain as her knee buckled under her.

I ran the few steps separating us. "Are you all right?"

"Well, no, not really." She tried to put weight on the leg and winced.

"Is there anything I can do?"

"Well, you could sit beside me. I thought I might just stay here a bit, pretend to admire the view."

Again, I liked her. I sat down and together we watched a string of gardeners carrying green plants across the atrium into the dining hall.

"It just keeps giving out on me. I know it looks bad, but it's nothing really."

I thought it was probably the "looking bad" that bothered her, and rightly so. God help any leader who stumbles; a fall's invariably taken to be the outward and visible sign of inner collapse. Rubbish, of course, as any owner of a pair of middle-aged knees will tell you.

"Is it painful?"

"A bit."

She'd given in, for the time being at least, and was showing no inclination to move. After a while, she lifted the edge of a tapestry and began rubbing the wall. Only when she took her hand away did I see a row of bluish-grey handprints, perhaps five or six in all, running along the skirting board. "They're new," she said.

I noticed the tapestry was positioned unusually low and immediately remembered seeing other tapestries equally badly hung:

too high, too low, not centred on the wall. Were they also hiding handprints?

"Do they fade?" I asked.

"Eventually, but there's always more." She hesitated. "He kept the hands and feet to show their father, to prove it was his children they'd just eaten."

We sat in silence after that. I didn't dare dwell on the evil in this place, so I turned my attention to a living child who could still be helped. "I've been thinking about your daughter's skin."

"And?"

"There's one or two things I'd like to try."

"Good, good. I'll take you to see her now. I can't stay, but her nurse can tell you anything you want to know."

Cassandra would be waiting downstairs, getting more impatient by the minute; but I could hardly refuse a direct request. And anyway, I didn't want to refuse. This was my one chance to get back to doing the work I loved, to stop being Cassandra's maid, nurse, keeper—whatever the hell I was. So, not reluctantly at all—eagerly, in fact—I followed Clytemnestra down a corridor and into a room with drawn blinds. The blinds had holes carved in the wood so that honey-coloured circles of light lay all over the walls and floor, though the room was otherwise in darkness, and unbearably hot.

A soft-faced, sweating woman stood up as we came in. I couldn't see Electra's face, just a few strands of black hair spread across the pillow. Her thin body scarcely raised the sheet.

"Iras," the queen said, "this is Ritsa. She's going to give Electra something to help her sleep."

No mention of her skin or her weight; evidently only the sleeping draught mattered. The girl seemed to have been confined to this oven of a room since midday. I'd expected Clytemnestra to stay, at least for a few minutes, but she was off at once. No sooner had the door closed behind her than Electra sat up, hair straggly, face flushed, yawning to reveal the moist, pink interior of her mouth.

"Was that my mother?"

"It was, my lovely," Iras said, her tone placating, nervous.

"I wanted to talk to her!"

"I know you did, lovey, but she's busy."

"She said Daddy would like my dress, but he didn't."

"Oh, baby, it wasn't the dress, it was—"

"She *lied*."

"He was just tired, you startled him." Iras glanced nervously in my direction. "Mummy doesn't tell lies."

"She tells lies about Razmus."

"Who's Razmus?" I asked.

Electra immediately switched her attention to me. "He's the man Mummy goes to see after dark when she thinks nobody's looking."

Iras smothered a sound that could've meant anything, but I was guessing fear. She said, quickly, "Razmus used to guard the watch-fire behind the palace. You've got to post a guard because there's always some idiot who'll set light to it for fun. The queen used to walk up there of an evening to . . . to check everything was all right."

I nodded. She had a hundred slaves she could have sent.

"He's an old man," Iras said. "His feet stink."

"Because he's got insects under his skin," Electra said.

I turned to her. "Is that why he's the watchman?"

"Yes, they itch so much he can't sleep. I've got them too—I can't sleep."

"Are some bits itchier than others?"

She nodded.

"Can I see?" I moved a little closer to the bed and Electra held out her hands. Close to, they scarcely looked like human hands at all, more like the claws of a predatory bird; they had the same cracked yellow skin. "What about your chest? Does it hurt when you breathe?"

As she sat up, the sheet slipped down around her hips to reveal a body whose ribs stood out like the strings of a lyre. There were deep hollows round the collarbones and her breasts were flaps of empty skin like you see on old women close to death. She had none of the wariness, the fierce awareness of her body as a private place, that you normally find in girls her age. This body was a sword, tempered, honed, sharpened, designed to inflict pain, and she displayed it with pride. Between the small breasts, a huge, black bruise had begun to form. Looking down, she seemed to notice it for the first time. "That's where Daddy——" And then she burst into tears. She was looking over my shoulder at Iras, and I stepped aside to let them hug each other. Iras rocked and murmured and patted the sharp shoulders, but it was a long time before Electra calmed down.

"Iras, can you get them to send up some water so she can have a bath?" I pushed Electra's hair out of her eyes. "That'll help a bit, won't it?"

"And then can I put on my dress?"

"I think Mummy wants you to stay here," Iras said.

"I could still wear the dress though?"

"Oh, all right, I don't suppose that can do any harm."

Once Electra was settled, I tried talking to Iras.

"I hope you won't pay any attention to that nonsense about Razmus," she said. "He's an old man, he really does stink . . . She doesn't understand what she's saying."

I thought she understood perfectly well. There'd been real malice there. "I suppose you've tried everything?"

Iras looked blank.

"For her skin?"

"She has ointments, herbal baths . . ."

I asked to see the ointments, sniffed them, rubbed some into the backs of my hands. Nothing surprising, nothing I wouldn't have used myself, though I rattled off a long list of the herbs I was inclined to try, making sure some were sufficiently rare for her never to have heard of them, and all the time I was wondering what on earth could be done to tackle the real problem here. A girl cooped up all day with a doting but frankly stupid nurse, no friends, no fresh air, no exercise, no work, nothing that could possibly get her naturally tired—and now this request to give her a draught to make her sleep. Perhaps it was intended as a temporary measure; perhaps it was just tonight she had to sleep through?

"It's not easy, you know." Iras, full of her own woes.

I touched her arm. "No, I'm sure it isn't."

"It's always me gets the blame. She doesn't eat, my fault. Sticks a finger down her throat, my fault. If she gets out when she's supposed to stop in—"

"How does she get out?"

Silently, she pointed to the blind. "I can't watch her every minute, I'm only human . . . And she's as sly as a box of monkeys."

A giggle from the bed.

"Nothing to be proud of, young lady, you should be ashamed of yourself."

Crossing to the window, I pulled the blind open. There was one moment of pure horror when I looked down into the Lion Court far below, but once the first shock was over, I began to see it a bit differently. A sure-footed, agile girl with a good head for heights would be in no real danger negotiating that slope, especially if she were edging along between one window and the next. That way, a few minutes would take her to the safety of a flatter roof and, I suspected, an easy route down.

Turning back to Iras, I asked: "Have you been with her long?"

"Since she was born. And, you know, after Iphigenia died, the queen wasn't up to doing very much."

No, I thought, Electra had all the hallmarks of a child who's been abandoned to the care of slaves. As I left, I saw that she was nipping the loose folds of skin on Iras' arms, pleading with her to be allowed to go downstairs, get out . . . I doubt if either of them noticed me slip away.

Cassandra would be furious, I'd been gone so long. Bursting into our room, I pulled the necklace out of the jewellery case I'd hidden under the mattress, intent only on getting it to her as fast as possible, but the moment I felt the opals cold and heavy in the palm of my hand, I slowed down. This necklace had belonged to Briseis's mother; it had been her bride-gift on her wedding day, and there were so many memories attached to it—happy memories too. But there was no time to think about the past, I had to press on into the uncertain future, so I made my way to the back stairs and grabbed the rope banister.

Be careful on the staircases, Machaon had said, only half jokingly. *Watch where you're putting your feet*. The worst thing about the stairs was the near darkness and the sticky, chaotic webs that brushed against your face as you went past. I came out onto a strange corridor, or at least one I didn't remember. Somewhere close at hand, a child was crying, not in the normal way of small children, who cry almost as frequently as they laugh—no, this was the wail of a child who knows he's been abandoned, knows that no help or comfort will come and that more pain may come instead, but goes on crying anyway because there's nothing else he can do.

I could no more have ignored that cry than I could have cut off my own hand.

It seemed to be coming from three doors further along. With my hand on the latch, I paused for a moment; I won't say I knew what I was going to see, because how could I possibly have known? But I felt the terror of what lay on the other side. The cry came again; I pushed the door open and went in. The room was empty, blinds open, sky filled with flickers of summer lightning, the kind you get towards the end of insufferably hot days. Perhaps I breathed out, perhaps there was a moment of relief, but not for long. In the corner to the left of the window, a crib was beginning to take shape: a small boy, standing up, holding on to the bars. No crying, though, not now, just big eyes swallowing darkness. I started to walk towards him, but then, suddenly, barring my way, were other children whose skinny arms joined to form an arch that I'd have to dip under to get through. They were singing, singing as if songs could kill.

Here comes a candle to light you to bed, here comes a chopper to CHOP OFF YOUR HEAD!

Laughter. Wild and whirling laughter. I couldn't help anybody in this room, not even myself. So I backed away, stumbled out into the corridor and banged the door shut behind me, feeling as if I'd just closed the gate of hell.

25

The sound of a door slamming somewhere close by drags her back to full consciousness. Blinking at the ceiling, she's amazed she managed even a few minutes of half-sleep, but then she'd barely slept at all the previous night. A couple of hours, if that. Her knee hurts. Raising her leg, she holds it in both hands, hearing the crepitus Ritsa had noticed. She inspired confidence, that woman—her hands were cool and capable, she took the pain seriously.

Not like that arrogant girl.

It's not your knee.

So, what did she think it was? Doubt? Fear? Indecision? The sheer impossibility, now the moment had finally arrived, of sticking a knife into Agamemnon's chest? If Cassandra could have listened to her thoughts last night, she'd have been certain that's what it was; but then Cassandra wasn't a mother, she couldn't imagine what it was to feel a mother's guilt.

I should have known.

Abruptly, she's falling back into the past, as she often does, only it isn't the past, it's the present, more real than anything around her. She's never succeeded in freeing herself from that time, slips into it quickly and easily, between one breath and the next.

I should have known. Because from the moment they arrived in Aulis, nothing had felt right. For a start, there was no formal welcome, no visits from Menelaus, Odysseus, Nestor or any of the other kings. No Machaon. And, above all, no Achilles. "He's been very strictly brought up," Agamemnon said. "He won't expect to see her before the wedding day. Not even then—he'll expect her to be veiled."

She had to accept that, since she didn't know Achilles, but still, it did seem odd. No visit, fair enough—but no messages, no gifts, not even flowers or fruit . . . ? "Are you he sure he wants this marriage?" she asked.

"Of course he wants it! Apart from anything else, he wants to be my son-in-law."

"He's very young to be getting married. How old is he? Seventeen?"

"He's his father's only son and he's going off to war. Obviously, it makes sense for him to try to get a child before he goes."

"Do young men think like that?"

"This one does. He's exceptionally far-sighted."

Iphigenia was tired after the long journey and went to bed early. As soon as she was sure her daughter was sleeping, Clytemnestra set off to walk down the path to the beach. It was late, very quiet. The moon came and went on the surface of the water. Since she'd been warned not to enter the camp, where there were several cases of suspected sweating sickness, she turned to the right through a patch of dense forest, coming out on to a tussocky hill overlooking a bay where curiously hesitant waves rolled in but seemed reluctant to break.

There were two young men in the bay, which was otherwise deserted, and they were racing each other, one on foot, one in a chariot. She watched, compelled by the runner's attempt to transcend the limitations of the human body. Perhaps, as they came towards her along the beach, the charioteer was holding back his team, because the race ended in a draw. "You won," the runner said. "No, I think it was you."

By now, she knew who the runner was. The son of Peleus, swift-footed Achilles, whose speed defined him. A gift from the gods, people said, though seeing him like this, bent double and retching into the sand, she thought his speed was not simply a gift. My god, he worked at it. Curious now, she slid down the last slope of sand and walked towards him. He seemed startled to be greeted by a woman old enough to be his mother, apparently, judging by her manners, respectable, and yet out walking after dark, unveiled and alone. He bowed low, greeted her courteously—no small feat since he'd only just finished vomiting—and turned to introduce his companion, who was called Patroclus. Achilles seemed to defer to him, which surprised her a little, for there was no difference in age and the advantages of status were all on Achilles's side. They talked about horses for a time, but the conversation, though never unfriendly, was distinctly odd. "Well, I'll see you tomorrow, then?" she said eventually and wished them goodnight.

Achilles looked slightly puzzled but bowed again. And still, no mention of the wedding.

At the top of the hill she turned and looked back. The exceptionally far-sighted one had found a clump of seaweed and was chasing his friend along the shore, the pair of them yelling like ten-year-olds. *It's wrong*, she thought. *There's something wrong.*

Returning to the half-derelict farmhouse where they were staying, she went straight to Iphigenia's room to check that she was still asleep. The sound of her quiet breathing kept time with the breaking of waves on the shore, as the tide swept inexorably in. She sat by the bed, tempted to wake Iphigenia and talk about what she'd just seen, but it would have been cruel to disturb her. She needed her sleep with such an important day ahead.

"I should have shaken you awake and dragged you out of there."

She's so used to talking to Iphigenia and getting no reply that it's a shock to find words taking shape in her mind—if that's where the words are. The image she has is of autumn leaves forming fleeting patterns on the ground before they're whirled up by a bitter wind and carried off again.

"It wouldn't have done any good," the leaves are saying. "They'd have followed us and brought us back."

"I should have protected you."

"You weren't to know. Nobody could've guessed what they were planning."

"I was your mother. I should have known."

"You've got to stop blaming yourself."

"I am so tired."

A small, cool hand insinuates itself into her hand. "Not long now—then we can both sleep."

26

For once, Cassandra didn't demand to know why a simple errand had taken me so long. "I've just been inspecting the b-bathhouse," she said, with the slight stutter she developed when something excited her. "And you'll never guess what I found."

She took my arm and pulled me into a room at the far end of a short corridor, and I must admit it was remarkable; I'd not seen anything like it in Lyrnessus, or Troy either, for that matter. The bath was huge—not free-standing, as baths normally are, but sunk into the floor. Flower petals floated on the surface of the water, but what really caught my eye was the scene on the far side of the pool. A heap of dark fishing nets, a smattering of lobster pots, even an upturned boat—the kind poorer fishermen use for short trips up the coast. To the right of the pool were two massage slabs, and behind them, fixed to the wall, a shelf holding precious oils. Scents of neroli and sandalwood lingered on the air, disguising, though not banishing, a pervasive smell of decay.

"All new," Cassandra said. "Built for him coming home."

I looked around. "A lot of thought's gone into this."

Cassandra hooted. "*Ye-es!* Come on, you haven't seen the best bits yet."

She dragged me across to the massage tables. All I wanted was to get out as fast as possible; I was terrified of being found nosing about, but I was curious too. On the back of a chair were robes in a deep blue shade, richly embroidered in silver and gold. A light linen shift lay on the seat, no doubt intended to be worn underneath, to protect Agamemnon's skin from all that metallic thread. Cassandra was staring fixedly at both garments. I couldn't understand the intensity of her gaze until I realized she was looking for a weapon, or more generally trying to work out how Clytemnestra planned to kill a man so much stronger than herself. It wasn't only his physical strength that would be a problem; there was also the speed of his reactions, his hyper-alertness to any sign of danger. He was a battle-hardened veteran of a long and brutal war—I kept coming back to that, I couldn't get past it. Men came back from that war changed in all kinds of ways, and they brought the battlefield home with them. Many a man has killed a dearly loved child because it crept up behind him and he hit out before his eyes had time to connect with his brain.

Looking up, I found Cassandra watching me.

"Do you see?"

"No," I said, stubbornly. "I don't see."

"She's going to use the nets. She gets him lying on his stomach, massages his back—and then, when his eyes are closed, she grabs a fishing net and throws it over him. He's helpless—only for a couple of minutes, but that's all she'll need. She can do whatever she likes with him after that. That's why it's so clever—*don't you see?* Everything's hidden in plain sight."

Oh, I saw all right. Suddenly, the quiet room was full of blood and rage, and yet, still, a large part of me remained unconvinced. Mentally, I measured the distance between the massage slab and the nearest pile of nets. "She'll need to be bloody quick." I was remembering her pacing up and down in the courtyard outside Iphigenia's tomb—and yes, she was light on her feet, as big women often are. Strong, too. Shoulders broad, surprisingly muscular upper arms . . .

Strong enough? Fast enough? I didn't think so. "And suppose he's *not* got his eyes closed? I reckon she's got less than a minute before he's on to her—and those nets are heavy. And he's not gagged, remember, he can still yell—the dining hall's just the other side of that wall."

For once, Cassandra seemed to be listening. "You're right," she said, slowly. "There's got to be something else." She walked across to the clothes and, with a little jump curiously reminiscent of a fox pouncing on a mouse, picked up the linen shift and shook it out. For anybody who knows anything about weaving, that garment was a work of art, the cloth so fine it was almost transparent, but it would be strong. One of her hands—I could see it clearly through the cloth—was burrowing into a sleeve. "*Ah!*" she said. At first, I couldn't see what it was she'd found, but then, as she came towards me, waggling her fingers, I realized her hand was trapped inside the garment. The sleeve had no opening.

Quickly, I checked the other sleeve—no opening there either. For one stupid moment I wondered how such a mistake could possibly have happened, but only for a moment. I'd seen garments like this before—though the ones I'd seen were made of canvas and stained with spat-out food and vomit. They're often used to restrain people whose mental affliction makes them a danger to themselves and others. It takes time for the trapped person to understand he's trapped, and in that time the dangling ends of the sleeves can be pulled tight behind him and knotted at the back. Once they're tied, he's trussed up as securely as a fly in a spider's larder.

"What do you say now?" Cassandra asked.

I just shrugged. "He can still shout for help."

"Oh, give her some credit. Music, singing, banging on tables? And they'll all be pissed." She was looking round the room again. "What I can't see is a weapon. I suppose she could bring it with her."

"Or he could. Don't forget he'll be wearing a sword."

"Don't they have to hand them in?"

"I think you might find that doesn't apply to him."

Candles were burning all over the room and yet the place felt dark. And that smell of something old and dank seemed to be getting stronger. Cassandra, still searching for a knife, was lifting the folds in the blue robe, her every movement precise, delicate. No trace now of the tremor that, in the worst days of her frenzy, had made her hands shake so badly she couldn't raise a cup of water to her lips without spilling it. Altogether, I thought she was in a strange mood—not frightened, as I was, but not calm either. If I had to choose one word, I'd say "exalted."

I looked again at the heap of nets, the scented oils, the massage slab, the linen shift waiting. "Everything about this is vile."

"Aren't you forgetting what he did?"

"No, Cassandra, I am *not* forgetting what he did."

That might sound like nothing, but it was a surprisingly sharp confrontation. It didn't help that in the aftermath of seeing the children, I was in a state of emotional turmoil too, though not, in my case, excitement—much less exaltation. No, what I felt was dread, not of any one specific threat, but of everything, equally—as if a translucent membrane that had protected me all my life had been ripped open, leaving me exposed to all the sharp edges in the world.

At last, Cassandra, finding no weapon hidden in the robes, jerked her head towards the door. I was only too glad to follow her. Outside, in the corridor, she turned to me. "Did you get the necklace?"

I stood on tiptoe to put it round her neck—she was a couple of inches taller than me—and noticed, as if for the first time, how white and sunless the nape of her neck was. And how vulnerable. When I'd finished freeing a stray hair that had got caught in the catch, she turned to face me, and I caught my breath, because the flames had already begun to dance. *Look, they're doing it!* Briseis used to say when she was a little girl watching her mother get ready for a feast. She always loved that moment when the warmth of her mother's skin brought the opals to life.

"It belongs to her really, doesn't it?"

Typical of Cassandra, that, answering the unspoken thought.

"They were given to you," I said.

We returned to the atrium, which was rapidly filling up with mainly grey- or white-haired guests, all of them agog with expectation. The dining hall was still closed, though promising sounds came from behind the shut doors: lyres, pipes, drums, even the sudden fierce blaring of a battle horn. The old men loved it. If they'd been horses, they'd have been lifting their tails and cantering down the meadow. But one of the younger men—there was a group of them who'd served under Agamemnon at Troy—stared wildly around at the sound of the battle horn. "Easy," one of the other young men said, putting a hand on his shoulder, while another laughed. A moment later, I lost sight of them, as another group of grey-haired men pushed their way through the crowd in search of drinks.

People had started fanning themselves, it was so hot. "I wish they'd open the doors," one of the old men said. He sounded peevish; perhaps the slaves serving wine weren't moving fast enough. Almost at once, as if somebody had been listening, the doors to the dining hall were thrown open. Servants carrying jugs were moving up and down the tables, but what really interested people was their first sight of the musicians. The bard was on his feet, standing with his back against a pillar as if he needed its support. He was trying out short bursts of song, consulting with the lyre player closest to him and then singing the same phrase again. The song seemed to be a lament for dead flowers, for the passing of summer, but also, by implication, for the dead.

"Can't somebody tell that fucker to cheer up?" one of the counsellors said, raising his voice loud enough to be heard in the hall.
"We did win the bloody war, you know?"

Rumbles of agreement. They started looking around for the
queen, whose job it was to put things like this right—and then
forgot about it as the next wave of guests arrived. But come to think
of it, where was the queen? She should have been here by now, wel-
coming the guests.

"What did I tell you?" Cassandra said. "She's losing her nerve."

I couldn't see it. The woman who'd sat up night after night,
weaving a straitjacket to restrain her husband while she killed him?
Though even now, a small part of my mind was searching for an
alternative explanation, something, *anything*, that would make this
situation feel less threatening. Could there be an innocent reason
for those sewn-up sleeves? Some men like being restrained; it excites
them to be helpless, humiliated, beaten. Not Agamemnon, though,
I'd never heard anything like that about him—and believe me, I
would have heard. I'd listened to and tried to console many of the
girls he'd slept with, including my own Briseis.

I don't know how many people noticed the queen's absence, but I
was very aware of it. At last, just as I was edging my way through the
crush to get Cassandra a cup of wine, I caught a glimpse of Clytemnestra in the dining hall talking to the bard. Minutes later, a cheerful
song with a good, thumping rhythm filled the atrium, accompanied
by a forest of walking sticks beating time.

I handed Cassandra her cup. "Shall we go outside? It's boiling
in here."

We stood for a moment at the top of the steps, looking down
across the Lion Court to the gate where dozens of armed men were
milling around. More arrived as we watched.

"What's going on?" Cassandra said.

I just shrugged. For all we knew, the guard was strengthened at this hour every night, though considering the country was at peace the palace did seem to require an inordinate number of guards. A blast of louder music from inside the atrium made us turn round. "Perhaps we'd better go in?" I asked.

"Not yet, I need some air."

It was a lot cooler outside; I felt a ripple of drying sweat on my skin as we drifted down the steps and round the corner into the gardens beyond. As we passed the door to the herb garden, Machaon came out and greeted us. He'd spent the afternoon working in his shed—and looked like it too, with smudges of dirt on his hands and face. He glanced at me. "I've made you up a salve for Electra."

Slowly, we strolled back to the Lion Court. In our absence, a table had been placed at the top of the steps and three bored-looking young men stood behind it, collecting swords from the guests. This was the usual practice in Greece, where the combination of swords, short tempers and strong wine might make for sometimes unpredictable evenings. A queue had formed, stretching well down the steps, and Machaon, who was wearing a sword, joined it. A couple more counsellors arrived and stopped to greet him, slapping him on the back and even, one of them, ruffling his hair as if he were still the boy they obviously remembered. From the interior came a buzz of laughter, music, singing and chatter, growing louder by the minute. Cassandra and I lingered at the foot of the steps, reluctant to go in. As we watched, a middle-aged man, clearly in a position of authority, came out from between the pillars and spoke to the young men behind the table.

One of the late arrivals said, "What's he doing here? He can't be coming to the feast, surely?"

"Well, you wouldn't think so, would you?" Machaon said. Seeing us look puzzled, he explained, "That's Aegisthus. He's no friend of the king."

"Aegisthus?" Cassandra asked. "Isn't he the brother of the children Atreus killed?"

Machaon shook his head—not in denial; it was more a warning to keep her voice down. I got the impression nobody in the palace ever mentioned the murdered boys. Nobody talked about them, or grieved for them; nobody even acknowledged their fate. No wonder their handprints stained the palace walls. So many people here must have been complicit in that crime, if only by ignoring it and moving on. Many of these old men shuffling up the steps would have been loyal friends of Atreus—or served under him, at least.

Dimly, I was aware that somebody had joined our little group, but I didn't turn round; I was too interested in Aegisthus, who'd come further down the steps and was speaking to somebody in the queue. He was dark, morose looking, with a broken nose and a white scar bisecting one eyebrow. Nothing like you'd expect a prince of Mycenae to be; he looked like a back-street fighter. A hard, pitiless, wolfish man. He must have been a baby or not even born when his brothers died, but that wouldn't have saved him. His whole life would have been shadowed by the duty to avenge their deaths, because blood feuds last for years, passing from father to son to grandson, sometimes outlasting the memory of the original crime. Once the cycle of revenge begins, there's no way out. So, why was he here tonight? He could take no pleasure from Agamemnon's safe return.

Behind me, I heard Machaon say: "You've *got* to get rid of him."

"I know. I *know*."

Agamemnon's voice. Instantly, I backed off, going to stand a few steps behind Cassandra.

"It's not easy. He's been making himself useful. There was fighting along the border a while back—nothing much, cattle raids, that sort of thing, but he dealt with it. The queen's got a lot of remarkable qualities, but the one thing she can't do is pick up a sword."

"So, he was her attack dog?"

"He was . . . useful. And don't look at me like that. Do you think I'm the only man in Greece who hasn't heard the gossip? I tell you one thing—*I* don't believe it. And I've got more and better spies inside the palace than anybody else."

It was a surprisingly frank exchange, I thought, given the difference in rank. After a few more desultory remarks, Agamemnon threw his arm across Machaon's shoulders and was obviously getting ready to leave, but then suddenly stopped and raised a forefinger. "There, do you hear that?"

A bird was singing somewhere in the woods outside the palace walls.

"Nightingale. I missed that when I was in Troy."

As he listened, Agamemnon's face was transformed. No longer the victorious king returning in triumph to his native land, but a tired, middle-aged man, glad to be home and looking forward to a good night's sleep in his own bed. At that moment, I think I felt the loss of my home as intensely as I've ever felt it, and I regretted sharing an emotion as simple as the love of home with a man I hated and despised. I didn't want him to be human, I resented having to see him like that. As far as I was concerned, he was the butcher of Troy, the man who'd ordered the massacre of children and seen it carried out; but there he was: alive, contented, pleased to be home. With a final pat of Machaon's shoulder, he began to walk up the steps, stopping every few yards to clasp the hands that were being held out to him, laughing, joking, greeting the old men by name, asking after families, herds, crops, and children who'd been born since he left. Finally, with a sea of grey hair and beards surrounding him, he arrived at the top of the stairs, where one of the young men standing behind the table had the temerity to ask for his sword.

"Not a chance, son," Agamemnon said. "This was my father's sword."

Pulling it from the scabbard, he raised it high above his head, turned it three times in huge, sweeping circles—drawing predictable cheers from the crowd—and then vanished into the lighted atrium beyond.

27

As soon as we were back inside the brightly lit atrium, Machaon caught sight of the dirt streaks on his tunic.

"I can't go into dinner like this. I'll have to go and get changed."

With that, he ran up the stairs, taking them two at a time, clearly delighted to have been given an excuse to at least postpone taking part in the celebrations. I wondered why he was so reluctant. He was a sociable man, he loved good food and wine—perhaps even loved them a little too much. Was it grief for lost friends? Patients who might have survived, but didn't? There'd be many people hiding themselves away tonight and some of them, hearing the drums and the blaring battle horns, would pull the covers over their heads and pray for sleep.

I looked around for the queen and found her standing in the doorway to the dining hall. Once, even as recently as last night, her appearance would have changed the atmosphere in the room, making the overconfident tentative, the articulate struggle for words. I'd seen it happen so many times, whenever Agamemnon or one of the other kings walked into a room. Kings must walk through life in a bubble of silence. Cheers, of course, banner waving, bursts of applause—but that's not the first reaction, nor the most important. The really telling tribute to the powerful is the hush they create whenever they enter a room.

Tonight, there was no hush for Clytemnestra. Nobody crowded round her, no ambitious men vying for advantage, no supplicants begging for favours. She stood at the entrance to the dining hall, as she must have done on so many evenings in the last ten years—and was ignored. There was something disturbing in it: that total draining away of power.

By contrast, Cassandra was the centre of attention. Men's eyes turned to follow her and many of the glances were frankly speculative. They knew who she was—and they knew what she'd become: Agamemnon's concubine, his bed-girl. *Lucky bastard*—you could hear them thinking it. Most of them were pig-ignorant—I won't say all, because I believe in being fair, even to the Greeks, but most were inclined to despise Trojan women, as if we'd chosen the lives that were thrust upon us. One young man, fancying his chances or perhaps just showing off to his mates, walked up to her with a swagger. A bit of chat—a few decidedly sleazy grins—and then he reached out and picked up one of the opals, cradling it in the palm of his hand like an egg. In passing, as if inadvertently, he touched her breast. "I love opals," he said, rubbing the stone until the fires inside it stirred. "Is it true they turn black?"

"I think that depends on who's touching them."

A familiar voice. The opal-lover spun round to find Agamemnon looming over him—looking amused, but with a hint of threat behind the smile. Forcing a laugh—a curiously falsetto yelp, though his voice had been deep enough a minute before—the young man bowed deeply and backed away. Agamemnon leaned forward and kissed Cassandra on the cheek. Perhaps out of a need to demonstrate ownership, but all over the room you heard a hiss of indrawn breath. For a king to kiss his concubine in the presence of the queen was unheard of. One or two people exchanged furtive glances, but most stared straight ahead. Cassandra stood her ground but flushed; she must have been aware that the glances directed at her were hostile now in a way that they hadn't been before. She withdrew to the shadow of one of the pillars and I followed. "Arsehole," I said, and for once I didn't mean the king.

Disengaging himself from a group of counsellors, Agamemnon went across to Clytemnestra and the two of them stood with their backs turned to the atrium, talking, though nobody was close enough to hear what they were saying. The bard was coming to the end of a song, but when his voice faded into silence, the singing seemed to go on, a treble descant coming from the court outside. Nobody commented, nobody turned to look; but Cassandra, immediately, as if she'd been summoned, walked towards the sound. I followed, and we stood together at the top of the steps, looking down into the Lion Court, whose stones, scoured by the full moon, were entirely deserted. Even the young men who'd been collecting swords had gone, and yet still the shrill voices went on. *Here comes a candle to light you to bed . . .*

"I can't stand much more of this," I said.

"No, I know what you mean. This is a terrible place." She peered at the roof ridge high above our heads. "No wonder they dance."

Back inside the palace, I saw Clytemnestra walking towards us. Cassandra bowed low; I took the regulation step back, but then, to my surprise, the queen acknowledged me first, before turning to Cassandra. "The king wants you to share his bath. Just keep an eye on him and follow him when he leaves. He'll be waiting for you in the bathhouse." Her voice was flat, as if she were impervious to the humiliation of delivering such a message, but how could she be? Sending her on this errand was a calculated insult. "The feast doesn't start for another hour," she said. "But I daresay you'll think of something to pass the time." And with that she was gone, pushing her way between groups of people who no longer parted automatically to let her through.

Agamemnon was attempting to free himself from the sycophants surrounding him, but as often as he tried to move on, he was pulled back, another compliment, another request. Clytemnestra rescued him, explaining that the king needed a short break before the feasting started; he'd been so busy meeting old friends he'd hardly had time to wash off the dust of the road. She was good: warm, convincing, tactful, cosseting every ego there except her own. And it worked. Agamemnon was free to walk towards the bathhouse and Cassandra followed. A frisson of vicarious excitement ran through the crowd. Nobody believed Agamemnon had been seized by a sudden passion for cleanliness; they were all happily imagining lustful scenes to come. Young men, envious; old men, wistful—and beneath it all, contempt for the Trojan whore. They'd forgotten she was a priestess, because it no longer suited them to remember. The young man who'd groped her breast under cover of admiring the necklace pointedly turned his back on her as she walked past.

At the entrance to the short corridor, Cassandra turned to face me. "Go now, Ritsa. There's no need for you to see this."

"No, I'm—"

"You can't. Not now."

Looking back on that moment, I ask myself: What did I think was going to happen? I remember details: the shadows under Clytemnestra's eyes—did that woman ever sleep?—the bold young man's falsetto laugh and, more clearly than anything else, the bard's androgynous voice soaring above the cackling of old men. I remember all that, and yet I can't tell you what I thought was going to happen next. I only knew I had to stay with her. So, despite what she'd just said, I did follow her, until the door at the other end swung open and released a mist of steam. Suddenly, emerging from the damp heat, there was Clytemnestra, one bare white arm raised to block my way.

"Leave her, I'll take care of her now."

A glimpse of the room beyond, the smell of melting tallow strong enough to turn my stomach. And then Cassandra raised the fingers of one hand in a half-gesture of farewell and followed Clytemnestra through the door.

28

The air's damp, and so hot every breath hurts her lungs. Same smells, though: the briny tang of the pool; beneath that, the taint of rotting wood, or worse. Turning to Clytemnestra, she says, "You dug too deep." The words don't register; nothing seems to be going on behind that alert, blank gaze. "I'm on your side," she whispers, trying to reach out, but again, nothing. Together, they watch Agamemnon pull his tunic over his head. All that bare, pink flesh, so vulnerable. "I want him dead as much as you do."

No reply, just the same dead-eyed, predatory stare. Cassandra looks around the room, her eyes flicking from one place to the next, checking to see everything's in the right position, almost as if *she'd* set the trap: oils, scrapers, towels, fishing nets, linen shift . . . But still no weapon, or none that she can see. She has a sudden sick fear that Ritsa had seen this place more clearly than she did, and that Clytemnestra's plan, whatever it is, could easily go wrong.

Meanwhile, Agamemnon, as carefree as a boy on the first day of the summer holidays, strides towards the pool.

Clytemnestra's hand closes round her arm. "Come on." Her fingertips are cold, her nails long enough to be felt as a row of crescent moons digging into the skin. Half pulled, half dragged across the room, she's in time to witness Agamemnon's delight as he sees the pool, the nets, the lobster pots, the upturned fishing boat—he's as excited as a child on a real beach. Naked, he walks down the steps and immerses himself in the flower-strewn water. A scattering of rose petals here and there, but mainly lavender, great purple rafts of it swirling into fresh patterns with every movement he makes. He flips over onto his back, and his swelling cock breaks the water like a seal.

Sprigs of lavender sticking to his skin, purple buboes on his neck, his groin . . .

Lord of the silver bow, hear me! Lord, whose arrows fly in darkness, hear me, hear me . . .

A purely automatic response—years and years of training went into that prayer; though surely now, at this moment of all moments, she can be free of that? She remembers the ravens strutting around the temple courtyard, their flight feathers clipped so they couldn't escape, and, silently, she recites their names: Lethe, Acheron, Styx . . . All named for rivers of the underworld, except her favourite, Koronis. Their names had been a prayer, a litany that in the hours of darkness never failed to soothe. Better to linger over their names than pray to Apollo, who's brought her here to die.

Looking down into the water, she imagines how it'll feel to step naked into it, and realizes she can't do it. She needs layers of cloth to protect her from a world that's full of sharp points, hard edges, things designed to stab and kill.

But Agamemnon's tugging at her skirt. "Come on, get in." Another more determined tug. "Get it off."

No. She tries to step back, but he's having none of that. Grabbing the hem, he pulls her down into the water, and the skirt balloons around her as his fingers delve painfully inside. Skewered like that, stuffed like a goose, she tries to fight him off—oh, but he likes that, he prefers them feisty, provided their resistance is easily overcome. Water's sloshing into her mouth, forcing her to gulp it down or choke. Breathless, she panics and tries to push him off her, but he's much too heavy. Jowls quivering, he thrusts himself into her and his weight presses her down hard on to the edges of the steps. Every thrust is the blow of an axe breaching the palace gate. She sees Priam crumpled at the foot of the altar steps, the sword he was almost too frail to lift, fallen from his hand. Children thrown from the battlements seem for one second to fly like birds, then Agamemnon jerks, the city burns, smoke from the blazing citadel stings her eyes, though as she comes slowly back to herself, she realizes it can't be smoke, there's nothing burning here, except candles warming the bowls of massage oils. Agamemnon collapses on top of her, buries his face in her neck. Looking up, she sees Clytemnestra, hovering like a bathhouse slave by the side of the pool, a white towel draped over one arm. How long has she been there? She stares at her over Agamemnon's freckly shoulder and Clytemnestra turns away.

Indifferent now, Agamemnon lifts his weight off her and stands up, his pubic hair coming to a point. As he climbs out of the pool, Clytemnestra wraps the towel around him and leads him across to the massage slab, where she invites him to choose the oils he wants.

"Nothing too soporific," he says.

Cassandra lets herself sink until her head's almost submerged, softening the sound of music from the dining hall. It's strange to think that on the other side of that wall eighty or so men are eating and drinking—and no doubt beginning to wonder what's keeping the king. Shutting her eyes, she realizes she can see, through her closed lids, Clytemnestra pick up a bowl, pour a little oil into the palm of her hand and let it trickle on to Agamemnon's back. Cassandra opens her eyes and blinks hard several times, startled, because what just happened isn't possible. Even with her eyes open, she can't see Clytemnestra's hands, though she can tell from the movement of her shoulders that this is going to be a brief, powerful massage. She swims to the side and hauls herself out onto the steps. From here, she can hear Clytemnestra's voice, high and clear—nothing odd about that—but Agamemnon's rumbling replies seem to come from deep inside her own chest. She feels the vibration of his voice in her ribs, almost as if that brutal, businesslike coupling had achieved what even the most passionate and devoted love-making routinely fails to achieve: the union of two minds.

A cheer from the dining hall. Agamemnon struggles to sit up. "I've got to get a move on."

"They'll be all right," Clytemnestra says. "There's plenty of wine."

She needs to get a move on—unless, of course, getting Agamemnon's most loyal supporters ataxic is part of her plan? At that moment Clytemnestra's nails rake down Agamemnon's spine from the nape of his neck to the cleft in his arse—hard enough to hurt. *Careful*, Cassandra thinks, feeling the pain in her own flesh.

"Sorry, was that a bit too hard?"

"No-o," Agamemnon replies, though doubtfully.

"Shall I start on your front?"

Normally, this would be the prelude to the climax, but that ship's already sailed. Swimming a little closer, she sees Clytemnestra standing by a chair, stroking the blue robe that's draped over its back. "I had this woven specially for tonight."

"Nice," he says, looking down the length of his torso at his disappointingly flaccid dick.

Cassandra shuts her eyes and sees through their closed lids Clytemnestra lean in and trickle oil on to Agamemnon's chest hair, though a moment later she feels Clytemnestra's hands gliding in circular movements over her breasts. Her lids are heavy; she has to force them open, but even when she's wide-eyed and staring the strange sensation remains. Closing her eyes again, she feels Clytemnestra begin the long, slow movement from collarbone to groin, trying not to look at the queen, because that face, at least seen from this angle,

is frightening. He's not happy; not happy, not aroused, not even titil-
lated, in fact, he seems to be sinking into despondency. Her chest
feels heavy with his pain, and he'd been so good earlier, so cocky, so
full of himself, fucking his concubine in front of his wife, and yet
now with those broad, capable hands sweeping across his genitals,
it's like being a naked, squirming, newborn baby again—or a corpse.
Men begin and end their lives as helpless lumps of flesh in the hands
of women, and all the years between—power, success, wealth, fame,
even victory in war—are merely a doomed attempt at escape.

"No, it's no use," Agamemnon says, sitting up and walking his
buttocks to the edge of the slab, "I can't keep them waiting any
longer."

Clytemnestra accepts that at once. "You'll wear your father's
sword?" Casually, not hurrying, she moves across to the table.
"You'll need something on underneath that robe. There's a lot of
gold thread in the embroidery, you won't want that next to your
skin."

Cassandra's so close she can smell his skin, not just the oil but
the dampness that lingers in its folds and creases. He picks up his
father's sword—a short, ceremonial sword, not a battlefield weapon
but capable of killing, which is why they have to be surrendered—
and turns it so the candle flames run up and down the blade. For
a moment, he's mesmerized, and Cassandra with him, but then he
slides it back into the sheath. Whatever it is, this curious binding
together of two minds, two bodies, it's not going away. What he
really wants now is sleep, but he still has an evening of carousing
to get through. *Oh well*, she hears him think, somebody'll get me
into bed. Looking up, he sees Clytemnestra holding a linen shift.
"I thought you could wear this," she says. "Underneath. It's so light
you'll hardly feel it."

Obediently, like a small boy, he lifts his arms and lets her drop
the folds of cool linen over his head. He makes no comment on the

exceptionally fine weave, because he's never in his life had to settle for less than the best, but he enjoys the feel of it, breathes a sigh of contentment as it settles on his shoulders. Another burst of cheering from the hall. "They sound happy enough," he says. The bard's singing a rather jolly song now—can't remember the words, but he hums the tune, as his fingers search for the openings at the end of the sleeves. Can't seem to find them and the cloth's so light it sticks to his oily skin. Frustrated, tetchy, he pushes harder, and manages to get a few inches further along, but the sleeves seem to go on for ever. Why are they so long? Irritated, he flaps the ends. What do they think he is—a bleeding ape?

"Are they a bit long?" Clytemnestra asks, cooing like somebody's demented granny. "Come on, I'll roll them up for you."

He holds out his arms; even now, there's no fear, only bewilderment because he can't get his hands through. But then, in one smooth movement, Clytemnestra slips behind him, pulls the sleeves towards her and ties the loose ends behind his back. Something about the movement of her hands tells him this is a proper sailor's knot, not the sort a woman would use to fasten off her embroidery. And with that realization, he moves in a single breath from bewilderment to terror.

"Clytem—?"

Twisting round, he sees she's gone. She can't have gone—where is she? A second later, when she reappears, she's dragging a fishing net behind her, which makes no sense, no sense—and even when the net descends over his head and shoulders, even when he feels the coils begin to tighten around him, *still* it makes no sense. Only when he sees her pick up Atreus' sword does it start to make a kind of sense, the kind that cooks children and feeds them to their father.

"*Look*." She's holding the blade in front of his eyes. "Look, darling," she says again—the same demented cooing sound—"*Daddy's sword*. Yes, that's right, Daddy's sword. Do you remember what

Daddy's sword does?" And then, abruptly, in her normal voice, "Do you remember? Do you remember how she called you Daddy just before you killed her? Why don't you call for your daddy now?"

Grasping the hilt in both hands, she raises the sword of Atreus high above her head. For a second, there's perfect stillness. Then all the candle flames in the room begin to gutter as the blade descends.

And Agamemnon screams.

29

I couldn't keep still. Nowhere was the right place, though to begin
with I'd simply crouched down outside the bathhouse door. It was
quiet. On the other side of the wall, I could hear the dining hall filling up, but there was no sound from the bathhouse. The corridor
itself was quiet; there was nobody coming or going. As long as I
stayed here, I would be completely unobserved.

But I was restless, desperate to find out what, if anything, was
happening, so after a while I ventured out into the atrium.

The guests had gone in to dinner, but the area was thronged
with fighters standing around in small, tense groups. Aegisthus, the
man Machaon had pointed out to me, lounged against one of
the pillars, apparently relaxed, though his eyes were wary. Despite the
scar on his face, he was an impressive-looking man, though there
was something not quite right about him, something that set him
apart, even among his own men. An internal warping, that's what
I sensed, though would it even have crossed my mind if I hadn't
already known his history? To be the brother of those children, to
have the duty of exacting revenge for their deaths imposed on you
from birth . . .

Music, punctuated by bursts of laughter, came from inside the
hall where Agamemnon's most loyal supporters were getting deter-
minedly drunk. Toasts were exchanged—*we did this, we did that, nobody*

thought we could do it, but we did!—and every toast more incoherent than the one before. At this rate, they'd have to be carried out.

Nothing like that in the atrium, where Aegisthus's men were armed, disciplined, silent— and sober.

The bard was taking a break, but the lyres and flutes played on— gentle, nostalgic music, but with the occasional dance tune thrown in for a bit of liveliness. Now and then, they cheered the men who'd fought at Troy, by name, the living and the dead, drumming on the tables and stamping their feet—then applauding themselves to the rafters as each celebration reached its peak. Money worries, failing crops, bad roads: all left at the door, along with their swords. Even Agamemnon's prolonged absence was a source of amusement, rather than disquiet. "Where's the king?" "In Troy." "Bet he is, up to the bloody hilt!" And another song: *"Hold him down, you Argive warriors, hold him down, you Argive chiefs—chiefs, chiefs, chiefs . . ."*

Only then, as sometimes happens in crowded, noisy rooms, an inexplicable hush fell. People stared at each other, aware of the strangeness of the moment and unable to account for it, starting to give little, slightly embarrassed laughs. And into that silence suddenly a man was screaming in pain and fear for his life. A few of the younger fighters immediately jumped up—I saw Machaon on his feet at the far end of the hall. Nobody could tell where the cry had come from. They looked at the walls, into the atrium, finally into each other's eyes, but they found little reassurance there. Was it Agamemnon? That was the possibility in everybody's mind, but though the voice was unmistakably male there was nothing to identify it as the king's. And then it came again, this cry weaker than the first. General uproar; men trained for battle since they were boys clawed at their swordless hips before snatching up knives from the table. Nobody seemed to know which way to turn; the bathhouse was so new, most of them probably didn't know it was there. And it didn't help that they were drunk. Meanwhile, Aegisthus's men surged forward, pushing the guests who were hesitating on the threshold back inside, then shutting and barring the doors.

Turning, I ran towards the bathhouse, meaning to drag Cassandra out, by her hair if need be, but before I reached the end of the corridor, the door burst open and Agamemnon staggered towards me. I say "Agamemnon," but I didn't at first attach a name to the thing that confronted me, skin slick-silver, scored by the dark coils of the net. A few paces away from the door, it tripped and fell, flapping its life out at my feet. And behind it, bending to peer into its bloodless gape, Clytemnestra, the queen, brandishing a blood-stained sword.

Everything about her was red: breasts, arms, belly—

"You killed my baby!"

He looked up at her, perhaps trying to say something, but only bubbles of blood came frothing from his mouth. She plunged the sword under the swelling arch of his ribcage, angling the blade upwards to be sure of piercing the heart. Then she fell back, her hair straggly with sweat, as if she'd just that minute given birth.

She must have been aware of my presence, but she didn't speak. Together, we waited for the next breath, exchanging speculative glances as the seconds limped pass. That breath never came. Instead, a vast silence yawned open, spreading as if to cover the entire world. Until it was broken by a single word.

"Mummy?"

The queen stared at the dark-haired girl in the red dress. "It's over, darling, you can sleep now, we can both sleep—"

"*Mummy?*"

Clytemnestra looked dazed. Then, as the full horror broke over her: "*Electra?*"

"What's wrong with Daddy?"

"Electra, what are you doing here? *Iras?* For god's sake, where is the woman?"

She was flailing about, trying to hide Agamemnon's wounds, trying to cover her breasts, finally, realizing nothing could be hidden anymore, reaching out to put her red hands over Electra's eyes. The girl reared back, but not fast enough to stop bloody fingerprints daubing her face. Turning her head from side to side, Clytemnestra's gaze fixed on me. "You—yes, *you*. Take my daughter away."

I ignored her. Dodging around her outstretched arm, I pushed the door open, bursting into a fog of steamy air. At first, I couldn't see Cassandra, but following a trail of bloody smears found her lying on the pool steps, half in, half out of the water. I flung myself down beside her, searched for wounds, finding one directly under her ribcage and another, slighter wound, more of a slash than a stab, in the pit of her stomach, just above the pubic bone. She was bleeding out, fading fast, and there was nothing I could do to stop it. Plumes of blood smoked and swirled in the water all around her. Sliding my arm under her head, I cradled her, picking strands of wet hair out of her eyes. Now, when it was too late, I knew I loved her.

She tried to focus on my face. "Is he dead?"

"Yes."

"*Good.*"

I couldn't stop the anger bursting out. "Why you? She didn't need to do this."

"She did—we have to die together. The gods require it."

"Then fuck the gods."

She raised a hand to her neck. "Take it."

I shook my head.

"No, go on, take it. It's hers, you know it is, it's never been mine."

Her eyes closed. I thought it was over but then she opened them again. "Do you know," she said, smiling, "I think the gods enjoy themselves?"

This time her eyes filmed over, quite suddenly, as a bird's eyes do when it dies. I'd never seen another human being die like that, never before—or since.

I sat with her for a moment, her head, heavier now, still resting on my arm. Then I pulled her dress down as far as it would go, because I knew the next people to touch her body would show it no respect, no gentleness. Shouts came from outside the room, along with a tramp of marching feet. I took the necklace from around her neck, being careful to free each individual hair that had got caught in the catch, not pulling, not tugging, even though I knew she'd never feel pain again.

Then I put the necklace inside my tunic, next to my skin, and the stones were still warm.

30

Immediately outside the bathhouse door, taking up the whole width of the corridor, lay Agamemnon, netted like a monstrous fish. No sign of Clytemnestra, and somebody must have taken Electra away, or else she'd bolted. I knew I was going to have to move, and move fast. Even in the short time I'd been standing by Agamemnon's body, my sandals had stuck to the bloodstained floor and every step I took after that produced an audible squeak. As I crept past the dead king, the lamplight fell on his staring eyes, but he didn't blink or turn his head away. How quickly, how easily, a man becomes a thing.

Clytemnestra was in the atrium, talking to Aegisthus, and seeing the two of them together like that, I thought it made sense: this wary alliance of two people intent solely on revenge. People were beating their fists against the barred door, but feebly, making no more impression than hens in a henhouse. I hung back and waited to see what would happen next. At last, Aegisthus nodded to his men, who immediately formed two lines leading up to the hall. Departing guests would be forced to walk between those two lines of heavily armed men and, presumably, be asked to swear allegiance to the queen—accept whatever cock-and-bull story she and Aegisthus might concoct between them. I felt sure her instinct would be to shout what she'd done from the palace roof, but she had her son,

Orestes, to consider—and he was still, as far as anybody knew, on his way home. None of the people in the hall had witnessed anything. The vast majority were elderly men who'd been too old to fight ten years ago when Agamemnon left for Troy. Now, they were confused, unarmed, disorientated, leaderless and very, *very* drunk. Probably most would swear allegiance to the queen and her son, the legitimate heir.

Once the doors were open and the rather pathetic little procession of grey-haired, befuddled old men had started, I walked at a steady pace along the atrium, keeping close to the wall, then pounded up the stairs. Inside the room I'd shared with Cassandra, I stood with my back to the door, the sound of my gasping breaths feeding my fear. *Slow down, breathe . . .*

I had to find the jewellery case because I was going to have to bribe my way out of here. I knew I'd hidden it again when I came to fetch the necklace, but my mind was in such turmoil I couldn't think where. Under the bed, probably, that was the obvious place—obvious to every light-fingered little toerag in the palace, I should think. I lay down and scrabbled about in the dust, disturbing several large spiders, one of whom, a female full of eggs, ran across the back of my hand. At last, my fingers closed round the case. No time to check the contents now. I needed a change of clothes: my tunic was daubed with Cassandra's blood where I'd cradled her head in my arms. Emptying the bag onto the bed, I selected a nondescript garment made of good-quality cloth, the sort of thing the wife of a prosperous merchant might wear. Stripping off, I pulled it over my head. My hair was spiky with blood, but there was nothing I could do about that. I found a veil and pinned it into place, my hands shaking so badly I stabbed myself several times before I got it fixed. There. Quickly, I put my hand inside the jewellery case, selected a plain gold ring that I slipped on my finger, then stowed the case away inside my tunic. I was ready, or as ready as I was ever going to be. *Cassandra*, I kept thinking, continuing the conversation we'd started in the bathhouse, the one that had been terminated by her death.

Once dressed, I looked out of the window. The palace was so vast, and the lives of slaves so separate from those of their masters, that it was possible news of Agamemnon's death might not yet have reached the kitchen yard. Patches of dried blood from the morning's slaughter buzzed under a bristling pelt of flies. No carts came in while I watched; the movement, now, was away from the kitchen door towards the gate. There was one driver obviously getting ready to leave and, knowing I had to seize the first opportunity, I ran down the back stairs so fast I tripped several times, each time burning my hands as I hung on to the rope banister. Somehow, I reached the ground floor intact, and forced myself to walk—again, very slowly—across the atrium and out into the yard.

Pulling my veil across my face, I strode confidently towards the cart. I was aiming to appear respectable, moderately well off but not rich, and I had no difficulty doing that—after all, I was merely impersonating the woman I'd once been, for most of my adult life. Only, that night, the circumstances were against me. Prosperous, respectable women don't hang around kitchen yards after dark, unattended by their maids and begging for a lift. I was on shaky ground and I knew it.

The driver turned when he heard my footsteps. He was a middle-aged, rather cynical-looking man, probably not averse to earning a bit on the side—probably not too particular about how he did it either. Ideal, for my purposes, but he wouldn't be easily fooled. I needed to get to the harbour, I said, and unfortunately, I needed to leave straight away, so would he mind giving me a lift? He looked doubtful—I'm sure he could detect the note of desperation in my voice, though I did my best to hide it—but his eyes lit up when I offered him the ring, nothing special about it, but still worth more than he could easily earn in a year.

Grinning broadly, he got down from the driver's seat and helped me up into the cart. Hessian sacks, giving off a powerful smell of root vegetables and soil, were stacked up by the bench seat. Even in the grip of my immediate fears, that smell took me back to the storage room at the hospital, to a semicircle of candles arranged around a sacking bed. He climbed onto the driver's bench, slapped the reins and we lurched forward. Putting both hands behind me, I braced myself against the jolting of the cart, while my mind flooded like a rockpool at high tide: an old man's mottled hand tapping out the rhythm of a song, green boughs being carried across the atrium into the hall, and the bard's voice, androgynous and somehow heart-breaking, soaring above it all.

Hauling myself back to the present, I stared at the carter's back. He had massive shoulders, the cloth of his jerkin strained tight across them. He'd only seen the gold ring, but he was sharp enough to guess I'd be carrying other things of value. Once we were through the gate and onto the narrow road leading to the harbour, it would be a simple matter for him to grab the case, cut my throat or just throttle me and throw me in a ditch. Nobody would notice I was missing, or care if they did. So, I began to chatter about Andreas and the *Medusa*. Was she still in the harbour? I asked.

No answer. He was looking towards the gate, where a group of fighters—Aegisthus's men, not palace guards—were checking the carts ahead of us. Every time a cart was cleared, we rumbled forward another few feet. The fighters were walking up and down the line, sticking their spears into any sack not obviously empty, no doubt hoping for screams of pain, though so far all they had to show for their efforts were a couple of dead hens, which they promptly confiscated. When one of them looked directly at me, I forced a smile, though god knows what ghastly rictus I produced.

Another cart waved through. Out of the corner of my eye, I caught a movement at the top of the palace steps: Aegisthus, dwarfed, as everybody was, by the immense white façade, was running down them. Meanwhile, the driver in front of us had been ordered to empty his boxes. "What, all of them?" "Yes, all of them!" The guards gave him no help, just placidly watched him struggle. By this time, Aegisthus was halfway across the court. The last of his boxes inspected and cleared, the carter climbed back into his seat and gathered up the reins—and, at that exact moment, Aegisthus shouted: "Close the gates! Nobody out, nobody in."

"Fuck," my driver said.

Fuck, I echoed, silently.

Slowly, the huge gates began to close, moonlit fields and winding road shrinking till only a sliver of the outside world remained. Then that, too, vanished.

"That's it, I'm afraid," my driver said. "Nothing I can do about it, not tonight anyroad. See if they open up tomorrow. I'll keep an eye out for you." He was looking worried. "I wonder what's going on."

He glanced up at the palace, and then at me, as if he thought I might know something. I just shook my head. Clambering off the back of the cart, I strolled away, longing to break into a run but forcing myself to amble along as if I hadn't a care in the world. I'd taken two sacks from the cart and, checking to see the carter wasn't watching, wrapped one around my shoulders and the other, apron-like, around my waist, transforming myself into a kitchen slave, a pan-scraper, floor-scrubber, brusher-up of maggoty messes in the yard. I had no idea where I was going, but there were shouts from inside the palace, followed by the sound of splintering wood, so I certainly wasn't going in there. When I drew level with the door of the herb garden, I opened it and slipped inside.

Shutting it behind me, I turned and stared into the deeper darkness underneath the trees until the shadow-shapes began to shift and come to life, as they always do if you stare long enough. I blinked several times, and when I looked again, I saw the garden as it really was: not the snakepit of my imagining, but a place of narrow gravel paths and flowering beds. My hem swished against the plants as I walked, releasing a snowstorm of small, pale moths. Passing the bench where Machaon and I had sat only hours earlier, I wondered what had become of him. If there was any attempt at resistance, he'd be in the thick of it. Armed or not, Machaon would fight.

The night-time scents of the garden brought with them the comfort of long familiarity, but the moment I opened the shed door a raw smell of mouldy roots grabbed me. I stood on the threshold and looked around. Nothing was exactly where it had been before, and at first this was disorientating, even slightly eerie, but then I remembered Machaon saying he'd spent the entire afternoon cleaning the dust (and, presumably, the handprints) off his workbench, and generally sorting things out.

There was a sacking curtain at the window, so I reached out and pulled that back. Now, with the light of the full moon streaming in, I felt confident enough to walk across to his bench. There were traces of the work he'd been doing that afternoon: a pungent smell of freshly chopped thyme, a jug of wine, and beside that a pot of what looked like skin salve. I picked up the pestle. Normally marble feels cool even on the hottest day, but this didn't. He'd been gone for hours and yet the pestle felt as warm as if he'd only just put it down.

Cassandra, dead; Machaon, quite possibly dead—so where did

that leave me? Shaken to the roots of my being—but free. With those two gone, nobody owned me. *I* owned me now. Suddenly, the space around me felt too big, the garden and the moonlit kitchen yard, empty and threatening. The storeroom, I decided. A small, safe place with sacks of vegetables I could pile up against the door. I'd be able to sleep there. Nonsense, of course, I wouldn't be any safer in there than I was out here, but I thought I might *feel* safer: there's a lot to be said for curling up in a small, womb-like space. Empty sacks for a bed—I'd noticed them earlier—though no circle of comforting candles to guard it. There were candles on the workbench, but I had no way of lighting them. First, I raised the jug to my mouth and drank a little of the wine, enough to send a surge of spurious courage coursing through my veins. And then, yawning, as much from tension as tiredness, I groped my way to the storeroom and opened the door.

Immediately, under the raw smell of earth, I detected a complex, familiar smell—strong enough to make me hesitate, but then I told myself not to be so stupid. As I stepped into the room, a hand shot out from behind the door and seized my throat. I was pulled sharply back while his other hand clawed my hips and chest, searching for weapons. I jerked my elbow back and heard a grunt as it connected with his ribs. Twisting free, I ran into the other room, across to the window, hands wet, fingers black in the moonlight. Looking down, I started scrabbling frantically at my tunic but couldn't see where the blood was coming from.

"Not you, you idiot. *Me.*" Machaon, of course. "I'm sorry," he went on, "I thought you were one of his men. All I could hear was you blundering about."

He was breathing heavily, and obviously in great pain. Pulling him closer to the window, I saw a tear in his tunic with a red stain sticking the edges to his side.

"How bad is it?" I asked.

"Bad."

He'd know. Carefully, I eased the cloth away from his skin. The wound was six or seven inches long, I couldn't tell how deep. "That could do with a few stitches." No gut, no needle, no nothing. "Do you want me to have a go at cleaning it?" Even that could be argued both ways. I was thinking that if I disturbed the early stages of clotting, I might be doing more harm than good. "I need to see what I'm doing. I suppose I could light a few candles from a torch in the kitchen yard . . ."

"Too risky, and there's no time. You'll just have to do the best you can with what we've got."

I fetched water, clean cloths—and, searching the storeroom, located a bag of salt. I found myself staring at the hessian sacks piled high against the wall, my memory supplying a circle of lighted candles. Dipping my hand into the jar, I scooped out the largest handful I could manage and added it to the water. Going back to him, I pressed a clean cloth hard on to the wound. We were standing close to each other, touching, though we didn't meet each other's eyes. I was thinking he hadn't done anything he didn't have a perfect right to do. I was his slave; he owned me body and soul. I didn't make the rules, but then neither did he. If there was anything unusual in his behaviour, it was the extent of the kindness he had shown in the run-up to that night.

Raising the cloth pad, I waited for fresh blood to appear. Was it slower than before?

Cleaning the wound was excruciating, and took a long time. He grunted once or twice but otherwise stared into space.

When I finished, he said, "Look, just bind it up. I've got to get out of here."

Another search, this time for bandages and scissors. He could probably have pointed me straight towards them, but he was sitting with his head bent, wrestling with the pain. Brave man, I thought, but then I'd never doubted his courage. I couldn't find any scissors, so had to settle for a knife. Suddenly, I saw Agamemnon's wound in front of me, red-mouthed and gaping. Who could blame the queen for doing what she did? Not me—I know what it is to lose a child. And who would blame me if I killed Machaon? What he'd done to me in that storeroom—even though he'd had a perfect right to do it—stripped me of dignity and hope. I'd get away with it, I knew that. I wasn't afraid of being found out. If I stabbed him through his wound, there'd be no way of telling how he died—and with everybody reeling over Agamemnon's death, nobody would be trying to find out. The question was: did I hate him? Did I hate *enough*? And the answer was *yes*. Oh, I admired him: the relentless hard work, the care for his patients, the compassion—and he had been kind to me, very kind, ninety per cent of the time. He'd protected me, from everybody except himself. I picked up the knife and went back to him; I was thinking: *Why not?* One stab—that's all it would take. I looked down at him, sitting hunched over in his chair, and noticed a bald patch on the crown of his head. He was so tall I'd never seen it before.

A sudden flashback to the hospital: Machaon striding up and down, smashing his clenched fist against the palm of the other hand, incandescent because a boy who'd been wounded in the final assault on Troy had died of his wounds five days after the city fell. "What's the bloody point?" he'd said, turning to me as if he thought I might have the answer. Now, looking down at his bowed head, I said, "Do you think you could lean forward a little?"

Part of me wants to say I couldn't do it, but that's not true. I could have done it. Very, *very* easily, I could have done it. I *chose* not to.

What followed was an awkward business, me struggling to wrap the bandages around him, him doing his best to help but stiffening up all the time. He was a big man; at one point I got a mouthful of chest hair and spat it out. He was resting his hands on my hips, just to steady himself, nothing else, but I felt an irrational spurt of anger remembering how he'd gripped my hips that night. It was a relief, to both of us probably, when the final knot was tied.

"I expect you know more than I do," he said, easing his shoulder on the injured side. "*Is* he dead?"

"He's dead."

"Did Aegisthus kill him?"

"I don't know. I only saw the body."

He looked stricken. Of course, he'd lost a close friend, a comrade-in-arms—his king. Looking up at me, he said, "I don't suppose I could have a cup of wine, could I?"

"Better not."

He had the wiped-out look of somebody who's seen his entire world collapse. Well, I was very familiar with that feeling. I examined the bandages for sign of fresh bleeding, but I couldn't see any. No point asking him for his opinion: he was stiffening up so badly that, even with his arm raised, he couldn't twist round far enough to see his side. I was trying to think what else I could do to improve his chances. Perhaps the bandages could be more securely tied? I cut into the hem of his tunic, tore off a long, circular strip and used it to strap his chest. There's something exhilarating about the sound of ripping cloth, slightly shameful too—or at least at that moment I felt there was.

"What will you do?" I asked.

"Now, you mean? Get out!"

"The gates are closed."

"I'll go over the wall at the back. I know the ground, I grew up here, I can find my way in the dark. I won't go anywhere near the roads."

For one insane moment, I thought I could do that, but a woman, travelling alone in a strange country, at night, with a Trojan accent? I'd have "escaped slave" written all over me, and anybody can do what they like to a runaway slave.

"I'll go to my father's—*if* it's safe, obviously. I won't risk leading them to him. And after that, I don't know. Find the resistance, I suppose. There will be one. He's not going to get away with it, there'll be masses of people ready to fight—"

"And they'll need a healer."

He laughed, only to wince and clutch his side. "Yes—back to the grindstone, I'm afraid."

A trickle of blood had started now. Pushing him back hard into the chair, I leaned my full body weight on the wound. When I stepped back, the bleeding seemed to have stopped again. I considered him. "You can't go looking like that." His robe was torn and bloody, in itself a reason for suspicion if he was caught before he reached his father's house. I fetched a sack from the storeroom, cut head- and armholes into it and helped him put it on. "There," I said. "You could pass for a farm labourer, just about, long as you keep your mouth shut." I wetted a cloth and wiped the blood off his face. "You'll need a knife."

"I've got my sword."

"You can't eat with that. Here, have this." I handed him the knife. "There's plenty more."

At the door, he said, "Take the salve to Electra. If you can do anything to help her, you'll be safe. You know, if you're clever, if you play it right, there's a niche for you here."

The pain he was in, it said something that he thought about my safety. I watched him limp away, his shadow briefly long and black across the moonlit path. Suddenly, I couldn't bear to part from him, and ran after him.

He turned to face me. "Is Cassandra dead too?"

"Yes."

"Why would he kill her?"

We walked together to the gate. He opened it, slipped through and, in the blink of an eye, was gone.

————————

Returning to the storeroom, I curled up on the sacks and tried not to mind when invisible insects ran across my bare legs. Spiders, probably—or woodlice brought in with the soil that would be clinging to roots and tubers. Chuggy-pigs, we used to call them, when I was a little girl. Drifting off to sleep, I was startled by a loud bang, very close, only a few feet away from my makeshift bed. I struggled to sit up, but there was nothing there to account for it. The noise was in my head. Fearfully, I waited for a repetition, but it never came and gradually I settled down again. I was longing for sleep, but was terribly, terminally awake. I thought about Machaon's wound and wondered what the chances were of him getting to his father's farm. Fifty–fifty? I couldn't put it any higher than that. I remembered the wound in Cassandra's belly, so clearly aimed at her unborn child. It was bizarre, that wound, that the queen had taken the time to do it—and let Agamemnon escape from the bathhouse, rather than finishing him off while she had the chance. Everything suggested a woman flailing about, out of control—and that frightened me.

And then, in the darkness, I felt Cassandra by my side.

"It's all right," she said.

"All right for *you*. You got what you wanted."

"Yes, I did, didn't I?" A hint of laughter. She laid one slim, cool hand on the side of my face. "Sleep now."

31

Lying in bed, sunlight filtering through the blinds, she thinks: *Nothing's changed. Nothing has changed. Except that now he's—*

The next word escapes her. She knows perfectly well what it is, but can't say it or even think it. Which is a pity, because it *is* a fact, and facts are all she has. The fact is, Agamemnon's lying in a small courtyard adjacent to the dining hall, stark naked and staring straight into the sun. Naked, because she won't let anybody cover him up; staring, because she won't let anybody close his eyes. The fishing net's gone, the linen shift's gone, because, as Aegisthus says, how the bloody hell are you going to explain those sleeves? But so far, she's refusing to let his body be moved—or Cassandra's, who lies beside him, also naked, staring vacantly into space. She doesn't care about the girl—they can move her any time—but she wants Agamemnon just as he is, with that sugary, rancid smell coming off his bloated skin.

Vengeance should end with death, or so people say. But why should it, when grief doesn't end with death? Years ago, kneeling beside her daughter, she'd brushed the coils of dark hair out of her eyes and the movement disturbed the flies, which rose in a black, angry, buzzing cloud. Cradling Iphigenia's lolling head on her arm, she tried to bat them away, but she couldn't; they just got angrier, even more persistent, their tiny, emerald heads glittering in the sun. "We've got to cover her up," one of the maids said, and Clytemnestra took off her tunic and wrapped it around Iphigenia. It didn't matter that she was naked, because there were no men left on the beach except a priest, and he turned his head away. Together, she and her women tucked in folds of cloth around Iphigenia's head and feet, so the flies couldn't get at her.

Clytemnestra said, to nobody in particular, "He didn't even stop to bury her."

"He couldn't," the priest said. "The minute the wind changed, the men stampeded for the ships. He couldn't stay here. He's got to be at the head of the fleet."

Downstairs, in the courtyard, she stops to look at what's left of her husband. *Of course you had to be at the head of the fleet,* she thinks, or says. She doesn't always know when she's speaking her thoughts aloud. *You couldn't let anybody else be first, could you?* Her eyes range down his body from the top of his head to his feet. Hairs like ivy clinging to his thighs. A forest in his groin. She could chop his dick off if she wanted to. There's nobody to stop her. Stuff it in his mouth. Apparently, that was quite a common battlefield mutilation at Troy—no doubt with Agamemnon's encouragement, or tacit approval, at least. No point telling *him* vengeance should end with death, not when there's such a delightfully easy way to make your enemy look ridiculous—and very, *very* dead.

A shadow appears beside hers on the white stone and Aegisthus's voice breaks in on her thoughts. "You can't leave him here like this."

"Who's to stop me?"

"For god's sake, woman, your son's coming home. What's he supposed to make of this?"

"He won't come now."

"Why won't he? His father's been murdered—yes, it's a tragedy, it's a disaster, but we've caught the killers, they've been executed, everything's back under control. What's to stop him coming home?"

"Do you honestly think anybody believes that?"

"Nobody saw you kill him—except her." He jerked his head at Cassandra's body. "And she's dead."

It's not true. That woman, Ritsa, the one who used to work with Machaon, she saw her. But does it really matter? She's a slave: even if she talks, nobody's going to listen to her, nobody of any importance, anyway. Cassandra, yes, that might have been a problem—though Cassandra wouldn't have betrayed her. She wanted him dead. And Ritsa? Well, she's a Trojan—probably she wanted him dead too. If she tells Aegisthus that Ritsa saw her deliver the final blow, he'll have her killed. Wouldn't hesitate, not for a second. But it's not necessary—and, more importantly, it's not his place to take decisions. Electra's more worrying, though she didn't see him die, thank god. She came on the scene a few minutes too late for that. Nobody else could have seen anything, that was the beauty of that corridor—you could walk past the end, and unless you happened to glance in that direction, you'd see nothing. And it was dark.

"And the girl?"

Aegisthus, crashing into her thoughts. "Cassandra? What about her?"

"Only that she needs burying! They're not going to last long—"

"—in this heat."

She's on the beach at Aulis, where words no longer make sense.

"You've got to bury her."

"No, I'm taking her home."

She hears herself say it, notices, in a calm, detached way, that her voice sounds different. It seems to have developed its own built-in echo, the words bouncing off the inside of her skull. A numbness is beginning to creep over the surface of her skin, but bringing with it a startling mental clarity. Everything she sees is clearer, brighter, more distinct than it's ever been before. Behind Iphigenia's head, there's a ladybird on a leaf and she knows—not believes, knows—that that ladybird will be with her for ever. The sun will always shine on its red shards and they'll never part to reveal the black wings underneath. It'll never move from that leaf, never fly away home, no matter how many times you tell it that its house is on fire and its children are gone.

"We'll need a cart," she says, amazed at the practicality in her voice. "And something thicker to wrap her in." She pats the tunic. "This won't keep them out."

Nothing kept them out.

———

Aegisthus's hand, gripping her arm. "You can't just let things slide like this. Either you start giving orders, or I do."

She looks down at his fingers and slowly detaches her arm. He steps back at once, but she can see him watching her. He hates her, because she killed Agamemnon, when that death rightfully belonged to him. No doubt he feels emasculated or something equally ridiculous—and perhaps she should be worried about that, or afraid, though fear seems to be one of the emotions she's mislaid. He *is* dangerous. And his desire for revenge won't stop with Agamemnon's death, particularly since he's been denied the satisfaction of killing him. Though what would satisfy him? Nothing. The hunger for retribution can't be satiated; one episode of bloodletting merely supplies the justification for the next. And the next.

Kill Orestes, marry Electra, seize the throne: would even that be enough . . . ?

"Leave me," she says, and sees on his face that he's tempted to disobey, but then, abruptly, he turns on his heel and walks away.

He's right about one thing, though: she's going to have to move the bodies, give them some sort of burial—obviously nothing formal, nothing public. She'll tell people the king was buried at night in the family mausoleum, with all due reverence and ceremony but, given the ongoing crisis, quickly and quietly. Probably people will accept that—and really, is anybody going to go down there into the vaults with a crowbar to investigate?

One last look before she lets them go. Cassandra first, because she's bewildered by that death, and hurt by it. She never intended her to die. Didn't want her hanging around the palace either, mind, but that needn't have been a problem: she could've been sent off to a temple at the back of beyond where nobody need ever have heard of her again. But looking down at that slim, white body, only the truth will do. I hated her, in the end. Standing by the side of the pool, watching that stinking old goat grunt and sweat his way to a climax, she'd felt the pain of being discarded. Even though the thought of him inside her made her sick, it still angered her to be so contemptuously set aside. And that anger, that jealousy, corrupted everything. Killing Agamemnon was always about justice for Iphigenia: not even revenge—justice. And right at the end, to have that purity of intention contaminated by their filth . . . Because there they were, the two of them, Cassandra's mouth open to show all her little pointed teeth, not even trying to pull away, as he pawed at her groin.

No, she can't bear to look at Cassandra, who injured her in ways she can't begin to explain.

Agamemnon, then. Look at him. The density of him, the thickness, the breadth, the heft . . . None of the words is precisely the one she wants. Opacity? That's the one that keeps recurring, though it makes no sense; it's not as if he was translucent in life. Out of the corner of her eye, she sees Aegisthus, hovering, waiting for her to take the decision, to give the order. Deliberately, she turns her back on him. As the sun rises higher, the buzzing grows louder. Flies, hundreds of them, drunkenly zigzagging from place to place. One lands on Agamemnon's face, starts to explore the dark caverns of his nostrils—a favourite place for egg-laying, as she remembers only too well. Another fly crawls into his open eye. She waits for him to blink or turn his head away, but he doesn't, of course he doesn't, he can't, because he's—

And suddenly, the word she's been struggling to use all morning is hers again. Dead. Because he's dead.

"All right," she says, turning to Aegisthus. "You can take them away now."

32

It wasn't hunger that drove me out of Machaon's workshop the following evening so much as my need to know where Cassandra had been buried—*if* she'd been buried. It was just as likely she'd been put out with the rubbish.

I waited all day in an agony of indecision, unable even to answer the simple question of how frightened I needed to be. My mind was a whirlpool of uncertainty, of fear and more than fear. At times, it was closer to panic. But this had started, not with the deaths of Agamemnon and Cassandra, but before that, when I opened a door on the top corridor and came face to face with the children. With their hatred, their failure to make any distinction between male and female, Trojan or Greek, because they blamed the entire adult world for betraying them. Everything that had happened to me since then had simply been added to the horror of that encounter. So when I tried to grapple with the reality of my situation, I found it very hard to know which impressions I could trust.

Obviously, I kept returning to that moment in the corridor when I'd seen Clytemnestra angle the sword to deliver the killing blow. We'd been alone; nobody else could have seen what had happened. Electra had arrived minutes later and I suppose it was just possible she might have seen something. Nobody else. So that left the queen. I didn't think she'd fear me; nobody really cares what a slave sees—the system would be unworkable if they did. Would she mention me to Aegisthus? If she did, he might well play safe and decide to have me removed, and he'd do it, with no more compunction than a man stamping on a cockroach. But would she tell him? I had no idea.

But my need to know what had happened to Cassandra remained. So, just as the shadows started to lengthen, I filled a jug with rainwater from the butt and set off for the palace. I was feeling braver than I had earlier because I'd managed to have a nap and eat something, if only a couple of overripe pears.

From behind one of the pillars, I peered into the atrium. Quiet, amazingly quiet. Holding the jug in front of me—it's surprising how few people question your presence if you're carrying something—I went into the dining hall. Slaves had been set to work to clean up the mess, though the job was far from complete. There were still red puddles on the floor—blood, or wine? So many blobs of sodden, pink bread were islanded in the spillage that I was inclined to think wine. Closer to the high table, at the far end of the hall, where smashed furniture had been used to build a barricade, I was less sure. Some of the fighters, young men back from Troy, had made a stand here. Aegisthus certainly hadn't had a bloodless victory.

On the table next to me, a loaf of bread had mysteriously survived the ruckus, so I grabbed that, together with a half-full jug of wine. Several other jugs had some wine left in them so I added that and then, abandoning the jug of water I'd brought with me, looked around for anything else I could take. Propped against one of the benches was a walking stick whose owner had abandoned it, no doubt shedding decades in his desperation to escape. I took the stick too, though I'd no idea why, and then a few places further on I found a platter with slices of meat! A bit leathery round the edges, but perfectly edible—and certainly better than brown pears. I stuffed the food inside my tunic and ventured further into the hall. I walked across to where the bard had stood with his back against a pillar, and saw a solitary lyre abandoned on a chair.

Still clutching the jug, I left the hall and walked up the stairs to the main corridor where a dozen slaves were engaged in what looked like routine cleaning. None of them so much as glanced at me. Everybody was hard at work—*busy, busy, busy*—and it took me a full minute to notice how peculiar it all was. A maid repeatedly flicked a duster at cobwebs festooning a corner of the ceiling; it didn't seem to bother her in the least that the duster never got anywhere near the webs. Another woman, on her knees, was rubbing a damp cloth over the muddy floor. A lot of men's feet must have marched along here recently, you could see their footprints, and the tiles certainly needed a good clean, but she had only the dirty cloth—no bucket of water to rinse it in—and so she was merely spreading dirt from one side of the corridor to the other. My strongest impression—and my abiding memory from that evening—was of an elaborate pretence of normality that convinced nobody. Scratch an inch beneath the surface, and nothing made sense. It wouldn't have surprised me if the staircase leading from this corridor had ended in mid-air.

A *stomp-stomp* of marching feet and there, coming towards us, was a squad of Aegisthus's men. *They* weren't pretending to be busy; they had a proper job: instilling fear in everybody who crossed their path. The cleaning woman scrabbled out of their way. I flattened myself against the wall, getting a whiff of sweat and the warm leather of their jerkins as they tramped past. In a minute, they were gone, leaving us frozen in their wake, as motionless as people painted on a frieze.

Somebody touched my arm. Turning, I saw a woman I'd known in Lyrnessus, Charis—was that her name?—she'd been in the bread queue that morning when we heard the news of Iphigenia's death. The morning the fear started. At first, though she held on to me, she didn't speak, just stood there, working her tongue around the inside of her bottom lip as if trying to locate a mouth ulcer. "Well," she said, at last. "Been a long time coming, this. Perhaps it'll quieten down a bit now."

I realized she meant the palace, though it didn't feel quiet to me. Stunned, yes—but not quiet.

"You know she's buried him?"

"The king?"

"Bet you can't guess where? That scrubby little bit of waste ground just outside the wall. Opposite the steps, you know, where you go down?"

That was unnecessarily detailed, almost as if she were giving me directions. "Do you know if Cassandra's buried there too?"

"Yeah, same grave—if you can call it a grave. Same hole in the ground, more like. Priam's daughter—and not a prayer said over her. Might as well have chucked her on the rubbish dump."

I knew then what I had to do. Even if the gate was opened tonight, I still wouldn't be able to leave.

Back at the shed, I rested for a moment, bracing myself for the risks I was about to take, then gathered bread, wine and herbs together—oh, and the walking stick, to beat off Aegisthus's men. Yes, I know, I *know*—but it did make me feel slightly better. I waited for darkness, which descended swiftly, the smouldering sun abruptly extinguished like somebody pouring water on a fire. I even imagined I could smell the sour, cindery smell that this leaves behind. A few wisps of sunset-cloud lingered, but not enough to obscure the moon, which rose high and magnificent above the tallest trees. I listened. Every herb garden I've ever known has been frequented at night by people pursuing illicit desires behind the screen of darkness. The herb garden at Troy was notorious. But I thought that with any luck continued uncertainty and fear would keep people in their own beds tonight, and so it proved. I waited in silence, but nothing moved except for the rustling of small creatures in the grass.

When I judged it was late enough for the kitchen yard to have cleared, I took the bread and wine, pulled my veil well forward and left the safety of the garden. There was always the possibility that guards had been stationed at the grave to arrest anyone reckless enough to pay their respects to Agamemnon. Because by now the whereabouts of his grave would be known. If Charis knew, then all the slaves knew—and their masters too. You can't keep secrets in a palace.

Reaching the top of the steps, I peered into the shadows underneath. Carefully, because the steps were treacherous with damp moss, I edged my way down, reached the bottom safely and pressed myself flat against the wall. On my right were two long, low mounds, possibly a mass grave for plague victims. Most towns in Greece have them from the tragedy of twenty years ago. Straight ahead of me, at the top of the hill, was a circle of white ash where the watchfire must have been. A stream, fringed with tall ferns, rushed down the hill, chuckling and gurgling over its stony bed before spreading out to create an area of boggy ground.

Directly opposite, just as Charis had said, was a heap of upturned earth: raw, red clay, no attempt made to create a smooth surface, clods just piled up and scattered everywhere. A botched job, done in haste. Had they even dug deep enough? It would have been hard work digging in this water-logged soil; they mightn't have bothered to give the dead a more than barely adequate covering. Feeling uncomfortably exposed, I walked forward, knelt on the muddy ground and began saying the prayers for the dead. Like every other woman my age, I knew them off by heart, so I was able to gabble through them, paying minimal attention to the words. A small part of me wanted to laugh. *Eternal rest?* No chance. *Peace?* Not in my lifetime. *Light perpetual?* Too much bloody light already—I was praying for the moon to go in.

So, I got through the service, though I can't claim to have felt any emotion more devout than fear. I'm not sure I even felt grief, not really, not then. Perfect love casts out fear. Hmm. Perfect fear's quite powerful too. My thoughts, my mood, changed from minute to minute. Most of the time, I just felt angry. With the gods, yes, obviously, but mainly with Cassandra, who I still thought could've lived if she'd wanted to. Perhaps that wasn't true; perhaps she was doomed from the moment Agamemnon said he wanted her to share his bath. But no, she'd wanted to die; she'd chosen death and she'd got what she wanted.

The cold was striking up through my knees; my hips were starting to ache. I thought I'd better stand up while I still could. I was nearly, though precariously, upright when I heard footsteps and turned to see a figure, draped in black, coming down the steps. The back of my neck prickled, but then something about the set of the shoulders said, *Electra.* She came towards me, pushing back her veil. For the first time I saw her as she really was—not the fake child I'd seen pinching the loose skin on her nurse's arms, but a girl on the cusp of womanhood. Looking down, I saw she was carrying a silver tray with jugs of oil and wine.

"Will you show me what to do?"

No way could I refuse such a request, so, together, we mixed the libation and then she knelt and poured it onto her father's burial mound. I wondered who had told her where to find her father's grave and how many people knew he was here, because really it was madness, giving him this dishonourable burial. Vengeance pursuing him into the grave. I said the libation prayers again, though with even less conviction than before, because I'd noticed a movement on top of the hill. Somebody had emerged from the shadows and was standing inside the circle of white ash. When I looked again only seconds later, he was gone. Meanwhile, Electra, still kneeling at the foot of the grave, was racked with sobbing. I remembered Clytemnestra saying: *She could walk past her father in the street, she wouldn't recognize him.* I must say, at that moment I shared something of her mother's irritation, but whoever Electra was grieving for—and it may well have been herself—her grief was undeniably real.

Another movement on the hill. Cautiously, so as not to attract Electra's attention, I looked more closely. He was a smudge of shadow against the white ash, though there was light enough to see he was broad-shouldered, thin-hipped, moved quickly—everything about his body suggested a young, vigorous man. Electra hadn't seen him—her head was bowed in prayer—but then she looked up the hill, and I realized she knew he was there, she'd known all along.

Her brother? Or somebody else she knew and trusted? It was much more likely one of Aegisthus's men, in which case we were in serious trouble.

"Come on," I said, seizing her arm. "We've got to go."

I could hear his cloak swishing through the ferns as he ran down the hill. Minutes later, there he was, up to his ankles in the marshy ground, ignoring me, staring at her. She got to her feet and for a time they simply looked at each other, not even taking a step forward. As I gazed from one face to the other, I could see they were brother and sister. Something about the eyes, the eyebrows even . . . This should have been a touching moment, two children of the same father, united in grief. He held out his arms; she ran into them and raised her mouth to his. Nothing could have prepared me for the naked sexuality of that kiss. It was shocking—and not merely because of its unrestrained passion, but because there was something predatory about it. The way he folded his arms around her and fastened his lips on hers reminded me of a hawk mantling its prey.

After a while, he raised his head and they began whispering together, Electra still fast in the circle of his arms. At last, he let her go and knelt in front of the grave, where she immediately joined him. There was no talk of peace now, no prayers for eternal rest: they prayed for war, for vengeance on their father's murderers, urging Agamemnon to rise from his grave and join them in their holy quest.

When they'd finished, Orestes stood up and seized Electra by her thin arms. "She's got to die—you know that, don't you?"

"Yes."

To consent, so readily, so easily, to your mother's death. I was looking at her face as she spoke, and I swear to god I saw the Furies' claw-marks on her skin. "Electra," I said, "you should go back to the palace now."

Orestes turned to look at me. Until that moment, he'd ignored me, assuming, I suppose, that I was merely one of his sister's maids.

"Who's this?"

"She's all right."

He seemed to accept that. "I've got to go anyway." Again, that predatory movement of his head as his mouth fastened onto hers. This time, I looked away.

She stood at the top of the steps and watched till he was out of sight, then, together, we walked round to the main entrance.

"Did Iras know where you were going?"

"I don't think so. I don't know."

I thought Iras probably knew a great deal more than it suited her to say. We found her waiting outside the door of Electra's room. "There's warm water," she said. "You can have a bath."

Electra smiled and nodded. Behind Iras' back she mouthed, *Thank you*, and closed the door, leaving Iras and me face to face.

"She's very close to her brother, isn't she?"

"Oh, yes, very close." She made it sound so cosy. "She was in a terrible state when he went away. I mean, she's always suffered with her skin but nothing like that. It was a real flare-up." She looked down the corridor. "When they were little, he used to sleep just along there, but you could never keep him in his own bed, he was always crawling across the roof and getting into bed with her."

I remembered the drop, imagined a small boy doing that perilous journey in the dark.

"I used to come and find them asleep in each other's arms." Perhaps she caught my expression. "Nowt wrong with that, they were only children."

Until they weren't.

There was nothing I could do to help anybody here. As I left, I touched Iras's arm because, after all, none of this was her fault. I walked quickly, head down, intent on getting back to my refuge in the herb garden. I needed time to think, but every time I told myself that, my thoughts immediately vanished, like fish when you throw a stone in a river. I suppose I was in shock, but everybody was, perhaps even the queen. Almost as if my thoughts had summoned her, I saw Clytemnestra coming towards me up the stairs. Flattening myself against the wall, I looked down at the floor as slaves are trained to do, hoping, expecting, that she'd ignore me, but instead she stopped. I could hear her breathing.

"You've been to see Electra?"

"Yes, I thought I'd just check in on her."

"And?"

"She seems calmer. Older."

A snort of almost laughter. "Oh, I think we all feel that."

We talked about Electra's skin, the various salves and herbal baths and other treatments we might try. Bullshit, basically, because we both knew what ailed Electra. Clytemnestra's eyes never left my face. I was braced for her to mention the last time we'd met, when I'd watched her kill the king, but she made no reference to it. Of course, she was astute enough to know she didn't have to. It was there, between us, as immovable as a boulder. She was going to have to say something, though.

At last, looking straight at me, she said, "I know you've lost your mistress and . . . and I'm sorry about that. But there's a place here for you, if you want it. My daughter needs a healer and I think even more than that she probably needs a friend. I need somebody to . . . to keep me informed. Iras is no use."

Her gaze had become, if possible, even more intense. She was making me feel uncomfortable, but I forced myself to look steadily back at her.

"I'm very loyal to the people who serve me. As long as they're loyal to me."

She was offering me a deal and not one that I could easily refuse. "It would be a privilege."

"Right, that's settled then." She nodded, pleasantly enough, and walked on. I continued downstairs, outwardly calm, inwardly squirming. Clytemnestra seemed to be in complete control of herself and of the situation, but in my mind a red mouth opened. I mean the wound at the pit of Cassandra's stomach. It wouldn't have killed her—it was hardly more than a slash. But still, there it was, and it spoke to me of a total loss of control. Oh, I'm sure Clytemnestra believed she just wanted justice for Iphigenia and how else could she get it when Agamemnon was judge and jury in his own cause? And yet at some point, the quest for justice had slipped into a morass of hatred and revenge. It was all there in the second wound.

She wasn't to be trusted. And no, I don't mean I couldn't trust her to deal fairly with me, I mean she couldn't be trusted to act predictably and rationally in her own best interests. Whoever decided to bury Agamemnon on that wasteland was mad. Had to be—and yes, it was probably Aegisthus, but she'd let him do it. Somebody would have seen them digging the grave and guessed who it was for, because palaces are like that. Whatever happens, somebody always sees.

It was a relief to be outside, to look at the moon, to try and detect in that perfect disc the first signs of waning—though the children would always be there, no matter what phase of its cycle the moon was in. Right from the beginning, this had been about children: the children Atreus fed to their father, the boys slaughtered at Troy, the baby in Cassandra's womb, and now, finally, perhaps—but nothing was final in this never-ending cycle—the children of Clytemnestra and Agamemnon, agreeing that their mother must die. The moon was high and full as I walked across the Lion Court, closing my ears and my mind to the shrill voices of children singing.

Lying on my sacks in the storeroom, I tried to sleep, but when I closed my eyes, I saw Orestes kneeling by his father's grave, dedicating himself to avenge his father's death. No choice, no hope, the Furies would plague him till he killed his mother, then drive him over the edge into insanity *because* he'd killed her. And so, from generation to generation, the wheel turns.

On the edge of sleep, I saw black birds, hundreds of them, wheeling and turning in a white sky before spiralling down to their roost. A soothing sight, but then, before I saw anything else, I heard the scrape of claws on tiles—and there they were, the Furies, landing on the palace roof. Helplessly, I watched as they linked talon to talon, hand to hand, moving their cracked, yellow feet in an endless, ancient dance. They had no eyes, or none that I could see, but then they don't need eyes—they can snuffle their way from one bloodletting to the next, never any shortage of victims, and every cause is just.

I felt Cassandra close beside me in the darkness.

No wonder they dance.

33

Next morning, I washed, dressed, tried in vain to tame my hair, and set off for the Lion Court. It was already crowded and, at first, I couldn't see why until I realized the guards were getting ready to open the gates. A tense moment: people stood around, alone or in small groups, not talking, not even looking at each other, until a guard on the wall shouted and waved his spear. Slowly, the great gates began to open and carts carrying fresh food began to come through.

I didn't expect the gates to be open for long. They'd do the bare minimum needed to replenish stocks and then the palace would be locked in again. Three carts were being driven through to the kitchen yard and I walked in that direction, rapidly, head down, hoping to persuade one of the drivers to give me a lift when he left. I'd just turned the corner when I heard a man's voice shout: "Hoy!" I went on walking—whoever he wanted, I knew it wouldn't be me. But then the shout came again and this time I looked round. I don't know what I was expecting, one of the guards, probably, coming to haul me off to prison—or worse. But no, it was my driver. I walked towards him, forcing myself to move slowly because too much haste might attract attention. I was still terrified, but without knowing what exactly I was frightened of, or how frightened I should be.

"Hello," I said, holding the side of the cart. "I didn't expect to see *you* again."

"Why not? Said I'd be back. They opened the gates for an hour yesterday. I looked around for you."

It must have been when I was at the grave.

"C'mon, hop in. I've just got to unload this stuff."

This stuff seemed to be mainly fish. "I've got to fetch something first."

"Go on then, but be quick."

I ran all the way back to the shed. By now, I was so used to the garden being deserted that it was a shock to see an old man sitting on the bench under the apple tree where I'd sat with Machaon.

"Just picking something up," I called, casually, as if he might be interested.

He didn't reply, just sat there placidly chewing mint leaves, probably more to cleanse his palate than anything else, because as I walked past, he spat out a green, well-masticated wad.

Inside the shed, I grabbed the bag from the storeroom, delved deep into a sack of withered onions to retrieve the jewellery case, and then—this was the last thing I did before leaving—snatched up a pestle and mortar from Machaon's workbench. Not as a memento—I was in no danger of forgetting what had happened here—more as a kind of pledge to myself for the future. The pestle nestling in the palm of my hand gave me instant, visceral pleasure: *If any man loves the tools of any trade, the gods have called him.* I reckon that goes for women as well.

Midday now, and the heat was searing, though with rumbles of thunder to warn that the weather was about to break. The approaching storm was visible in the virulent green of the leaves. The birds were busy too: short, urgent, noisy flights from tree to tree, getting stuff done before it became impossible to fly. I lugged the clothes bag to the kitchen yard, waited while the driver finished unloading the fish, then threw it into the well of the cart and climbed up after it. Sweat streamed down my sides, though that was probably nerves as much as heat.

I'd no sooner settled than the driver turned round. "Is it true?"

"The king? Yes."

"He's dead?"

I nodded.

"You know that for a fact, do you?"

"I saw his body."

He made a curious *phuph* sound, as if every bit of breath had been knocked out of him. "It's a moment, that is."

It was odd. When Agamemnon died, I'd been standing so close to him that I could smell that strange, intimate, not entirely pleasant smell you get in folds of hot, damp skin. Perhaps that's why his murder felt like a family tragedy: terrible, yes, for some of the people who knew him, but intrinsically small-scale, domestic, confined to a tight-knit group of people in a cramped space. Now, in that winded sound, I heard for the first time the shock waves that would spread throughout the Greek world and far beyond.

For a full minute after that, the driver stared into space, then he gathered up the reins and drove into the Lion Court, where we joined a short queue of carts waiting to leave.

My thoughts turned to what I'd do when I got to the town—*if* I got to the town. My only reference points were Andreas and the *Medusa*. "You can put me down by the harbour wall."

"I'll do no such thing, I'll get you on the ship. If Andreas found out I'd just dumped you, I'd never hear the last of it. Good bloke, but you don't want to cross him."

In the time it took him to tell me that, another cart had been cleared. I watched it trundle through the gate. At least, now, I was sure of a bed for the night—and yes, I did wonder briefly whether Andreas would be in it. The relief was short-lived; the closer we got to the gate, the less hopeful I felt until I was sitting there, dry-mouthed, knowing—not suspecting, mind you, *knowing*—that the same thing was about to happen. We'd get right to the head of the queue, and then the gates would close. The guard came towards us, stopped, said something over his shoulder to the other guards, came on again. Casting no more than a desultory glance over the empty sacks, he stepped back . . .

There was some kind of consultation going on between the guards. I looked towards the palace, expecting to see Aegisthus running down the steps, but there was no sign of him. I leaned forward, trying to make out what was happening in the shadows under the Lion Gate. Gradually, it became clear that we were being held back so that somebody of importance could enter. A slur and clatter of horses' hooves on stone, a glint of eye-white in the gloom and then a young man rode into view. I recognized him immediately, though yesterday evening by moonlight I'd had only an indistinct impression of his face. It was his body I remembered. Today, he looked, not less powerful, but certainly younger. A hint of adolescence still: a gawkiness he'd outgrow in a matter of months. If he lived.

Orestes.

The name passed from mouth to mouth as softly as a sigh. No cheers, no shouts of acclamation, nothing like his father's reception a few days before. The death of the king overshadowed everything, even the return of his son. At first, we all waited for the escort of armed guards to follow him through the gate, but there was only one young man who urged his horse into a trot until they were once more riding side by side. An equal, then: a friend, not a servant. But where were the guards? Both men were armed, but so is everybody who ventures on a long journey over lawless roads. For Orestes to ride into the Lion Court with only one companion was extraordinary. He seemed to be saying: *This is my home, this is the safest place in the world. Why would I need a guard?*

At the foot of the palace steps, they dismounted. Two guards came running to lead the horses away. At the last moment, before beginning his long climb up the steps, Orestes threw an arm across his friend's shoulders and pulled him close. Clytemnestra had come out from between the pillars and was standing waiting at the top of the steps. Every eye was on Orestes as he started to climb, steadily, never hurrying, never hesitating. I remembered how Agamemnon had stumbled because the red cloths stopped him from seeing where he was putting his feet.

It would have been natural for Clytemnestra to run down the steps to meet her son, or at the very least to wave and call his name; but she did neither, just waited for him to reach her. At the last second, before they embraced, his shadow fell across her face. We heard the murmur of their voices, though we were too far away to make out individual words. After a while, Clytemnestra turned to welcome the other young man, who'd been standing back at a tactful distance to give Orestes time with his mother, and then the three of them—four, if you include Aegisthus, who I thought I glimpsed waiting in the shadows—disappeared into the darkness of the palace.

Immediately, people came to life, smiling, talking, speculating. Another big moment—a good moment—the young king returning home. Something was flapping on the roof—birds, crows probably, carrion feeders attracted by the smell of blood from the kitchen yard. The cart jerked forward and I was so startled I nearly lost my balance and had to grab the rails. The shadow of the Lion Gate passed over us and we emerged into a day of racing clouds, gusts of rain-flecked wind that snatched the breath out of your mouth and, in the far distance, beyond Iphigenia's tomb, glimpses of the sea.

34

On our way back to the harbour town, the driver didn't seem inclined to talk and for that I was grateful. I knew I was going to have to construct a story to explain how I'd seen Agamemnon dead but without witnessing his murder. It didn't take me long to come up with a plausible version of events. After Agamemnon's death, slaves had been rounded up and made to march past his body, as a mark of loyalty and respect, before being strictly confined to their quarters. The story was simple, entirely credible—and I was only going to need it for the next few days. After that, everybody would know what had happened—or the official version of it, at least—so nobody would bother to question me. But, in the short term, *this* was the version of events I was going to have to give consistently to everybody who asked. Even Andreas.

By the time we reached the harbour, the tide was out so there was no decent veil of water to hide the *Medusa*'s warty sides. Close to, in the stormy yellow light, the hull was warped, dented and barnacle-encrusted, snot-green seaweed dangling from Medusa's face. Was she even seaworthy? She didn't look it. But she'd got us through one storm, and with any luck she'd get us through the next.

"Andreas?" the carter called.

A shadowy figure crossed the deck, and there he was, leaning over the side, red-haired, peppery, aggressive, difficult—somehow, unmistakably difficult even now, when he was grinning from ear to ear. "Come on up." He reached out as if to help me on board.

One thing I've learned over the years: you're always alone on a rope ladder. This one was wet, and slimy from long immersion in water. I gripped as hard as I could, but my fingers kept slipping. At the top, Andreas's calloused hands dragged me onto the deck. The carter followed; it was obvious from the way he greeted Andreas that they were old friends. I wondered how differently my story might have turned out if that hadn't been true.

In those first few minutes back on the *Medusa*, I felt numb. No joy, no relief, not even grief for the loss of Cassandra, though I was intensely aware that the last time I'd stood on this deck I'd had her by my side. But nothing dredges up memories like a familiar smell—and, as we went below, the smell in that passageway was like nothing else on earth. I remembered how, on that first night, Cassandra had put her hand over her mouth, and immediately I was fighting back tears. I tried not to let it show, but Andreas guessed I was struggling. He got me along the passage and into the dining room, where the table was already laid for a dinner, lamps and candles lit. He poured wine into the largest cup I'd ever seen, and sat beside me while I drank.

"Is she dead too?"

"Yes. Apparently, she was with the king when he died."

Apparently. I was so proud of myself for having the presence of mind to say that, and simultaneously ashamed for not telling him the truth. Andreas touched my shoulder—only to withdraw his hand immediately as if he feared it was too intimate a gesture. "She was a remarkable woman," he said.

And I felt he'd understood her, that in the evenings we'd spent together at this table he'd been more perceptive about her, perhaps more perceptive about my relationship with her, than I'd allowed myself to be.

"I loved her."

"Course you did."

So much of my relationship with her had been clouded by my resentment at being her slave. And her arrogance. I wasn't so immersed in love and grief that I was prepared to acquit her of all blame.

There were voices coming from the kitchen. "Have you still got crew on board?"

"No, that's me sister. She brought some food over."

A minute later, a small brown woman bustled into the room, wiping her hands on her apron before holding them out to me. "Kari," she said. "I don't suppose Andreas has told you who this is, has he?" She nodded to the carter, who grinned and squirmed. "That's Alcar, our sister's husband."

Naturally, I offered to help with the cooking, but she wasn't having any of that. "No, you sit yourself down. Must've been bloody awful up there."

Not long after, we were all sitting around the table. My lack of first-hand knowledge about who was responsible for the king's death frustrated them, but at least left them plenty of room to speculate, which they did. Aegisthus—that's what everybody thought. Neither of the men could imagine a woman overcoming an experienced, battle-hardened fighter like Agamemnon, so Clytemnestra was automatically ruled out. "I bet she was in on it though," Andreas said. "Everybody said her and Aegisthus were having it off."

I tried intermittently to join in the conversation, but my head was aching and for a large part of the time I seemed to be in two places at once. They'd be getting ready for dinner in the palace, Clytemnestra in her rooms, attended by her maids. I wondered if Orestes had been to see the bathhouse. Perhaps not. The massage slab and the fishing nets would be objects of horror to him, because he was perfectly capable of working out how the murder must have been done. And Aegisthus? Would he be sitting down to eat with the family? I doubted it. Clytemnestra would want him to stay out of sight. So, he'd be—well, what would he be doing? Walking the corridors, alone, a living embodiment of the evil that haunted the place. But perhaps that wasn't fair? Closing my eyes, I saw Clytemnestra's children kneeling in front of their father's grave, praying for revenge. If they were victims, then so was Aegisthus, who'd been a baby in the womb when his brothers were killed.

By the time the plates were cleared away, I was almost nodding off. Brother and sister embraced. Kari invited us to eat at her home the following evening, and Andreas went up on deck to see her down the rope ladder and into the cart. Alcar was going to drive her home.

Left alone, I looked around the table as slowly the room filled with shadows. It was a relief when Andreas returned.

"I've put you in there," he said, pointing to what had been Agamemnon's room. I guessed that was where Andreas himself normally slept. From that moment on, I was intensely conscious of the cabin door behind us, though whether he was equally aware of it, I'm not sure. Certainly, there was no move towards it. I suspected he'd gone into full *I am a gentleman* mode. His sister urging caution? No, I didn't think so—it was Andreas through and through. It would have been intolerable to him that a woman who'd taken refuge under his roof—or rather, masthead—should not be able to enjoy a good night's sleep in a comfortable bed without fear of molestation. Oh, I respected his integrity, but at the same time the last thing I wanted was to spend the coming night alone in the bed that Cassandra had so recently slept in.

But I couldn't make the first move, and he wouldn't. So, after a run of increasingly long silences, I pleaded tiredness and we said a civilized goodnight. Closing the door quietly behind me, I sat on the bed and took the opal necklace out of the jewellery case. I always liked looking at it, though I was never tempted to put it on. I knew it wasn't mine to wear. Instead, I cradled one of the stones in the palm of my hand, waiting for my blood heat to stir the flames. Perhaps, one day, I would see Briseis again and be able to give her mother's necklace back to her. With Andreas' help, that would be possible.

Sheltered by the harbour walls, the ship was peaceful, the floor rising and falling as gently as breath. I returned the necklace to the case and put it under the bed. Nothing for it now but to slide between the sheets, stretch out my legs into the cold spaces where Agamemnon's and Cassandra's bodies had lain, and try to sleep. But something was niggling away at me, some thought I'd had about Cassandra that no longer seemed fair or true. In that conversation I'd had with her in the storeroom when I was on the verge of sleep, I'd said, "You got what you wanted." I was angry with her because I thought she hadn't wanted to live—and even to this day, I am still, intermittently, angry. But I don't think now that she got what she wanted. I don't think any of us did. The women of Troy, the mothers who watched their sons hurled from the battlements, what did they want? Justice for their boys—and revenge too. Revenge for their own suffering, for the spoiled hopes. And I suppose you could say, "Well, they got revenge." Agamemnon, the man who gave the order to kill their children, was dead.

Does it really matter that none of them struck the blow that finished him, that he was killed by a Greek queen avenging an entirely different crime?

Yes. I think it does matter.

Justice. Revenge. Call it what you like, it turned out, in the end, to be a prerogative of the rich and powerful. The best those slave mothers could hope for was survival—and not all of them managed that.

I don't claim that that night on the *Medusa* I thought about this clearly—or at all, in the terms I'm using now. What I felt was a deep uneasiness, a restlessness. I knew I wouldn't be able to sleep, and I knew I didn't want to be alone. So, after tossing from side to side for half an hour, I went back into the dining room where Andreas was sitting at the table as I'd left him, drinking the last of the wine. Barefoot, moving quietly, I put my arms around him from behind and buried my face in that springy pelt of hair. "I don't want to be alone tonight."

Turning round, he reached up and touched my face. "You don't have to be."

And then, holding hands like two naughty children, we crept into Agamemnon's bed. Love-making was easy, with none of the awkwardness of our first night, as if somehow in all the chaos and danger of the last few days, our bodies had remembered and gone on learning.

Afterwards, on the brink of sleep, I saw Cassandra again, crowned with laurels and bay, walking through fields of white asphodel, alone. Just as I felt I couldn't bear it, she looked back at me and waved. Prayers had been said, libations poured: she could cross the river now. I wouldn't be seeing her in quite this way again.

Meanwhile, there was Andreas, every breath ending on a whistle, every second breath beginning with a grunt. I didn't mind, I even liked it. Pressing my face between his shoulder blades, I wriggled my arm around him, and slept.

35

Moonlight spilling like acid on the white stones of the Lion Court. The children singing.

Standing at the top of the steps with the lighted atrium behind her, Clytemnestra shivers. "I want to see my father's grave," Orestes had said—almost the first thing he said after entering the palace—and so she took him down the stairs into the candlelit darkness of the mausoleum. The air heavy with incense and the scents of late-summer flowers. Orestes knelt at the foot of the tomb and vowed to avenge his father's death, every prayer addressed to the gods but intended for her. He's here to kill her; she knows that—it's the only reason he'd risk his life by coming home. He doesn't believe the story of his father being assassinated by rebels, since caught and executed, and why should he? Nobody else believes it. And he has, or shortly will have, Electra's own account of how their father died.

Does he even believe his father's buried under that stone? She watched him pull out a knife, hack off a lock of hair and put it on the slab. Then he stood up, tall and straight, taller by a couple of inches than his father had been, ready to leave the tomb and face whatever there was left to face.

She went first. On the top step, where the treads are crumbling, she stumbled and would have fallen if Orestes hadn't put out his hand to steady her. An adult son's gesture of concern for an ageing mother, instinctively offered, politely received. Meaningless.

He's waiting for her now, in the lighted atrium behind her. At least Aegisthus has not appeared. Orestes can't stand the man, but it's going to be difficult to get rid of him: he's useful, and he knows too much. And anyway, they're related, though for a moment she can't remember how. Cousins, or something. She's very tired: when she closes her eyes, her lids scrape over eyeballs that no longer have the comforting wash of tears. Will she ever cry again? And really, does it matter? What is there left worth crying about? Though she does feel a momentary tweak of grief for Orestes as he used to be: stroppy, defiant, passionately loyal to the father he didn't know, blaming her because he wasn't allowed to go to Troy.

Now, in his place, there's this poised young man with impeccable manners, who bows over her hand before raising it to his lips, whose eyes are the grey of a winter sea. Turning, she looks over her shoulder into the lighted atrium, and there he is, pacing up and down, waiting for her to appear. Should she go in and try again to relate to him? No, she decides, not yet.

The moon rises higher; the children's voices are shriller now— that high, fierce, pure note you get in very young boys. She sees shadowy figures emerging from a mist she hadn't known was there till now, a whole crowd of them. These aren't just the children Atreus killed, so who are they? Boys who died in Troy, following their mothers as they trudged behind Agamemnon's victorious chariot all the way from the harbour wall to the palace gate? What else could they do, these desolate children, except stick close to the only security they'd ever known?

Crawling and waiting, crawling again, they creep towards her up the steps, red-eyed, white dust on their skin and in their matted hair, black blood clotted around their untreated wounds. Here they come, swarming out of their ruined city, chanting one of their silly little rhymes, full of names she doesn't recognize: *Here comes a candle to light you to bed* . . . Glimpses of swollen tonsils and half-erupted teeth, as they yell into her face: *And here comes a chopper TO CHOP OFF YOUR HEAD!*

And then, immediately, as if they've frightened themselves, they begin to back off, retreating down the steps, glancing over their shoulders as they go, acknowledging their lack of power. They reach level ground and there, one by one, they step into holes in the moonlight and disappear.

Broken as they are, these children are not the Furies, who never back off, never retreat, acknowledge no limits to their power. Unfortunately for her and for Orestes, it's the Furies who, with claw and dreadful brow, attend them now. Bracing herself, Clytemnestra goes into the atrium where her son, who suddenly looks painfully young, his jawline blurred with soft down, stops pacing and bows. She gives him her hand to kiss; he raises it to his lips, then bends to kiss her cheek. She lets him lead her into the dining hall where she knows Electra will be waiting.

As she passes, slaves turn to face the wall, but there's nothing new in that. Slaves are trained to look away. What's new is the behaviour of her counsellors. Once, they'd have been vying with each other to catch her eye; now, not one of them willingly meets her gaze. There's a group of them straight ahead. Aware, now more than ever, of the image she must present, she straightens her shoulders, becomes once again the queen—widowed, yes, but still powerful, a fortunate woman, looking forward to spending an evening in the company of her children. And she is looking forward to it. Let the Furies scrape and clatter their clawed feet on the roof; their moment will come, and soon; but not tonight. Tonight is hers.

AUTHOR'S NOTE

I'd like to thank Clare Alexander for many years of encouragement and sound advice, first as my editor at Viking Penguin and more recently as my agent at Aitken Alexander Associates. Simon Prosser has been throughout a most enthusiastic and supportive editor and publisher. No author could have a better team and I know how lucky I am.

I would also like to thank my daughter, Anna Barker, for being an insightful first reader.

ABOUT THE AUTHOR

PAT BARKER is the author of seventeen novels. *The Ghost Road*, the final volume of her Regeneration trilogy, was awarded the Booker Prize, and the trilogy is regarded as being among the greatest historical novels of all time. Her novel *The Silence of the Girls* was shortlisted for the Women's Prize for Fiction and the Gordon Burn Prize in the UK, and won the Independent Bookshop Week Book Award in 2019. She was made a Commander of the Order of the British Empire (CBE) in 2000. She lives in Durham, England.